MISADVENTURES IN A WHITE DESERT

This is the story of how Patrick Woodhead and two friends set out to ski to the South Pole. Despite forgetting their skis, they managed to cross 1,100km of the forbidding Antarctic interior and in doing so became one of the youngest and fastest teams ever to reach 90 degrees South. And all with the help of some very large kites . . . Battling egos, exhaustion and the fear of peeing at minus 55 degrees, the team fought their way across the ice, following in the footsteps of their heroes. Patrick's story gets down to the bare bones of polar exploration, but essentially, it's about three friends trying to keep it together in the harshest environment on Earth.

PATRICK WOODHEAD

MISADVENTURES IN A WHITE DESERT

Complete and Unabridged

ULVERSCROFT
Leicester

First published in Great Britain in 2003 by
Hodder and Stoughton
London

First Large Print Edition
published 2005
by arrangement with
Hodder and Stoughton
a division of Hodder Headline
London

The moral right of the author has been asserted

Photographs © Commonwealth Antarctic Expedition
Map by Chips Woodhead

British Library CIP Data

Woodhead, Patrick
Misadventures in a white desert.—Large print ed.—
Ulverscroft large print series: non-fiction
1. Woodhead, Patrick—Travel—Antarctica
2. Large type books 3. Antarctica—Description and
travel 4. Antarctica—Discovery and exploration,
British 5. South Pole
I. Title
919.8'9'04

ISBN 1–843955–561–0

Published by
F. A. Thorpe (Publishing)
Anstey, Leicestershire

Set by Words & Graphics Ltd.
Anstey, Leicestershire
Printed and bound in Great Britain by
T. J. International Ltd., Padstow, Cornwall

This book is printed on acid-free paper

For Robyn — 'may the sun shine on your face and the rain fall softly at your feet'

CONTENTS

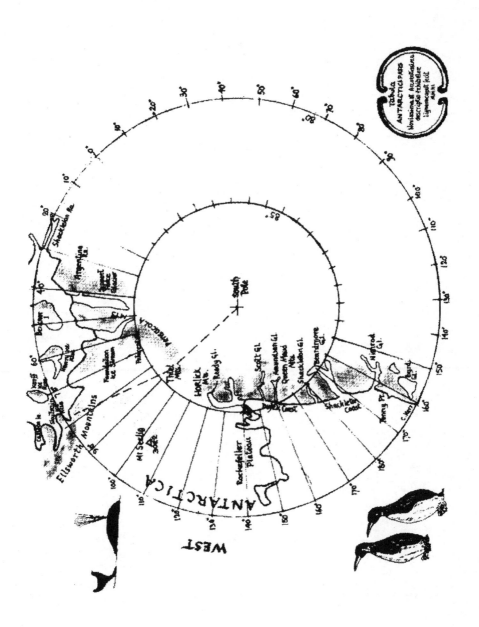

1

Jumping with Both Feet

It's dark, my legs are starting to cramp up, and I am all alone. Things do not bode well for the South Pole.

Only three days before I leave for Punta Arenas, I am in the least likely, not to mention most embarrassing, situation I have been in for weeks — I am stuck in the wardrobe at my parents' house. While ferreting around for some old ski gear, I have somehow managed to let the door close and lock behind me.

After unsuccessfully trying to dismantle the latch with a coat hanger, it is slowly dawning on me that my only hope of escape is to be rescued by my mother. I put my head in my hands and groan at the absurdity of it all. It could not have been more than two hours earlier that I had reassuringly hugged her and told her not to worry. I was no longer a teenager, I had said. I was able to look after myself.

With a simple click of the wardrobe door, all hope of looking like a tough, or at the very least credible, adventurer is now gone. I'm twenty-six years old — I really shouldn't have to be dealing with this kind of thing.

Sitting in the dark, waiting for rescue, I think back over the last year and the strange turn of events which led me to this wardrobe. For some reason the old adage 'Be careful what you wish for' seems to spring to mind. A year of constant fretting and an unhealthy amount of self-doubt since it all started has made me sure of just one thing. At the start of this whole adventure, I really had no idea what I was getting myself into.

As with most young guys, we kind of needed to make our own mistakes. And the way we set about organising our expedition to Antarctica certainly reflected this. We seldom took advice from people or listened to them when they expressed the odd word of warning. To an impartial observer, it might have looked as if we knew what we were doing, that there was some God-given duty we were fulfilling. Unsurprisingly, the truth could not have been more different.

We stumbled up to each hurdle, anything from the logistics to the finances, and then simply tried to blag our way across. There was seldom a plan or any real sense of planning. However, we did have the desire to do something, and that desire was extremely strong. Combined with stubbornness, ignorance and a vague ability to think on our feet, it was a surprisingly effective combination.

I've always thought that the mid-twenties are a dangerous time for most males. Their testosterone levels have come down only a little since the heady days of being a teenager and, by virtue of the fact that they look respectable in a suit, real businessmen sometimes take them seriously. This often results in two things. They have an outrageously inflated opinion of their own capabilities and, more frighteningly, a means of acquiring the necessary funds to make things happen.

Some might say that Tom and I were typical mid-twenties and had a rather ambitious, or even unrealistic, approach to organising expeditions. A criticism I could certainly live with. But, in our defence, there was some basis to it all. We had done a few trips previously and, after each, our horizons seemed to expand. From weekends climbing in the Alps, we moved up a few levels and started longer and more ambitious projects. Like voracious children our appetite seemed to grow as the years passed and soon the South Pole itself had come under our cross-hairs.

Where it really started, though, was in a

six-inch-square garden in one of the grimier suburbs of Bristol. For about the last half-hour I had been listening to a car going backwards and forwards down the little street I lived on. Every so often there would be a grating sound as the person evidently tried to change gear, and then a gentle crunch — a bumper nudging into the side panel of another car.

I had been trying to ignore the noise and get on with some work when eventually my curiosity got the better of me. Outside, along the row of back-to-back gardens, all the various neighbours had come out of their houses and were watching a girl trying to park her car. With coffee or a half-eaten piece of toast in hand, they all stood and stared, far more interested in watching than helping.

I peered across at the car and recognised Nadia, a girl from the university, whom I had met before and who was a veritable legend in the world of bad driving. Not only was she dangerously unskilled, she was also persistent, as the scrapes on the side of her car amply testified. In the garden next to me, a tall guy in a dressing gown was lazily eating a large bowl of cereal and, like the rest of us, wondering what all the commotion was about.

As her rear tyre mounted the kerb and

came dangerously close to a lamp-post once again, the man eating the cereal looked at me with a sheepish grin. With a nod, we both crossed over to the little gate at the end of the garden and on to the road. A few hand signals and some gentle tugging of the steering wheel later and Nadia's car came to rest. When the keys were finally pulled out of the ignition, an almost eerie calm came over the little neighbourhood. Slowly, everybody started to retreat back indoors.

After our good deed for the day, the man in the dressing gown introduced himself as Tom Avery and we started talking. With a wonderful morning sun, there didn't seem to be any great rush to get indoors and we chatted for the next half-hour or so. It soon became apparent that Tom had an abiding passion for adventure and exploration, which, I later learnt, bordered on mild obsession.

He was reading geography at university, and his knowledge of little-known republics and unexplored jungles was practically encyclopedic. He could talk at great length about rock formations or glacier movements and, if we didn't stop him in time, would often try to do so. While climbing in the mountains, we would regularly find him on his hands and knees, intently studying a small bit of rock. In view of our lack of interest and the suffering geology can cause, he tried to keep his enthusiasm to himself. However, as we used to spend such a great deal of time in the mountains, there was naturally quite a lot for him to get excited about.

Another of Tom's characteristics was his unfailing diplomacy. During all the years I have known him, I have only ever seen him lose his temper on two occasions. The first was during a climbing expedition, when a tiresome documentary producer insisted we name a mountain after his production company. The second time was when I pulled his younger sister.

When we left university three years later, Tom was visibly torn between towing the family line and getting a nine-to-five job or pursuing his real interest and heading off to far-flung places. With few realistic career prospects in the latter course, he joined an accountancy firm and bought himself a couple of pinstriped suits. For eight months, he tried desperately hard to get excited by the prospect of auditing financial books, but soon he came to the inevitable conclusion that the best in life was passing him by.

A few months later, a letter arrived for me in the post. Attached to the underside of the paper was a badly photocopied map and an arrow in thick red felt pen. It marked a point that said simply 'Here'. As we soon discovered, Tom had managed to find an entire mountain range that had never before been climbed.

★ ★ ★

This was to be the first of our adventures together.

About three years after that letter arrived on my doormat, Tom and I were sitting in our local pub. It was a Sunday afternoon and nothing seemed to be moving very fast. I stared vacantly out of the window, watching the drizzle come down like a gentle mist. The drab sky merged with the ashen buildings and all the colours seemed to bleed away into the general greyness. It was one of those lethargic, energy-sapping afternoons.

We had just returned from a climbing trip and were enjoying the pleasure of a well-earned pint. After a few minutes, Tom leant across the table in a conspiratorial manner and said he had an idea for another expedition — the South Pole. As he went into detail, I smiled with a total lack of interest, the memories of ice and cold far too recent for me to take him seriously.

'Why not?' he persisted, sensing I was just about to change the subject.

'Because it's over a thousand kilometres' skiing to the pole!' I replied wearily. 'It'd take us about three months and all the while we'd be horrendously cold. Besides, we couldn't possibly afford it.'

I looked at him and couldn't believe his timing. We had just got back from the mountains and the last thing I felt like doing was trudging off into the Antarctic wilderness. A hot meal and an offer of another pint would have been a far more appealing suggestion.

I fell silent and went back to staring mindlessly out of the window. Tom would soon forget about it, I thought. He was probably just throwing around a few grandiose ideas. However, as I should have learnt from all our previous trips, Tom has a drive and organisational talent that would put soldier ants to shame.

He had obviously spent a considerable amount of time thinking about the whole idea and, as with all these things, the next big hurdle was trying to work out who'd join him. Choosing an effective and cohesive team is incredibly important. If, for some reason, the combination of people isn't right, then no matter how successful the expedition turns out to be, you'll still have a miserable time. Or, as I heard someone once say, 'On a Polar

8

expedition begin with a clear idea which Pole you are aiming at, and try to start facing the right way. Choose your companions carefully — you may have to eat them.'

As Tom and I had discovered with expeditions of this sort, a lot of people say yes, but only very few will actually take the next step. As the realisation dawns on any would-be volunteer that they will have to jack in their jobs, spend weeks in the biting cold and basically subject themselves to financial ruin for the foreseeable future, their initial enthusiasm tends to wane. Even if someone is prepared to do all this, there's always the question of whether they will react well under extremely stressful conditions. Prolonged periods in freezing and often dangerous environments do tend to beat the niceties out of a person's character.

The other consideration is whether the potential teammate has any irritating habits. After a few weeks cut off from civilisation, simple things like snoring, slurping food or bad BO can be issues which escalate into near-homicidal proportions. It's much better to have done a few minor trips with them first, so at least you know that they won't get agoraphobia the moment you touch down in Antarctica.

Expeditions are always a great test of a

person's friendship. There are invariably occasions when you feel so scared, or so exhausted, that there are simply no barriers left between you and another person. After days on a mountain, you can be at your lowest ebb, the bare bones of your character laid open for all to see. The simple truth is that you just have no strength left in which to conceal them. It is extremely scary to expose yourself like that, mainly due to the fact that you're not really sure how either you or, for that matter, the other person will react under such circumstances.

With this in mind, the first person on Tom's hit list for potential teammates was a mutual friend of ours called Nick Stopford. The first time I had ever met Nick was during a terrible night on Mont Blanc, where one of our teammates came within an hour of dying from altitude sickness. That night had been the most scared I had ever been in my life — by a long way — and Nick had been there, right in the middle of it.

The whole disastrous trip to Mont Blanc had been in preparation for an expedition to a tiny, landlocked country called Kyrgyzstan in central Asia. At the time, Nick had just returned from climbing Mount McKinley in Alaska and thought this next expedition seemed like the perfect way to gain some good experience for an Everest attempt the following year.

From the outset, it was pretty obvious that there was the potential for a big personality clash between Nick and me. Although he was a strong climber and had a very genuine passion for mountains and exploration, to me he seemed extremely dour and serious all the time. He always seemed slightly patronising in the way he talked to me, viewing our expedition only as a launch pad for his Everest aspirations.

After the first few days' climbing in Kyrgyzstan, tempers were barely concealed and a deep unpleasantness was starting to fester between us. He found me as arrogant as I was unfriendly, and things looked as if they were firmly locked in a downward spiral. Fortunately, Tom had seen the potential rift developing and made a concerted effort to settle our differences. After a few bonding moments with some near-falls and a couple of crevasses, Nick and I slowly became friends. We soon discovered that although we could wind each other up with a few well-chosen words, we could also make each other laugh just as easily. Since then we have become superb friends, and he is usually the first person either Tom or I think of when planning any adventure.

The next person on Tom's hit list was a South African called Andrew Gerber. I had never met him before, but Tom knew him through a friend, who had reliably said that Andrew was 'well up for any adventure'. I raised an eyebrow sceptically at Tom. This didn't exactly sound like the most concrete of proof that he would be right for a sixty-day expedition in the harshest climate in the world.

On subsequent meetings, I learnt a little more about Andrew's background. He was born and raised in South Africa, living on a farm near Cape Town. Like all kids his age growing up in Africa, he had learnt to shoot and skin an antelope before the stabilisers came off his bike. Despite his very British accent (he had been at school and university in the UK) he still maintained that wonderful South African attitude that anything is possible.

Unlike the pessimistic British and their lackadaisical acceptance of their lot in life, for me South Africans seem to represent this eye-opening mindset, where almost anything can be achieved. I think it has something to do with the years of apartheid suppression and the subsequent emancipation of the South African blacks. While the majority of older whites all quietly lived in shame, the younger generation saw this great revolution, in which people who had been repressed and marginalised for decades suddenly got told that they could actually be whatever they wanted. I have never met a young South African who is not proud of their nation.

Although Andrew had never been on a long expedition, he had been on some extremely hard-core sailing trips, during which they spent weeks crowded below deck in rough seas. I guessed that this kind of pressured environment, where tempers can easily ignite, was a very good indicator of how someone might perform living in a two-metre tent for a couple of months.

I later learnt that Andrew was also an excellent downhill skier and exceptionally fit. The only thing that worried me was his ability to deal with the cold. As far as I could tell, he had spent the majority of his life in Cape Town, and the coldest place he'd ever been was Stockholm on a summer's day.

The waitress walked over to where we were sitting and gently laid the bill down on the edge of the table. She moved away, smiling apologetically at having interrupted Tom's monologue. As he started speaking once more, I absent-mindedly picked up the plastic folder and scanned through the bill.

By now, Tom was talking quickly and

passionately about what the expedition would actually entail. Names of mountain ranges, equipment brands and a million other bits of trivia seemed to pour out of him in one long, effusive gust. He described what Antarctica was like, the endless ice and the incredible cold. How his idea was to travel in the footsteps of some of the world's greatest explorers and, in doing so, undertake what was reputedly one of the most difficult physical challenges on the planet. Half listening, half daydreaming, I sat and tried to get my mind round the idea of skiing over 1,200 kilometres into the heart of Antarctica.

Out of all the information I had gleaned so far, there were several things that particularly caught my attention. Apparently, only twelve people had ever attempted the route he was suggesting, five of whom had died on the return journey. Barring injury and storms, the trip would take us approximately seventy-five days, passing across the Trans-Antarctic Mountains via the Beardmore Glacier — the largest in the world. Aside from the excruciating cold, Tom guessed the sleds would weigh about 200 pounds, we'd be burning calories equivalent to running a double marathon a day, and navigating crevasse fields so large you could lose an entire army. And all this with only one change of underwear.

I sat back in my chair and looked at Tom in disbelief. It just sounded impossible. The scale of what he was proposing was absolutely huge. Three long months of intense pain and drudgery, along a route which, at the risk of sounding melodramatic, only seven people had survived.

'Why have so few people attempted it?' I asked suspiciously.

'Haven't got round to it, I suppose.'

The answer struck me as particularly unconvincing. The idea was to celebrate the centenary of Captain Scott's 1901 *Discovery* expedition and retrace their original route. Back then, Scott's expedition had been man's first serious bid to reach the South Pole and explore Antarctica's interior. We wouldn't follow his exact route, as on this first attempt Scott had only made it a couple of hundred miles inland before being forced to turn back. Tom's plan was to then continue to the pole along the route of his later *Terra Nova* expedition of 1910.

'Don't worry, it's not as bad as it seems,' he said reassuringly. 'It's going to be nothing like the haphazard expeditions of the last century. For starters, we'll only be going one way.'

This was a good point. Once we arrived at

15

the South Pole, a Twin Otter plane would land on the ice and fly us back to civilisation.

'We'll also be using state-of-the-art polar clothing, which is nothing like those old-fashioned furs. There'll be a satellite phone for emergencies and a resupply halfway into the journey. Oh, I nearly forgot. There's also the kites,' he said, the beginnings of a smile spreading across his face.

Kites had only been used a handful of times before in Antarctica and, like kite surfers on the beach, we would use them to tow us across the ice. Kiting technology had radically advanced over the last five years and some polar explorers had covered incredible distances in a single day. They were notoriously dangerous and difficult to control, but, if there was a favourable wind, they could halve a team's time spent on the ice.

To me sitting in the pub, the whole concept seemed abstract and unthreatening. It was hard to visualise the actual distances involved when all I had to work from was a little map he had sketched on the back of a napkin. The patchy outlines and hazy ink seemed to gloss over the harsh reality of what was involved. The dotted lines conveyed nothing of the real scale and only led the eye to three words, written at the centre and underlined twice — 90 degrees South.

An hour or so later, I left the pub and strolled back down the road. The weather had not improved whilst I had been indoors, and with the early dusk any vestiges of colour that I'd seen a few hours previously had now disappeared completely. I put the collar of my jacket up, stopping the drizzle from going down my neck, and went over all Tom had said. I thought about Antarctica and how so few people had actually seen the bizarre continent, this white desert lying quietly at the bottom of the planet.

From a very young age, I had read stories about the early explorers in Antarctica. I always imagined them to be these wizened, fur-covered giants, fearlessly stomping off across infinite horizons. The endless miles of ice, which would be maddening to most people, just appeared to be the backdrop to some great game they were playing. They seemed unstoppable, as they attempted to raise their flag in the most inaccessible place on earth.

A few years later, looking back on these accounts, I thought that possibly they had exaggerated it all a little. Admittedly, I had never been anywhere near a decent ice cap at this stage, but I did get the sense that the stories had been hammed up a bit. Whether this was to satisfy a public desperate for tales of suffering and the odd amputation, I wasn't sure, but it all seemed so improbable.

As I read more, however, I realised that this simply wasn't the case. There was a message that rang loud and clear from every single polar book I had ever come across. Polar exploration, in the words of Apsley Cherry-Garrard, was 'at once the cleanest and most isolated way of having a bad time ever devised'. It didn't sound good.

Cherry-Garrard was part of Scott's 1910 expedition and wrote a book rather bluntly called *The Worst Journey in the World*. In the dead of the Antarctic winter, with unimaginably cold temperatures and twenty-four-hour darkness, three men travelled 120 miles in search of Emperor penguin eggs. The reason for them leaving at such an inhospitable time of year is that penguin males have to sit through the four months of Antarctic winter holding the egg on their furry feet. The poor buggers lose over 45 per cent of their body mass trying to keep warm, while sitting patiently waiting for the females to return in the spring. Emperor penguins evolved in the Antarctic, and even they have about the most miserable time imaginable waiting in howling winds for daylight to finally reappear.

Only science would be able to motivate

men to do something as idiotic as venture out in those conditions. Cherry-Garrard described in this book the relentless and desperate cold, which drove them to despair. On an almost daily basis, they would have to fight the urge to just lie down in the snow and gently end it all.

'Such extremity of suffering can not be measured: madness or death may give relief. But this I know: on this journey we were already beginning to think of death as a friend. As we groped our way back that night, sleepless, icy and dog tired in the dark, a crevasse seemed an almost friendly gift.'

However, this extreme journey had been made in the middle of the Antarctic winter. Any expedition we went on would set off in the considerably fairer climes of summer. Despite this reassurance, his account did little to calm my nerves. Books are often worse than any other type of medium. It's not like film, where the images sit slothfully on the retina. Words on a page seem to shoot up the optic nerve and force themselves into the recesses of the brain. By the time the imagination has got hold of it in its jaws and twisted it round a few times, Antarctica can turn from a slightly cold, big lump of ice into the epitome of hell on earth. I'd heard people talk about when hell freezes over. Maybe it already had, it was just that nobody had noticed.

The inescapable truth was that I had no idea whether I was capable of completing such a challenge. I had never been anywhere near the polar regions and had only these intimidating first-hand accounts to base any opinions on. It wasn't just the old explorers who painted such a picture; lots of modern adventurers also took great pains to describe how unpleasant Antarctica could be.

A few years previously, I had seen Sir Ranulph Fiennes talk at the Royal Geographical Society in London. He spoke about his great Antarctic crossing, when he and Mike Stroud skied for ninety-seven days, entirely unsupported by the outside world. To carry the enormous amount of food and equipment required, they pulled sleds weighing 450 pounds (the weight of two fully grown overweight men) and moved at a morale-destroying speed he called 'the polar plod'.

People in the audience seemed fascinated by the hardships he endured. He went on to describe polar travel as a constant mental battle between the strong and the weak side of a person's character. He said the only way to make it to the pole was to ignore the pain and suppress the fear and exhaustion. Sitting in the dusty old lecture theatre, I watched this tall, smartly dressed man speak and realised that, unlike that of movie stars, this was an inspiration that was tangible. It wasn't an actor pretending to be the hero, this was a real person standing only 20 feet away, and he told stories that would stretch the imagination of the majority of Hollywood directors. I listened with the same incredulous horror that I have when being forced to watch a scary movie.

It's curiosity which creates impetus. As I listened that night, and the images turned over in my mind, I felt an incredible curiosity build inside me. I wanted to see with my own eyes the things that had inspired such dread and awe in polar explorers. I wanted to feel first hand the strength of emotion Antarctica could evoke, but, being a teenager, I had absolutely no idea how to get there.

A few years later, I found something that made particular sense to me in the writings of the explorer Roald Amundsen. When he was fifteen years old, he stumbled across the works of Sir John Franklin. The lurid tales of hardship, murder and even cannibalism from this early British explorer sparked something in the Norwegian lad which would irreparably change the course of his life. He wrote in his book *My Life as an Explorer*,

'Oddly enough it was the sufferings that Sir John and his men had to go through which attracted me most in his narrative. A strange urge made me wish that I too would go through the same thing.'

It sounds pretty masochistic to wish to experience such prolonged misery and slowly starving to death in the High Arctic like Franklin is understandably not something that would attract most people. However, the suffering is really only a by-product of what people like Amundsen were searching for. It is this strange sort of extremity in life which they were trying to find, the emotions intrinsic to a human at the very edge of their character.

As I sat listening to the lecture, it was all too obvious that I was nothing like the explorers of the early twentieth century. Their names were engraved around the top of the lecture theatre and almost all of them had either died horribly, had crew members that had died horribly, or, at the very least, had lost a few limbs to frostbite.

Now I have absolutely no desire to start losing toes or, for that matter, any of my friends, but strangely I found that I did want to get a taste of this kind of life. People like Ranulph Fiennes or Borge Ousland may want to break records and compete at the highest level, but I just wanted to look into that window for the briefest of seconds. In doing so, I thought, perhaps I might understand what it actually is that they're all banging on about.

In the lecture hall, Fiennes started talking about how he often felt hampered and constricted by the lack of danger in modern-day society. He said that time and again he found himself just standing by, watching, as everyone seemed to go through life limiting risk and cocooning themselves in civilisation.

By deliberately subjecting himself to the mercy of the elements, Fiennes was able to feel more basic, primeval emotions, which, quite simply, made him feel more alive. It sounds a little clichéd, but it was a convincing argument — people don't head off to Antarctica to avoid risk, they go there because risk is exactly what they seek.

I watched him sitting calmly on stage, the question-and-answer session drawing to a close, and I felt a strange sort of envy. I wasn't jealous of his fame or notoriety, I was jealous because he had seen so many things that I felt I never would. He had experienced such an extraordinary life and done so much, while I would soon be drifting out of the lecture hall and back into obscurity.

That night was a long time ago, but I still clearly remember the jilted sense of longing. I realise now that when Tom put forward the idea of skiing to the South Pole I never really stood a chance of saying no. To my surprise I discovered that the idea of an expedition to Antarctica was still very much alive, albeit buried beneath the infinite piles of everyday life.

I am sure many others have felt the same sense of longing, just as I am sure some people will have no idea what I am talking about. The only difference is that Tom and I took the next step. I don't mean that in a self-congratulatory, slap-on-the-back sort of way, only in the sense that so many people let that moment or idea gently float off into the ether. For me, however, owing to the conviction of my friends, I suddenly discovered that ideas led places.

For some time now, a giant rock had been sitting at the top of a hill. Slowly, very slowly, it started to roll downwards.

2

First Steps South

'I believe every human has a finite number of heartbeats. I don't intend to waste any of mine running around doing exercise.'

— Neil Armstrong

As most people are well aware, the flight from England to New Zealand is very, very long. I began travelling on Friday, arrived on Sunday, and somewhere in between lost an entire day.

The plan was to spend a month training in preparation for the South Pole and, given the time of year, only the southern hemisphere had any decent snow. I had been trying to get fit back in London, with limited success, but there were other considerations too. We really needed to practise our survival techniques and crevasse rescue. The urgency of pulling a person out of a crevasse is somehow lost when trying to replicate the whole thing in a pub car park.

The others were all on a different flight and

so I was travelling alone. Long flights are always tedious, so I decided to put the time to good use and read a tourist information book concerning New Zealand. The first surprising fact was that the country appeared to be almost entirely predator free. I had assumed it was going to be like Australia, teeming with all sorts of deadly invertebrates, but to my great relief it was nothing of the sort.

In England our most poisonous snake is the adder, a bite from which usually requires that the victim seek medical attention within one week. In Australia, a person bitten by the deadly taipan has roughly three minutes before the poison takes effect. So basically, unless you're bitten in a hospital car park, there's not a great deal of point trying to do anything about it.

As I discovered, over the last 80 million years New Zealand has developed a unique environment, owing mainly to its distance from any other land mass. Only birds (and one species of bat) could reach such far-flung shores and, within a few thousand years, a third of them became either flightless or at least aerodynamically challenged. With no natural predators, birds basically filled the void left by mammals, and some grew to a colossal size. The book had all sorts of sketches of long-since-extinct animals. The most incredible was the ostrich-looking moa, a bird that weighed up to a quarter of a ton and was nearly 12 feet high. There was also the Haast eagle, which was the largest eagle ever to have flown on earth, with a ten-foot wingspan and talons the size of a lion's claws.

I read to my delight that there were virtually no snakes, the spiders were largely inoffensive and the Haast eagles long since extinct. In comparison to Australia, New Zealand appeared to be entirely innocuous. It did seem strange, though, that with an environment so suited to mammalian predators, there was almost nothing with sharp teeth.

★   ★   ★

At the airport in Christchurch, Nick and Tom were waiting patiently. Tom hadn't slept at all on the journey over and looked a little shell-shocked by the whole ordeal. While Nick had drunk his way through the complimentary wine and had slept all the way, Tom had spent the entire time being pestered by small children and listening to Nick's snoring.

We bundled him in the back of the hire car and set off for a town called Wanaka. In one of the least inhabited countries on earth, and on a road so straight it could have been made by the Romans, I managed to get booked for speeding. The policeman handed me the ticket and explained that I could pay the fine at the local police station or post office.

'Then again,' he said, smiling slightly, 'you could just leave the country and not pay the fine, like all the other tourists.'

'Thanks for the advice,' I said, and we parted happy in the knowledge that from an official point of view everything was above board.

Four hours later, and with Tom still without rest (nervous passenger), we arrived in the beautiful lakeside town of Wanaka. Andy had already been in New Zealand for a week and had given us instructions to meet in a bar called Shooters. The bar was packed with hard-core snowboarders with plenty of attitude and a lot to prove. We soon realised that cross-country skiing wasn't exactly the coolest sport in town, and so found Andy and gently retired to a corner of the bar.

It was great to have the whole team finally together, and everyone was looking forward to getting up into the mountains for some proper training. A few hours later, we all stumbled back to our hotel room, tripping over the ski equipment as we went. I think Tom finally slept at this point.

We were due to meet up with a mountain guide called Gotlieb at the end of the week. He had previously trained a Singaporean team that had made a successful attempt on the pole a few years back. With four days to go until then, we decided to ski up into the back country and get used to being back on the ice.

In Wanaka, we checked into the guide's office and started to tell the woman behind the counter about our plans for the next few days. This is standard practice in the French Alps, as if things go wrong a search party will know roughly where you'll be and can easily locate you. However, the dowdy receptionist didn't seem to understand any of this and completely failed to appreciate why we were telling her our movements.

'So you don't want one of our heli-skiing brochures, then?' she asked, staring fiercely over the top of her glasses.

'No,' said Tom wearily.

'What about hiring one of our guides for the mountain?'

'No, thanks.'

'Some equipment. You need some equipment?'

Again, Tom shook his head. Having slept only seven hours in sixty, he was still slightly simple and doing a lousy job of explaining the reason behind their miscommunication. After a couple more minutes, they parted angrily, both believing the other to be a complete idiot. If something did go wrong with our trip, I was pretty certain that the Wanaka guides office would be damned if they were going to move a muscle to come and save us.

Early the next day, we set off for a ski resort called Triple Comb. The sun was shining and the sky was a deep cobalt blue. The road took us all the way round Lake Wanaka, and really for the first time since arriving in New Zealand I started to appreciate why everyone had told me how beautiful it was.

We parked the car and sorted through our equipment. I hadn't shouldered a rucksack in some time and it was a pleasure I definitely hadn't missed. Without any real idea as to what we were doing, we decided to head off in the vague direction of a mountain called Shark's Tooth and see what happened. So, that's kind of how things went.

Within five hours we had skied ourselves into a steep couloir, got stuck and had to climb out. I was leading at the time and the snow was up to my waist. As I sank back in the deep powder, each step drained the energy out of me. Sweat poured down my face and my heart thumped noisily against my chest. Evidently, the training I had been doing around Hyde Park hadn't got me fit enough for this little climb. Christ, I thought, how is it ever going to get me fit enough for Antarctica?

I pushed myself as hard as I could, while trying to look as if I was taking the whole thing in my stride. I got to the summit and mopped my forehead before the others arrived. As they crested the ridge, I said something flippant about the climb. I tried to sound casual, but it's not easy appearing relaxed when your heart's beating like a sewing machine.

Mid-afternoon, we came across a tiny hut, looking lonely, perched high up on the side of the mountain. The little refuge had been built to accommodate heli-skiers, and it seemed like the perfect place for us to set up camp.

While we were putting up the tent, large olive-green parrots flew up and landed confidently close. They had bright red plumage under their wings and sharp polished beaks, and there was just something in their manner that suggested they were entirely unafraid of humans. Within seconds, they had landed on the rucksacks and were busy throwing all our equipment over the snow. It was quite amusing at first, until the little buggers really started to get stuck in. I went over to shoo one away and the parrot waddled back three or four paces, happy in the knowledge that he could fly and I couldn't. Then, as soon as I turned my back, he got back to the business of gnawing on my water bottle once again.

'They love rubber, apparently,' said Andrew matter-of-factly. 'They're called kea birds and they are supposed to be really intelligent.'

One of the keas had already got back on to my rucksack and had started the process of rummaging through it once more. Fantastic, I thought, I'm going to be outwitted by the only mountain animal that has a penchant for ski gear. I later discovered that kea birds have been known to attack adult sheep. If food is scarce, they land on the sheep's back, tear through its fleece and then peck out the poor animal's kidneys. That's a pretty sure-of-itself bird that will attack a fully grown sheep. As I watched the beak hack into the side of my water bottle, I decided never to lie on my face and remain still for any length of time.

That night it was seriously cold. The sky was completely clear and full of an incredible number of stars. The moon reflected off the snow and a beautiful panorama of mountains encircled our little campsite. Next to me, Nick was stirring the cooking pots when we felt the guy ropes bouncing up and down.

I zipped back the flysheet to see a kea bird tucking into the side of the tent. Did these things ever sleep? The night turned out to be very long indeed, with each of us (but mainly Nick — it was his tent, after all) having to shoo the birds away. Even in the pale moonlight, the keas had a contemptuous look which seemed to suggest they knew that however much we shouted and shone the head torches in their eyes there was not a chance we'd be getting out of our warm sleeping bags. As I raised myself up to bang the flysheet for the eighth time that night, I vowed silently to get my revenge. The next time I came up to the mountains, I'd be including a little catapult for just such an occasion and, just to add a little ironic justice, I'd use rubber pellets as well.

Slightly haggard through lack of sleep, we got up early and went off into the back country to try and find the Shark's Tooth. It was cold and windy when we got over the first ridge and my boots were rubbing a bit from the previous day's ski. From experience, I am paranoid about boots being uncomfortable, and the slightest twinge makes me nervous. I knew that the sixty days in Antarctica would be utterly miserable if I couldn't get the boots comfortable before I went.

After a few hours the sun came out and we had a glorious day's climbing up peaks and skiing down the other side. We had a huge valley of mountains to ourselves and the snow was fantastic. Unfortunately, the Shark's Tooth eluded us, as it was absolutely miles away, but we still skied from 9 a.m. to 5 p.m. with only about a twenty-minute stop all day.

Coming back to our tents, we dropped over a ridge and had to pick our way through some nasty couloirs. They looked steep and as if they avalanched on a regular basis. We tiptoed across the exposed sections and just hoped the snow wouldn't slide. Having been right next to my father when he was swept away in an avalanche a few years previously, they are something I've subsequently gained a healthy fear of.

Once again, we spent the night rattling tents and scanning the shadows with head torches. It became a matter of personal pride that I should catch the keas savaging the tents, and I had a sneaky feeling they were trying to trick us by flying off with loud squawks only to return silently minutes later. Like prison guards, our torches criss-crossed in the darkness, but our feathered adversaries managed to successfully ruin our sleep and my ski pole.

We had miscalculated with the cooking gas

and now had barely enough to melt the snow for water. Feeling acutely embarrassed to have made such a mistake, we had to hike our way back to the ski resort a day early. We were seriously thirsty by the time we finally arrived, but all refused to admit it. We had been trying to spend just three days in the mountains and had completely failed to do that. It didn't exactly bode well, considering we were supposed to be gearing up for 60 days in Antarctica.

★ ★ ★

After spending the afternoon recovering, we set off for Lake Tekapo the next day. We were about to meet our guide Gotlieb and start our polar training in earnest. The road ran through New Zealand's stunning scenery and, over each rise, another glorious view would unfold. The landscape had a rugged remoteness to it which reminded me of the Scottish highlands. Somehow, it combined incredible beauty with a bleakness that made it seem hostile and uninviting. I could easily understand why so many of the younger generations of Kiwis travelled abroad and ended up staying there.

Gotlieb was kind of what I was expecting, but with a few unusual twists. About five foot eleven with a grey beard and a bald head, he looked more like a contented office clerk than a polar explorer. However, from a few previous expeditions I had learnt my lesson about judging anyone by their appearance. Just because the guide happens to look more as if he should be wearing slippers than climbing boots didn't mean he couldn't kick your arse when climbing on the mountain.

After some initial introductions, we got down to the business of talking about what kit we would be taking to Antarctica. It was soon clear that Gotlieb was a self-confessed gear freak. He talked about tent poles and ski bindings the same way a classic car enthusiast talks about Ferraris. He handled things with fastidious care and had obviously spent hours thinking about their design. His eyes lit up with indulgent joy when he recounted how he had modified his sled by coating it in super-slippery resin for an expedition to Patagonia last year.

It was obvious Gotlieb liked things to be meticulous and highly organised. He loved talking about gadgets, little mechanical devices and any sort of modification to our equipment. He struck me as exactly the sort of person you'd want to have designing the side impact bars on your car. After studying our kit, he generally approved of the brands, but was obviously slightly put out that we had not made any of our own little adjustments. Clearly, he was looking forward to spending the next few hours arguing their pros and cons.

The morning was spent learning different theories about how to keep warm in the severe cold, put tents up in blizzards and maintain all our equipment. Over his thirty years as a guide, Gotlieb had acquired a whole range of subtle little tricks, which basically made life a bit easier when living in extreme conditions. By the afternoon, we were starting to feel a bit restless. So, with a strong wind blowing outside, we decided to go and test our newly arrived kites.

We had picked them up only the day before from a town called Timaru. Not sure whether the customs department would still be open when we arrived, we had telephoned the airport to see what time they closed. The manager, Bob, kindly informed us that he was just about to lock up the airport himself, but if it was urgent why didn't we pop round to his house, collect the package and complete the customs forms over a nice cup of tea. The rest of us waited outside while Tom filled in the forms and politely declined the offer of a second cup. When it came to customer relations, Heathrow just didn't have a patch on Timaru.

Tom had found a kite designer in the US who had just spent the last couple of years redesigning polar kites on Baffin Island. Polar kiting is not exactly a mainstream sport, but its evolution has been amazingly fast in the last few years, owing directly to the influx of people wanting to kite-surf. Over the last five years, the kites have become incredibly dynamic, the materials more complex, and new systems of control have been invented. The latest prototypes had just arrived from Baffin Island by FedEx.

As we took them out of the wrapping, the kites seemed extraordinarily light. They were apparently made of material designed by NASA for one of their space programmes. We immediately tossed the instruction manual to one side and started to unfurl the larger of the two kites.

Previously, we had all flown five-metre kites on a weekend course down on the south coast of England. All of us had quickly realised the power of these things. Even comparatively little kites can pull you off your feet and right across a crowded beach. They are awesomely powerful. As we unwrapped the 14-metre kite, the super-light canvas covered every inch of the floor and we all stood in silence, looking at the size of it.

'I'll be buggered if you think I'm going to clip that thing to me and stand out in the wind,' said Nick, echoing all our thoughts, and just to reinforce the point a gust of wind rattled one of the windows.

'Anyway, it looks more like a parachute than a kite,' he continued. 'Are you sure it's the right one?'

Tom picked up the manual and leafed through it for a couple of seconds.

'Looks like it,' he said. 'We're just going to have to be seriously careful out there. This wind might be a bit strong for our first day testing, but sod it. I'll go mad if I have to sit here and talk about kit modifications all day long.'

We walked to the banks of Lake Tekapo and stood for a moment, watching the winds scorch across the turquoise water. The long grass around the lake's edge was bent at a 45-degree angle and the trees rustled noisily.

We set up the five-metre on some flat ground by the side of a local hotel. I was to be the guinea pig. With a few gentle tugs on the kite lines, the thing launched like a Polaris missile and immediately started dragging me across the grass. Like some sort of demented water skier, I tried to hold on to the handles as it pulled me sideways. The others burst out laughing and then stopped when they realised there was a good chance I was going to hit the side of the hotel about 200 metres away.

Half hopping, half dragged, I tried to get the kite into the neutral part of the wind, but with little success. I looked on in horror as the fence line of the hotel rapidly approached. This was going to hurt. Suddenly, two pairs of hands grabbed me. Tom and Andy had finally caught up and were putting all their weight on my harness. Tom tripped on the uneven ground and ended up being dragged flat on his face through the mud, his arms outstretched, still holding on to the back of my harness. He later claimed it was sheer devotion to my well-being that made him cling on, but if I were being unkind I'd say he'd got his fingers caught in my belt.

After a few hours of practice, the flying started to get less erratic, but still, we could do little more than just hold the kite at the edge of the wind. The pull was just incredible. I watched as the kite caught another gust and yanked Andy completely off his feet. If we managed to get these things under control and had a few good days in Antarctica, we'd be at the pole in about a week. That is, of course, if we didn't break our necks in the first few minutes.

That evening, the weather report wasn't good. We were hoping to get up into the Fox

Mountains to start the practical side of our training, but the weather looked too bad for a helicopter to fly. The only positive aspect was that the weather fronts were irregular and we hoped that we might get a long enough break to fly up in the next few days.

Gotlieb had previously estimated that the drive to the heliport would take us about six hours. However, what he neglected to tell us was that he drove at roughly the same pace as a combine harvester. I sat in the car following him and I found it hard to relax. I could never understand people who were content to potter along at half the speed limit. Then again, perhaps this was some sort of test to teach us a lesson about patience and weather delays in Antarctica. Whatever it was, it was really starting to get to me.

Eventually, we arrived at a little village at the base of the Fox Glacier. The weather was completely shut in and there was no chance of going farther up the hill. We had all been eating huge meals to stock up before we went on to the mountain, and this further setback meant we all had way too much energy. The ominous black clouds made the air feel heavy and oppressive and did little to help alleviate our pent-up angst. We milled around for a while, before finally deciding to go for a walk in the surrounding rainforest.

For four days we hung around that tiny village at the base of the Fox Glacier waiting for a break in the weather. It was so incredibly frustrating to wake up each morning to see the blanket of cloud and the helicopters firmly locked up in the hangar. We would be leaving for Antarctica in just a couple of months and yet here was our training slowly being squandered by endless weather delays. This was the time when we should have been testing ourselves, our equipment and, most importantly, finding out whether we could work effectively as a team. I just had no idea whether I was capable of skiing to the pole, and having the days slip away from me while we sat morosely in our little hotel did little to relieve my doubts.

With cabin fever starting to set in, I decided to go for a run to try to dispel the general gloom that had come over me. I also wanted to be alone for a little while, so I set off for a beach about 10 kilometres away.

After following winding forest trails, I came down to a place called Gillespie Beach and looked upon the most glorious stretch of coastland I have ever seen. The mile or so of black-stoned beach was slightly hazy from the sea mist and bright sunshine. Huge cliffs, with waterfalls funnelling off them, rose up from the sand and disappeared into the rainforest behind. The scene looked prehistoric, like something out of *The Land that Time Forgot*, and it felt incredible to see somewhere so untouched.

It was wonderful to see something so spectacularly beautiful, with life and colour as vivid as I could remember. It was the diametric opposite of what I imagined Antarctica to be. I knew from the photographs that there would be mile after mile of ice, endlessly repeated as far as the eye could see. I knew that there would be nothing to trigger a thought, nothing to entertain the eye, as we spent the long weeks skiing south.

My image of Antarctica served only to heighten the impression of how rich this stretch of coastline was. I tried to store everything away in my mind and remember every last detail of the imposing cliffs and wonderful, pounding sea. The smell and sounds that I was finding so invigorating would be a distant memory in just a couple of months' time.

Standing, looking out to sea, I realised this was the first time I had properly relaxed in a few weeks. I had been feeling very tetchy of late, and had found myself having to bite my tongue on a couple of occasions to stop myself snapping at the others. I wasn't sure why. Possibly, it was the oppressive black cloud back at Fox village or some subliminal apprehension I was feeling about leaving for Antarctica.

Just the fact that I was feeling so pent up did not bode well at all for the expedition. Here we had been on top of each other for just a week; in Antarctica it would be two whole months of sharing a tiny tent. Once on the ice, there would be no escape or break from our teammates. I could hardly nip off for a quick run if I felt like clearing the air.

Every other expedition seemed to end up with its members hating each other by the time they got back to civilisation. Why should we be any different? It just wasn't something I had even considered when planning it all in England. Perhaps we would be risking our friendship as much as everything else?

Then again, I consoled myself, we would probably be too tired to bicker in Antarctica. Eight hours of exercise a day definitely has a habit of beating the fight out of you. Possibly, it was simply all the waiting which was getting to me now. Mooching around and squandering precious training days is something I have always been very bad at dealing with.

It was time to turn back, and I ran through the forest, arriving at the car park just as the sun was setting. Caked in mud and getting cold, I was just about to begin cursing the others for leaving me there when the headlights of our hire car came over the hill. Andy did an enormous handbrake turn right in front of me and swung open the door. Keen not to acknowledge that he had just pulled off a manoeuvre to make Starsky and Hutch proud, I said simply, 'You're late,' and we sped back to the hotel.

★   ★   ★

The next morning, Gotlieb handed round some much-needed coffee, as we had been out for a few drinks the night before. The weather was starting to close in again and it was looking as if we might have got out of bed early for nothing. With my head gently pounding, I watched the pilots sitting in the cockpit, radioing the control tower to confirm whether we could fly in these conditions. With a flick of a switch the rotors started to power up and I smiled. It was a goer.

We were the first and last flight to go up that day. The helicopter stayed under the swirling cloud and flew right up the glacier. We cruised just over the tops of the crevasses and towering seracs. Dropping over a mountain ridge, we came up to our landing site. By this time, the weather had closed in once more and everything looked uniformly white. We hovered tentatively and, as I looked down, it seemed to me to be impossible to gauge how high we were above the ice.

Suddenly, I felt cold air whooshing into the cabin. I turned to see Gotlieb open his door and then, to my horror, throw out my rucksack. That pack had everything I needed for the mountains, and to watch it tumble out of the helicopter and into the abyss left me speechless.

'To judge the distance for landing,' shouted Nick into the intercom, after seeing the bemused look on my face.

With the grey skies and grey snow, the pilot was using my rucksack to see exactly where the ground was. Fair enough, I thought, but Gotlieb could have used his own damn pack.

The skids gently touched the snow, and we jumped out to unload the baskets carrying all our gear. Within a couple of minutes the pilot gave us the thumbs-up and in a quick flurry of snow he was gone, leaving us all alone on the mountain.

With such unpredictable weather, we had decided to stay in a small refuge called Centenary Hut. It was completely snowed in when we arrived but, after a little shovelling, the door creaked open. Inside, it was big enough to accommodate a few mattresses, a little wooden table and a cooking area.

As we unpacked our equipment, snow blew up against the window and it was obvious we couldn't go for our planned ski tour. Instead, we decided to work on our survival techniques and plodded down to the flat area below the hut to practise making an igloo. Using a snow saw, we took turns carving out blocks and started to arrange them in a circular fashion. The bad weather made talking difficult, so we just got on with it and after two hours we had a fully functioning igloo. Drenched from being in the snow the whole time, we started to get cold and squeezing inside the igloo felt wonderful. The stormy weather was entirely shut out by the thick wall of snow and the light filtered through in a beautiful soft blue.

Previously, the closest I had been to an igloo was sleeping in a snow cave in the Alps. A snow cave is built on the same basic principles as an igloo, but is great deal less luxurious. I had been climbing with a friend, George, and his younger brother, Fergus, when we decided to find somewhere to sleep for the night. In the process, we very nearly killed ourselves. As we later learnt, with all these types of shelter it's vital to create proper ventilation, otherwise the cocoon of snow literally suffocates you.

We had built our snow cave and then happily sealed up the entrance and got on with cooking some food. While the pasta bubbled away on the stove, the gas gently drifted on to the snow cave's floor and after an hour or so I was feeling a little woozy. It was that same sort of heady, spaced-out feeling you get from sniffing board markers at school.

'Mate, I don't know what it is, but my head is spinning,' I said to George as he stirred the pasta on the camping stove.

'Yeah, I'm feeling a little light-headed as well. It's probably just the altitude or something.'

That was the last thing I remember that night. After a few mouthfuls of food, we all gently passed out.

In the morning, I woke up with a blinding headache. My face was sopping wet and the top of my head was stuck to the ice. I was still lying on my back but had moved in my sleep and the back of my head was right by Fergus's face. An entire night of his breathing had condensed on my head, making it soaking wet and slightly frosted. My hair was also neatly stuck to the wall of the snow cave. Confused and in a general state of discomfort, I slowly pulled my head off the ice. I can safely say that I woke up feeling more wretched and miserable than I have ever done since.

Owing to a bit of bad engineering, a chunk in the ice wall had collapsed during the night. Thankfully, this allowed some fresh air into our home-made gas chamber. Had that bit of wall not collapsed, I think we would have been one of the prime contenders for the following year's Darwin Awards. (The Darwin Awards are given to those people who manage to kill themselves in extraordinarily stupid ways. Darwin's natural selection theory comes into play as they remove their genes from the collective human gene pool and thus help the evolution of the human race.) However, the one amazing thing about sleeping in igloos or snow caves is the incredible light in the morning. As the sun shines through the ice, a beautiful soft blue light diffracts around you and it feels as if you're frozen inside a giant ice cube looking out.

The next morning it was beautifully sunny and the wind was gently blowing. We went back to the flat area to practise flying our kites. We unfurled the five-metre and, although the wind wasn't strong enough to really get us moving fast, it was still exciting enough. Leaning out on the harness, it was possible to ski at almost 90 degrees to the wind and we zoomed up and down the white expanse.

The wind dropped a little more and so we decided it was just about safe to bring out the 14-metre. As Andy unrolled the kite, it made the five-metre look like a baby. With one tug on the lines it whooshed into the air, and I was immediately jerked along behind.

I tried to edge my skis and manoeuvre the kite out of the main power zone of the wind, but it just seemed to sit there, dragging me faster and faster behind it. There must have been about 200 acres of flat snow but even so I soon felt as if I was running out of space. I tried to tack back to where the others were, but the massive kite had me completely at its mercy. A few seconds later and a few ominous-looking cliffs seemed to appear just in front of me.

I tried to tack once more and succeeded only in getting the kite directly above my head. This is theoretically the neutral zone of the wind, yet I was still being lifted off my feet. I immediately had visions of being sucked up into the sky and floating off over a mountain ridge, but then the kite dived to the left again. Off I went, back towards the cliffs. A few seconds later and the inevitable happened. The kite crashed straight into the rocks and the fabric and lines became tangled and snared.

I could see some of the lines already being sawn in half as they rubbed up and down the rocks. I shouted at the others for some help. They shouted back that they couldn't hear what I was saying, I did likewise, and for a couple more minutes we shouted incomprehensibly at each other.

Starting to get cross, I took off my skis, anchored one of the main kite lines and began to climb round the side of the cliff. The couloir started to get steeper and I quickly realised that I didn't have any crampons or for that matter a rope. I got to the top and looked at the sad wreck of the kite, its semi-inflated canvas flapping with each gust of wind. I thought about trying to untangle it myself, but it was right on the edge of the cliff and I really needed to be roped up and abseil down a little. I followed my tracks down and stomped over to the others, seething with rage.

'Why the hell didn't you guys come and help me?'

'Er, you didn't ask us to,' replied Tom a little defensively. After all, I was the one who had just trashed the brand-new kite.

'Well, it was pretty obvious by all my hand movements.' They all looked at me impassively, patiently waiting for me to apologise for destroying the kite.

'. . . and besides, the 14-metre is too big,' I continued. 'There's no point practising with it as we'll never be able to get it under control in Antarctica.'

Eventually, with Gotlieb anchoring me on a rope, I managed to unhook the tangled mess from the cliff. Miraculously, only three lines were severed and the kite itself was undamaged. Andy managed to repair it in an hour or two and then casually sailed around controlling it perfectly. I could be such an idiot sometimes.

★　★　★

During the night the pressure dropped ten millibars. Bad weather was here again. A decent ski tour was out of the question, so we decided to practise a few crevasse rescues. A snowstorm swirled around our little party as we tentatively picked our way across the glacier looking for a suitable place to practise. After about half an hour, we found a deep crevasse. Setting up all our equipment, we got ready to drop someone in.

Andy was first up and shuffled forward towards a tiny crack in the snow's surface. I was second on the rope and, having never dropped someone into a large hole, was pretty uncertain as to what was going to happen next. Andy weighs more than me, and I was expecting an almighty jolt and then a desperate effort to stop myself getting pulled in as well. Instead, as he went through the snow bridge, there was a pitiful tug on my harness and I found I could easily take the weight by braking with my skis.

What I had failed to appreciate was that when a person falls into a crevasse the rope saws into the side of the snow. This creates a huge amount of friction, which, in turn, absorbs all the impact of the fall. Unable to see anything owing to the storm, Tom and Nick shouted over, asking whether Andy had even gone in yet.

Normally, someone falling into a crevasse would be a life-threatening emergency. People would be shouting and rushing about, desperately trying to get the poor bugger out as soon as possible. But here, the point of the exercise was to try to get out of the crevasse ourselves. While Andy desperately tried to haul himself out, there was nothing really for the rest of us to do. We made a couple of anchors with the skis and then tied up the rope. Someone had brought a thermos, so we all went over to our packs, sat down and had a cup of tea. It was quite surreal to be sitting down and chatting, while one of our teammates was frantically dangling over a 400-foot drop.

Fifteen minutes later, Andy emerged, covered in ice and sweating profusely. He walked over to where we were sitting and watched us talking for a couple of seconds. Slowly, Nick noticed him standing there.

'All right, mate?'

'What are you guys doing sitting over here?' Andy said in disbelief.

'Having a cup of tea. Do you want one?'

'Shouldn't someone be holding on to the rope?'

'Well, we anchored it using a couple of skis and it seemed to do the trick. So we thought we'd have a quick cuppa while we waited,' replied Nick sheepishly.

'What if the anchors came out? There'd be nothing to stop the rope running through.'

'Well, I suppose that's probably true,' said Nick, 'but it felt pretty solid.' We all murmured softly in agreement. With Andy still a little shocked at our general lack of safety consciousness, we elected that from now on we would have someone attached to the rope at all times. It was a good idea, especially as I was next up.

Walking up to the little fracture in the snow and then jumping up and down is definitely one of the most unnatural things I have ever done. From the very first time you ever go into the mountains, it is relentlessly drilled into you to avoid crevasses. Almost everything a climber learns about glacier travel is geared towards one goal — how to avoid going into one of these holes.

I jumped up and down, but each time tried to land as softly as I could. Something in the rational side of your brain just doesn't allow you to try too hard. Suddenly, the ground went beneath my feet and I fell through up to my waist. For a couple of seconds, my legs kicked out into space and then, as I uttered a quick expletive, the rest of my body slipped through.

The rope snapped taut and I swung limply in midair. From where I had broken through the snow, light poured into the crevasse, illuminating a vast blue cavern about 400 feet deep. After the wind and snow on the surface, the crevasse seemed utterly still. Everything was quiet and the sheer walls of ice dropped down deep below me into the gloom.

My harness made a small creaking sound, which scared me enough to get on with the practice. It was a great deal harder than I had thought. Snow fell into my face from the lip of the crevasse and my rucksack pulled me off balance. My large outer mittens also made it difficult to set up the locking devices, which I needed to haul myself out.

As I inched my way up the rope, I noticed that my ice axe had gone. I checked all my clips and then looked down to find it had fallen about five metres below me. I swung to one side to get a better look and couldn't believe my luck. The ice axe was balanced on a tiny ledge sticking out from the otherwise perfectly smooth walls of ice. Somehow the weight of its shaft had stopped it falling into the abyss. I couldn't have balanced it there if I had tried.

I didn't have enough rope to get down to retrieve it, so I shouted for the others through the gap above my head. After a lot of bawling, the others finally stopped drinking tea and Tom's face appeared, looking inquisitively at me. After I had explained my embarrassing predicament, he smiled at me and said, 'Dickhead,' before leaving to organise some more rope to be lowered down.

The weight on the rope makes it cut through the lip of the crevasse and an ice axe is essential to hack away at the snow surrounding it. It has been known for over-zealous climbers, desperate to get out of the crevasse, to hack away at the snow only to find themselves inadvertently severing their own lifeline. I'd hate to die like that. It's like sawing off the branch you are standing on.

Each of us in turn had a go at trying to get out of the crevasse and learnt a great deal about the techniques required. I had no idea how frequently we would be crossing crevassed areas in Antarctica, but I knew there were enough of them to make it an inevitability. Crevasses were something I had always been terribly afraid of. I knew that if the initial fall didn't kill you, then the sheer walls of perfectly smooth ice would make escape all but impossible.

By dropping ourselves into the crevasse over and over again, I felt the fear might somehow be contained. If we were proficient with all the techniques involved, then maybe in Antarctica there would really be nothing to worry about.

Early next morning, I got out of my sleeping bag. I desperately needed the toilet and listlessly shuffled across the hut floor, trying to pretend that I wasn't really awake. With half-shut eyes, I put on my boots and opened the door. A huge flurry of snow, cold and general unpleasantness hit me, and as soon as my pathetically slow reflexes kicked in I slammed the door shut again. It felt as if someone had been waiting behind the door and had just slapped me with a wet fish. The outhouse was only five paces from where I was standing, but I just couldn't deal with padding through the snow and the spindrift going down my neck. I turned, resigning myself to the fact that I was going to have to endure a full bladder, and got back into my sleeping bag. 'Weather?' said someone in a groggy voice. 'Rubbish,' came my reply, and we all went back to sleep.

All day the wind blew, the snow fell and it was miserably cold. It would have been pointless and, in the zero visibility, dangerous to go outside. Instead, we spent the whole day in the hut, reading, playing cards and trying to keep warm. I found a book written by an American who had spent seventeen years in solitary confinement in prison, which certainly put my own confinement in perspective, and I tried to relax. It was frustrating not being able to exercise outside, but I had heard numerous stories of polar explorers spending days stuck inside the confines of their tent. Patience was not a virtue I possessed in abundance, so it was probably no bad thing that it was being tested in New Zealand.

The next day, we hoped for something better, but it seemed pretty unlikely that we were going to be able to ski out. The weather forecast on the radio the night before had been appalling — winds gusting 100 kph, new fronts and a lot of snow. It therefore came as a big surprise that the morning dawned bright and clear. We set off early, and after about two hours of skiing across the plateau we reached the top of the Hars Pass. Coming down past the Fox Glacier the route was beautiful, skirting alongside the incredible ice fall and skiing in soft powder snow.

After another couple of hours of skiing, we finally reached the end of the snowline and a small patch of flattened snow, no bigger than a couple of coffee tables placed side by side. Gotlieb got out his radio and within five minutes a helicopter arrived, landing perfectly on the impossibly small landing site. We charged down the valley, again keeping underneath the cloud, and managed to arrive in Fox village just before the next front came in.

After unloading all our gear, we drove into the village to get something to eat. I sat feeling a little ambivalent about how the training had gone. Partly it was the bad weather, which had prevented us doing more, and partly Gotlieb's reluctance to take any sort of risk. It seemed such a shame that the training had not been more gruelling. When I left England, I assumed that these few weeks were really going to test us. I wanted long days, cold weather and that contented, exhausted feeling by the time we were ready to pack up and go home.

Although we had certainly learnt good crevasse technique and some helpful pointers about the kit we should take, I just didn't feel that we had pushed ourselves physically. I had wanted to get a good idea of what it would be like to travel for days on end in Antarctica and, sitting in the restaurant, I didn't feel any closer. The simple reality was that only Nick, on his Everest attempt, had done anything like a sixty-day expedition. The rest of us had been nowhere close.

From a team-building perspective, it had been useful. We had all got on incredibly well and Andy had proved himself to be more than capable. However, apart from the night with the kea birds, we had hardly been under a great deal of stress, so it was difficult to tell how people might react under more extreme circumstances. If we rationed too little fuel or snagged the lines of our kite in Antarctica, I doubted help would be quite so easy to find. I wondered whether our tempers might fray a little more easily out there.

We arrived at the airport check-in desk with only half an hour before the plane left. As I sprinted through the terminal, a customs official stopped me and rifled through my bags. With a few shakes of his head and a

'You're old enough to know better', he removed some nail scissors from my washbag. Strangely, he said nothing about the fact that I was also holding a two-foot-long steel bar used for the kites, which would have made a formidable cosh. With only a few minutes remaining, we just made the last call on to the plane and settled down for the long flight home.

As the cabin lights dimmed and most of the passengers pulled up their airline blankets to get some sleep, I wondered whether I was ready for Antarctica. I shut my eyes and thought about it for a few minutes. I should probably be fitter, heavier and have some idea what it was like to pull a fully laden sled. My kiting skills were painfully inadequate and I had managed to drop my ice axe down the only crevasse I had ever seen the inside of. As my school report cards used to say, there was definitely 'room for improvement'.

I turned off the reading light and tried to settle down into my seat. The person next to me began snoring softly and somewhere near the back of the plane a baby started crying. It was another twenty-two hours before we would be landing at Heathrow. It looked as if it was going to be a long flight.

I turned uncomfortably in my seat and thought about it once more. Was I really prepared for Antarctica? Somehow, it just didn't feel likely. Then again, I thought, I don't think anyone is ever ready for that place.

3

Death by Sponsorship

'Money is better than poverty, if only for financial reasons.'
— Woody Allen

Make no mistake: trying to persuade someone to give you £180,000 is no easy thing.

Some people scoff when I tell them that raising sponsorship is undoubtedly the hardest part of an expedition. They picture climbing up mountains or traversing frozen wastelands to be unimaginably hard. In comparison to trying to prise money out of the tightly clenched fists of unexcitable executives, the odd mountain ridge is absolute child's play.

Sponsorship is an utterly exhausting process, perfectly capable of turning your hair grey with stress. This I know.

Unfortunately for us, the Antarctic continent is extremely remote. This fact alone makes any expedition to its shores mind-blowingly expensive. The logistics are staggering and so is the price of aviation fuel.

Since we had first made the decision to attempt the South Pole in that old London pub, we had exactly nine months in order to raise the necessary funds. This is not unlike someone asking me to come up with the money to buy a small house before my next birthday. It wasn't going to be easy. We could have all the enthusiasm in the world, but unless we had £180,000 in the bank, everything else was just scribbles on meaningless bits of paper.

Our Achilles heel was the logistics. We wanted to follow in the footsteps of Scott and Shackleton and, one hundred years ago, they obviously came in by boat. For their journey into the interior, their closest natural harbour was at McMurdo Sound on the Ross Ice Shelf. We could also have travelled by water, for a greatly reduced price, but that would have meant overwintering in Antarctica. The long dark of four months in minus-60-degree temperatures would undoubtedly have driven me mad. It had been known to happen to the old explorers, and they had had an entire ship's worth of men to talk to; we were just four.

So, it had to be by plane. To get to McMurdo by air is actually quite simple — if you're a scientist. From New Zealand, planes fly regularly across the Southern Ocean and refuel at McMurdo on their way to the pole. However, any request to catch a ride on one of these flights falls on deaf ears, owing mainly to an expedition that took place a few years previously.

Sir Edmund Hillary's son, Peter Hillary, led a team attempting to reach the pole and back to the coast again via McMurdo. After much negotiation, he had managed to persuade the scientists to fly them in. A few weeks later and everything had gone wrong. Food had been contaminated by fuel and the team's morale broke down entirely. It turned into a bitter, acrimonious affair, joyously followed by an already sceptical media and culminating in the Americans having to fly them back to the edge of Antarctica.

Subsequently, the scientists have clammed up a bit with regard to explorers and are reluctant to let anyone on their planes who doesn't have a PhD. This gave us but one choice — Adventure Networks International (ANI). That's not to say that ANI is an undesirable company, far from it, but two major factors meant that they were a poor alternative. First, they fly out of Punta Arenas in Chile and their closest landing strip on Antarctica was on the opposite side to where we wanted to be. Second, they are the only operators available to non-scientists, making negotiations on price more of the 'take it or leave it' variety. Their managing director, Anne Kershaw, was reputed to have the face of an angel and a business savvy that would put Rupert Murdoch to shame.

We spoke to Anne and agreed to meet up on one of her visits to London. It was a difficult occasion to dress for. We wanted to look relatively scruffy to have a chance at haggling over the price, but not so badly dressed that we looked entirely incompetent. Although an hour late and entirely unapologetic, Anne was delightful and seemed to have the answer to all our questions. When it came to discussing the price, it soon became pretty obvious that we were way out of our depth. Like two fresh-faced tourists haggling over a bribe with an African policeman, we found ourselves in one of those uncomfortable situations where both parties knew that one of us didn't have a leg to stand on.

From her handbag came a breakdown of the costs and we 'ummed' and 'erred' in a convincing sort of way. In truth, the huge amount didn't really faze me, as it was far more money than I could really appreciate. If she had asked to borrow a hundred pounds to get home, then I would have started to sweat, but £180,000 was so far out of my league that I didn't bat an eyelid.

After a forty-five-minute meeting, I waved goodbye with her last words ringing ominously in my ears. 'Deposit the money by the end of September and we'll sort all the logistics for you.'

I had to sit down and have a sugary tea. September was the following month. I've never felt so skint in all my life.

★ ★ ★

Pitching for sponsorship is a curious thing. It makes your self-esteem oscillate on a daily basis. One minute, a multinational's managing director is referring to you as a heroic 'polar explorer' (despite the fact that at this stage I hadn't been anywhere near either pole) and the next you are haggling with the secretary at a reception desk for five minutes of some minor office clerk's time. Some shake your hand with unrestrained enthusiasm, others sit in mute disdain, positively annoyed that your boyish antics have wasted so much of their time.

It is an utterly exhausting job trying to raise money, owing mainly to the fact that the people who have it naturally don't want to share it with you. Like one of those suicidally bored holiday reps at Butlins, you have to be constantly enthusiastic about everything, despite the fact that it looks as if you're about to receive your eighth rejection of the day.

We basically went for the 'sling enough mud' theory and wrote literally hundreds of letters to anyone who might have a vague interest in polar exploration.

Our original selection criteria for companies involved looking at the products or services they were marketing and trying to make some brilliant association with our expedition. Anything that mentioned the words 'snow', 'polar' or 'south' immediately came under fire. As the letters of rejection slowly came back, our links to different brands became more and more tenuous. We racked our brains to try to align ourselves with different companies' slogans, but the results often weren't inspiring. It got to the stage where we found ourselves trying to rhyme company names with geographical features in Antarctica. The work was unrewarding to say the least.

After several weeks of continued rejection and massive self-doubt, we got some interest from a couple of food and drink corporations. Being in our mid-twenties, we fell into that heavily clichéd 'young and fulfilling your dreams' image that big brands are always trying to promote. At each sponsorship meeting, Tom and I nodded enthusiastically about the latest demographic trends or brand identity initiatives, basically happy to promote almost anything short of the Nazi Party or tampons.

We already knew that if sponsors were prepared to give us money, then we would have to compromise a little. If you're famous or experienced you usually have to do so only to a small degree, but we were neither, and it soon became apparent that we would have to take what we were given. I had many a concerned moment thinking we would have to spend our time at the pole grinning inanely, while pretending to enjoy a low-fat yogurt in minus 40 degrees.

The only thing that consoled us was that throughout history explorers have had trouble raising finance. In 1908–9, Ernest Shackleton sailed to Buenos Aires fully aware that he hadn't raised sufficient money for the expedition. Captain Scott, Wally Herbert, Borge Ousland — all these titans of polar travel have had enormous difficulty finding generous sponsors, no matter how big their name or how noble their cause.

After three rather hopeful meetings, Snickers chocolate bars declared that they were seriously considering sponsoring us for £100,000. The marketing budget would have to be ratified by their head office in Switzerland, said their PR company, but the UK boys had given the all-clear.

I simply could not believe our luck. As we left their austere office building, Tom and I tried to look casual, as if this sort of thing happened every day, but only made it as far as the reception desk before bursting out laughing. It felt wonderful to have this affirmation that someone was finally listening, that they believed in what we were trying to achieve and, most importantly, that they were giving us significantly more money than I had ever seen in my life. Preparations could now begin in earnest.

I was particularly pleased that Snickers had come on board as the title sponsors, because about two years previously there had been a slight misunderstanding.

I had been on a climbing expedition with Tom, three other friends and some Russian climbers, in Kyrgyzstan. This landlocked and obscure republic used to be part of the old Soviet empire, tucked up against the Chinese border in central Asia. We had managed to find an entire mountain range that had never before been climbed and were attempting to put new routes up some of the highest peaks. It was a thrilling time, treading where no one had ever been before and having the honour of giving each of the mountains we climbed a name.

The highest in the range, Peak Kurumdy, was also unclimbed, but unfortunately had been named by a Russian surveying team many years previously. At 6,642 metres, it is one of the highest unclimbed peaks in the world. After ten days of trying to force ourselves up a very unstable ridge, we managed to reach almost 6,000 metres. With persistent storms and conditions worsening by the hour, we turned back from the summit, our tail firmly tucked between our legs.

A couple of days later we arrived in base camp. Our initial joy at having a chance to finally relax faded with the news that we had completely run out of food. Cut off from the outside world, all we could do was wait for our pre-arranged transport to arrive and spend the days moping around camp, lying on the grass feeling gaunt and unhappy.

One of the film crew, who until recently had never left inner London, sent us all insane by constantly complaining that he was hungry. Rather portly and obviously not the most abstemious of characters, he lumbered around camp constantly mumbling about his stomach. I could see the others eyeing him up dangerously and thanked my lucky stars I

71

wasn't the fattest kid in town.

We spent three days living off stock cubes and some wild mushrooms. I was lying on the grass, trying to remember what happened at the end of *Lord of the Flies*, when George, one of the climbers, came into the mess tent chewing on something.

With a huge grin, he explained how he'd had the brilliant idea of raiding the medical supplies and was happily chomping his way through a pack of antiseptic throat lozenges. We all pounced on the bag, eating our way through the most innocuous pills and happy to have something solid passing our lips. Imbued with this new-found strength, we decided to do one last climb before the truck arrived the next day to pick us up.

The morning of the climb, I was last into the mess tent and, as I ducked under the canvas, our Russian guide Anatoly threw me a Snickers bar. As the others were already there, I presumed he had had the good sense to hold back five chocolate bars just in case of such an eventuality and everyone had been given their share.

The day was glorious, with perfect snow conditions and warm sunshine. Despite the ideal surroundings, I felt weak from lack of food and regularly stopped to nibble at my precious chocolate. Then at midday we stopped for a rest and the others immediately began to crowd round me, salivating quite alarmingly. I suddenly realised that they were waiting for me to dole out the single chocolate bar. It immediately dawned on me that I was the only one Anatoly had given any chocolate to and now I had to tell the others that I had eaten the whole thing myself.

This may seem like no big deal, but to a group of guys half deranged from hunger and the side effects of the medical supplies this was the lowest form of betrayal. Their eyes looked at me with an exhausted disbelief that I hope never to see again. Since then, I have felt horribly guilty whenever I pass a sweet shop.

So two years later, by getting Snickers to sign on the dotted line and come in as the major sponsors for the expedition, I thought somehow I had been given a chance to atone for my previous mistake. By a strange twist of fate, I was being allowed to make up for that terrible day by providing money and as many Snickers bars as they could eat.

Two months after agreeing to come in as title sponsors, Snickers withdrew their support owing to 'internal problems'. I couldn't believe it; we now had to go through the whole sponsorship rigmarole again. As I phoned Tom and told him the crushing news, the guilt came rushing back. I vowed never to eat chocolate again.

A few weeks passed and, after several meetings, it looked as if an insurance company called Hastings Direct wanted to sponsor the expedition. I wasn't sure as to the exact link between car insurance and polar exploration, but given the current state of affairs we were in no position to be picky. Unfortunately, they couldn't afford the full cost of the expedition and so their managing director started speaking to a few other companies to drum up some support. As all our leads started to dry up, we focused all our efforts on trying to woo Hastings Direct.

With the sponsorship game there is a direct correlation between press inches and the opening of sponsors' wallets. Our solution was simple — we were going to have to get ourselves in the papers.

We shamelessly plastered our jackets with Hastings Direct logos and made phone calls to every TV and newspaper station we could think of. I soon learnt that talking to journalists is very much like fishing — you have to get them to latch on to some sort of interesting or original 'hook'. The problem was that I have always been an absolutely rotten fisherman. I have very little patience and, as far as I can see, it's a great deal easier using enormous great nets. With this in mind, we trawled through the lists of newspapers and glossy magazines entirely indiscriminate as to whom exactly we were targeting.

The plan was to lay down a wealth of information before the journalist could politely cut us off. The majority of my conversations went something like this.

'Good morning. I am part of the Commonwealth Antarctic Expedition. Have you ever heard of us?'

'No, sorry. Can't say I have.'

'Hmm. Surprising. Anyway . . . ' And then I would launch into this tirade of statistics, interesting trivia and royal personages involved. Hardly pausing to draw breath or even check whether the journalist was still on the line, I would let it all come out in one effusive burst. After I had exhausted my list of conversation prompts, I would wait for a response, imagining the captivated journalist to be scribbling furiously.

'Really, how interesting,' the journalist would invariably say, somewhat flatly. 'Why don't you send me something via e-mail?' Then an e-mail address would be given in such a perfunctory manner that I suspected they might be deliberately trying to mislead me. I doubted it would stay in their inbox for more than a nanosecond.

Occasionally, however, a paper would find interesting the fact that Tom would be the youngest Briton or that we were using kites to power us across the ice. During my first few conversations I was relatively modest and realistic about what we were attempting, but only a couple of hours later I had resorted to more desperate measures. I could hear myself massively inflating whichever part of the expedition they seemed to find interesting. It was alarming how quickly I had turned into this pushy, loud-mouthed character, who seemed happy to shamelessly name-drop at the slightest provocation. It's no wonder the journalists didn't want to talk to me. I wouldn't have wanted to either.

Tom was having a little more success and had managed to get himself on to the news programme *London Tonight*. I sat watching him on television, plastered head to toe in logos. I could see him starting to sweat in the hot lights. I watched, feeling nervous for him, and hoped to God that Hastings Direct would be impressed by the performance.

As he spoke, I thought about how ridiculous it all felt. Here he was telling the world (or what seemed like it then) that we would soon be embarking on this great, heroic adventure, and yet we were no closer to leaving than we had been when we first thought of the idea. We had not a single sponsorship pound in the bank. Nothing, not a penny, and here we were, a couple of weeks before leaving, announcing it to anybody who'd listen.

Looking back, I clearly remember how depressed I felt, watching the news programme that night. A wave of impotent frustration welled up inside me. At that moment, I suddenly realised how bleak our chances actually were. It just seemed utterly hopeless, as there was nothing else that could be done. Trying to come to terms with the fact that I had just wasted an entire year on a completely pointless venture took all the fight out of me.

Standing in England, a million miles away from where I wanted to be, I couldn't think of any plausible way to raise the money. As the presenter wished Tom the best of luck and he got up to leave, I thought that I should really start preparing myself for the inevitable. In a couple of days, I would have to return to the small wreck that was my professional career.

★　★　★

The day after the interview, Tom got a phone call from a guy called Andrew Cooney. After introducing himself, he promptly informed Tom that he intended to be in Antarctica that season. As he went on to explain, he was attempting to ski to the South Pole via the Ross Ice Shelf. This was going to cause a big problem for us. We had been telling all the potential sponsors and newsmen how little trodden this route was and how special we were for attempting it. Having another team skiing right beside us would have looked a little odd, to say the least. However, after they had talked a bit more, it appeared that Andrew had got his ice shelves mixed up and he was in fact skiing via the Ronne Ice Shelf on the opposite side of Antarctica. Tom sighed in relief.

Then Andrew announced that he was also billing himself as the youngest man aiming to reach the South Pole. This whole 'youngest' angle was one Tom had been flaunting to the press. So far, it had proved to be an effective way of drumming up interest. It wasn't a record that particularly interested him, but of all our hooks this one seemed to be working the best. Bugger. We were going to have to think of something else.

'So, how exactly are you guys looking to fund the whole expedition?' asked Andrew casually.

'At the moment there's a company called

Hastings Direct who are keen to come in as title sponsors,' replied Tom frankly. It was no big secret. We had just been on the news plastered in their logos.

Our exact situation at the time was that Hastings Direct were keen to come in as title sponsors, but didn't have the budget to fund our entire expedition. In an effort to make up the deficit, their managing director had been searching around trying to find some subsidiary sponsors.

We knew that if we had a big commitment from Hastings Direct then attracting smaller sponsors would be no great problem. Over the last few days, we had also been making some calls and some of the smaller companies we had spoken to were definitely showing a bit of life.

Andrew continued to ask about our sponsorship and how Hastings Direct were involved, but Tom decided to change the subject.

They talked some more, about equipment and routes, with Tom openly discussing all the progress we had made so far. From previous climbing expeditions, we had learnt how invaluable the exchange of information between teams and individuals could be. If one pair of boots was fantastically comfortable, while another pair immediately let you down, then it was obviously important to share that information and stop another poor sod making the same mistake. With about a hundred people having skied to the pole, it's hardly like Formula One, where every new invention has to be kept under wraps.

A few minutes later, they rang off amicably and Tom thought little more about it.

We got on with our preparations and started assembling the equipment we would need. Gore-Tex jackets had to be sent over from America, skis and bindings from Norway, and boots made by two little German brothers living inside the Arctic Circle. It would all take weeks to arrive and so, from a financial point of view, we basically put the whole lot on credit. Our only option was to hope for a refund if the sponsorship money never materialised.

Most manufacturers of outdoor clothing obviously cater for the more fashionable skiing market rather than the minuscule polar one. With so few people attempting either pole each year, it isn't exactly cost effective for them to produce clothing specifically designed for that purpose. The net result is that you have to make your own little adjustments to each bit of kit, which often involves knowing how to sew competently. It's therefore not uncommon to find hard, wizened polar explorers sitting in a group, crocheting for all they're worth.

All our alterations were designed to seal our clothing from the wind and cold, yet still allow enough air to circulate. This would minimise sweating and allow us to breathe freely. In addition to this, I managed to design my own 'willy warmer' which consisted of a windproof, fleece-covered flap that tucked neatly inside my trousers. Losing a toe I could live with, but I wasn't prepared to risk anything else.

As important as buying the right equipment is, it's no use if you're not up to the challenge physically. The weeks of writing sponsorship proposals and keeping up the pressure on marketing departments had left me unhealthy and more than a little puny. So far, the sum total of my fitness drive involved a few half-hearted jogs and mostly giving up smoking. It was pathetic, and the incredible speed at which time seemed to be passing seemed only to exacerbate the problem.

I had read about polar explorers training by dragging tractor tyres over the hills. This was supposed to be the closest equivalent to pulling a sled on the ice, but living in London I didn't have any hills, nor had I seen any tractors of late. However, after some haggling, I managed to get hold of some grubby old minibus tyres, which seemed close enough, and I thought the sand traps that run round Hyde Park might serve as hills.

I unloaded the tyres, fixed them via a long rope to my harness, and then set off. I meant to go for just one hour, as this was to be my first training session. It was hard work, much harder than I had expected, and soon sweat was beading down my face. Having never dragged a sled on the ice, I had no idea whether this was much harder or, heaven forbid, easier than what I would have to do for eight hours a day for sixty days. Suddenly the enormity of what we were trying to accomplish was made abundantly clear to me.

At first I didn't notice the stares. Then, about five minutes into the run, I looked up and saw little groups of people pointing and laughing. Obviously this wasn't an everyday occurrence in one of the royal parks. People seemed utterly bemused by what this red-faced Englishman was trying to achieve. As the tyres scraped and bounced over the ground, the sand kicked up behind me, engulfing dog-walkers and picnickers in great clouds of dust.

A rotund man in shorts and a jaunty panama hat stood by the side of the sand trap and seemed to be waiting for me to draw level with him.

'Say there! Young fella!'

I stopped and, breathing heavily, pulled the tyres up next to me to relieve the tension in the line.

'What you running around with those tyres for?' he asked in a thick American accent.

'I'm in training for the South Pole,' I said, wiping the sweat from my eyes and trying to sound as if I did this kind of thing on a regular basis.

'You're gonna drag car tyres all the way to the South Pole?' he asked incredulously.

'No,' I said, shaking my head and smiling. 'This is just the training. Out in Antarctica, I'll be pulling a sled.'

'Oh,' he said wistfully, and then added, 'So, what's going to be in the sled?'

'Food, gas, clothing, that sort of stuff. Everything we need to survive for about sixty days.'

He nodded slowly and then, with a wave of his hand, motioned goodbye. As a quick afterthought he added, 'Mind you don't get eaten by polar bears down there.'

'I'll be sure to watch my step,' I said, and with that, thought I'd better start running again.

After forty-five minutes my tyres were

completely full of sand and I was exhausted. I hadn't expected to give up quite so soon, and I had been forced to stop on the opposite side of the park to where my car was. It was getting dark and I was pretty sure no taxi driver would pick me up, given the current state of my 'luggage'. I unclipped myself from the tyres, ran back to my car and then drove back to pick them up. Trying to force them into the boot of my sister's little car, I forgot about the tons of sand they had collected. Fortunately my sister is still living in Australia and hasn't yet come back to the UK. When she does, she'll probably think that I've gone on a hell of a lot of beach trips.

The Hyde Park 'walk of shame' became a daily feature, although when Andy or Tom accompanied me it wasn't so bad. With two of us it was more obvious we were training for something, rather than being some random nut with a couple of car tyres and a bit of string. As the weeks passed, the training definitely became easier. We upped our running time and our lower backs became used to the load. It was a strange type of exercise, mainly because of the gradual but constant resistance. As with running a marathon, we were never really out of breath, nor sweating a huge amount, but the gentle resistance just seemed to sap the energy out of our thighs.

One morning, Andy and I were getting ready when a red-faced jogger stopped in front of us. With his hands on his knees, desperately wheezing for air, he falteringly explained how he came running every morning in the park.

'For weeks now I have been running here and couldn't work out for the life of me what was making these lines through the sand traps,' he said, his chest heaving up and down. 'Every day I would try to work out why someone would spend their time laboriously smoothing these sections in the sand.' He pointed to the track coming from the boot of my car to where we were standing.

We smiled and apologised vaguely for unintentionally causing him such grief.

'Every day it had me going,' he added, and with a smile he set off once more. This time, however, he had about him the satisfied air of someone who'd just solved the riddle of the crop circles.

During that same session, Andy and I were by the road that bisects the park when police motorbikes started stopping traffic in front of us. Moments later, a parade of cars came cruising past, in the centre of which was the Queen's. We saw Her Majesty staring languidly out of the window, until her eyes fixed on two idiots dragging tyres through one of her parks. This was the first time I had ever seen the Queen in the flesh, and for the briefest of seconds I saw her face bunch up in confusion as she wondered what on earth we were doing. I imagined Phil the Greek being woken from his mid-afternoon nap by a sharp nudge in the ribs and a demand from the Queen that we be ejected forthwith.

The other part of our training was to put on weight, and plenty of it. Almost every article concerning polar exploration goes into self-indulgent detail about the number of calories that a human body burns at high latitudes. The cold, strenuous exercise and length of the expedition often mean that explorers lose frightening amounts of body fat.

Books like *Mind over Matter* by Ranulph Fiennes certainly play on this theme and were enough to terrify us into wondering what was going to happen to us from a physiological perspective. Obviously, unlike Fiennes, we weren't attempting an unsupported crossing of the continent, but, given that he is billed in the Guinness Book of Records as 'the greatest living explorer', we were definitely worried. We had never so much as put a foot in the polar regions and, as such, thought we were going to age about sixty years, lose half our body weight and be missing the majority of our toes.

Fiennes' teammate, Dr Mike Stroud, had famously calculated that during one day on that expedition he burnt over 11,500 calories. Given that an average man consumes around 2,500 per day and running a marathon burns approximately 5,000, it meant that we were either going to have to consume an unfeasible amount of food each day or we'd need sizeable love handles to eat into.

At school I was always one of the skinny ones and viewed food simply as a means of refuelling. Previously I had assumed that trying to put on weight would be superb. I imagined the joy of settling down and gorging myself with cream cakes and chocolate biscuits. When fellow diners looked across, disgusted by the spectacle, I could smile back at them, the food loosely stuck in between my teeth, and explain that I was heading off to Antarctica. The reality of it all was quite different.

Everyone, from my mother to my girl-friend, from business colleagues to cousins, took it upon themselves to try to force-feed me. I could barely leave the house without someone trying to buy me a pack of lard or a string of pork sausages. Like a child being perpetually told to finish their plate, I would sit morosely at the dinner table, pushing the food from side to side. Invariably, my girlfriend Robyn would be watching like a hawk from the kitchen, while I sat despondently at the dinner table. With aching jaws, I would gulp down another mouthful, shuffling the food glumly around the plate and dreading the arrival of yet another high-caloried concoction.

I imagine it must be the reverse of someone trying to diet. Food became an utter nuisance, which was both time consuming and unpleasant. I had too much to get on with, and eating now seemed to occupy most of my day. One night, Robyn took me to an American rib restaurant in London, hoping to take advantage of the all-you-can-eat offer.

After an entire rack of ribs and a small tray of chips, I was starting to feel a little queasy. Leaning back to allow the kilogram of food to sit a little more comfortably in my stomach, I noticed a sign hanging behind her on the wall. It detailed the annual winners of the 'Rack of Ribs' competition held at the restaurant every 4 July. In the female category alone, a woman named Lisa 'The Hog' O'Reilly had eaten a total of seven racks in one sitting. I did some calculations and realised that was approximately six feet of continuous meat. Her boyfriend must be so proud.

The net result of such excessive gluttony was a total body weight increase of exactly five pounds. The only apparent physical difference was a small bump that had appeared on the bottom of my stomach. After three days in Antarctica it would disappear completely and I would be back to square one. If only I had saved all that money spent on food, I would have been able to fund half the trip.

★ ★ ★

Back in the office, Tom gave me a call to say that he had heard nothing from Hastings Direct. As we had discovered from Snickers pulling out and other sponsors gently falling by the wayside, when they went quiet was the time for us to panic. We understood the reasons for their silence a little later that day, when Anne Kershaw at ANI phoned.

'I've got some bad news,' she said sympathetically. 'I've just been contacted by Hastings Direct and asked to put a guy called Andrew Cooney down for the expedition to the South Pole.'

With that all our fears and suspicions had just been realised. All the effort we had spent, the hours and hours writing proposals, making calls and trying to get Hastings Direct on board, had just gone up in smoke.

'I know that you were hoping to get this sponsor yourselves, so I can only assume that this isn't the case any more. I'll extend the deadline for the first payment of the money, but I can only push it back a week at the most.'

With our most promising sponsor now gone, things looked bleaker than ever. The South Pole faded once again into a surreal and abstract notion. A place so far beyond my reach that it felt pointless even trying. The unlikely hopes I had set so much store by had collapsed without a fight. A year's work destroyed in a conversation that lasted less than a minute.

For the next two weeks before our flight to Chile, Tom did his best to persuade Hastings to continue to look at sponsoring our expedition. The problem, as always, simply came down to money. A single place on a commercial trip cost £35,000, whereas our expedition would cost five times that amount. There was no way they'd go for us.

Whilst I was out training a few days later, my mobile rang. It was Nick, calling to say that he had made the decision to drop out of the team. Unlike the rest of us, who were either quitting our jobs or didn't have any in the first place, he had specifically asked for three months' sabbatical from his accountancy firm. He couldn't risk taking that amount of time off and then have nothing to do if the sponsorship money didn't materialise.

Inadvertently, I had stopped just across the road from the Royal Geographical Society. As Nick spoke, for the first time I looked closely at one of the statues carved into the red-brick wall. It was Shackleton, in polar furs, his stone eyes staring out with an intensity I had never seen in anyone before. The look was mesmeric and conveyed a sense of purpose which ordinary life just does not require. I wiped the sweat and dust off my face and stared jealously into those eyes, which had seen things I so longed to see.

'What about you? What are you going to do?' asked Nick a little louder this time.

'I don't know yet,' I said vaguely. 'Just keep on trying, I guess.'

In the end I didn't even try to persuade Nick to reconsider. I could only agree with him that it wasn't worth the risk and that our chances of reaching Antarctica this year were diminishing by the day.

Over the next week, Tom, Andy and I reluctantly tried to come up with some sort of plan B. At this point it looked as simple as it did unsavoury; each one of us would attempt to raise sponsorship for himself and try to join a commercial trip leaving from Cooney's Ronne Ice Shelf.

One of my leads with Omega watches started to look promising, and although the amount they had proposed would make only a dent in the full price of the expedition from McMurdo, if plan B came into effect then it would give me personally enough to head off to Antarctica.

This whole situation reminded me of Shackleton's predicament in 1908. Desperate for backing, and trying to complete the Herculean task of financing an expedition in only seven months, he had exhausted every angle. By the time he set sail, he was up to his neck in creditors and had pre-emptively sold the book rights, film rights and anything else he could think of in an effort to get his *Nimrod* expedition sailing south.

For Tom, however, it was a different story. The only company he hadn't had a final rejection letter from was Hastings Direct. He had no personal fortune to dip into, nor an aged grandmother about to pop her clogs. If he borrowed the money from a bank, he would financially cripple himself for the foreseeable future, and that's only if a bank manager would lend him such an unsecured sum.

It was desperate. We had been working on this project together for over a year, and for Tom suddenly to have to stand by and watch me pack my bags seemed monstrously unfair. That evening we were in the kitchen at a party, away from the others, racking our brains as to what else could be done. One of our mutual friends staggered in and slapped me on the back.

'Good luck in Antarctica, lads.' He grinned inanely and then proceeded to quiz us intently as to how we could go for a pee in minus 30 degrees without getting frostbite.

We both smiled politely and I changed the subject as soon as possible. I could only imagine how Tom must have been feeling, sitting there, smiling at well-wishing friends. Come Monday morning, it looked as if I would be off to Antarctica while he went back to the day job. Tom and I avoided eye contact as we talked, while the laughter filtering into the kitchen from the next room only made our own predicament seem that much more awkward.

'Look, Tom, I'm really sorry how things . . . '

'Don't,' he interrupted. 'It's not your fault. Anyway, the main thing is that one person in the team gets to the pole. Even if just one of us goes, then the time won't have been wasted.'

Shit, I thought, I had better make it.

I left the party and walked through the park to worry about my own problems. If I was the only one who could raise the money, then there was a good chance I would be joining a commercial expedition, and that meant skiing in the same team as Andrew Cooney.

I knew only too well that the main reason I had enjoyed expeditions in the past was because of the friends that had been with me. They had always been there to share in the successes or help during a bad patch. I was certain Antarctica would be gruelling enough without having to go through the whole human dynamic of spending sixty days with complete strangers. Such interaction drives the housemates mad in *Big Brother*, so imagine what it can do to four people sharing a six-foot-long tent, beaten down by weeks in the cold.

The sad fact is that the majority of polar teams end up falling out with each other by the time they return to civilisation. Previously friendly teammates lampoon each other in the press or publish a raft of vitriolic articles. The mud-slinging goes back and forth, with much pointing of fingers and public airing of frustrations from their time on the ice. It happened with Fiennes and Stroud, Fuchs and Messner; even Scott and Shackleton were not immune. They all seemed keen to grind their axes and rubbish their teammates.

For me, the whole reason for making this journey was to see a place I had been fascinated by for years. I had little interest in spoiling the experience of a lifetime by having to deal with petty jibes and daily irritations.

Walking through the park, I breathed in the cold air and tried to think about something else. Nothing came to mind. Everything else just seemed to fade into obscurity. It was bizarre. My mind was consumed by Antarctica and I had never even been there.

Two weeks before the plane was due to leave, Tom called me in absolute disbelief.

'The MD at Hastings has just told me that he is thinking of sponsoring both Cooney and myself to go for the pole.'

'That's fantastic,' I said. 'We can go a slightly different route and then you'll only have to see him for a couple of days in Punta Arenas.'

'Wait. There's more,' Tom replied wearily. 'The MD also said that he wanted us to go together, as in the two of us forming a team and going the whole sixty days side by side.

He suggested that I should take him under my wing a bit and look after him while we're on the ice.'

'Why would he want you to do that?' I asked incredulously. The whole situation was getting absurd. How could Tom be expected to change teammates only a matter of days before we left?

'He wants us to do a lecture tour together after the expedition,' Tom continued meekly.

'The way I see it, you've got no choice. You either agree and have a crack at reaching the pole or you refuse and sit in London all winter wondering how the rest of us are getting on.'

He knew it just as well as I did. But by talking to me, Tom was just delaying the inevitable. As it would turn out, Andrew Cooney never got his sponsorship and would have to fund his expedition privately. Only a week before he was due to leave for Antarctica, Hastings Direct decided to withdraw their support of him. Tom, on the other hand, finally had his money.

Meanwhile, Andy had been fighting his own battles over in Cape Town. He had established that he would be the first ever African to ski to the South Pole and had presumed large corporations would jump at the chance to cash in on some of the media attention that would surround such an event. However, it was not so easy, as he soon discovered. It wasn't that companies weren't interested; it was the sum he was asking for when converted into South African rand that was the problem. With the current exchange rate it was an enormous amount.

Despite this economic barrier, he managed to gather a number of smaller sponsors together, leaving Andy with a further £14,000 to find. Four days before we were due to leave, he got a loan from the bank and wired the money directly over to Adventure Networks. More money than he had ever seen in his life, and he only managed to keep it in his account for a matter of seconds.

The run-up to leaving for Antarctica was predictably frantic. Tom's boots hadn't arrived from Norway and it was looking as if he'd have to fly to Oslo that weekend. In an effort to compile all the kit needed, Andy drove ceaselessly around England for two days straight. With each stop a new item of clothing would be tossed into the back of his Land Rover and he'd set off once more, his wheels barely coming to a complete standstill.

I had most of my kit organised by this stage and so took the night off from worrying and went for dinner with my girlfriend. With the whole sponsorship rigmarole and frenzied preparations, I had been seriously neglecting her. Over dinner, we sat quietly for the first time in months and the extent of what I had been putting her through dawned on me.

I realised that every one of our conversations in the last six months had only been half listened to, only half registered. While I had been perpetually thinking of skis, sponsorship and dates, she had been dealing with the worry of whether I would be badly frostbitten, be a totally different person when I came back, or for that matter whether I would return at all. For the person leaving it is so much easier, as they are focused and excited about what lies ahead. For the one staying behind, there is only frustration, anxiety and the perpetual reminder of an empty bed.

We sat just looking at each other for a while, enjoying the last time we'd be able to communicate so easily. She knew I felt sorry for the pain I was causing her, but she also knew there was no alternative, as staying in England doing a nine-to-five job would slowly suffocate me.

'Come on, eat the rest of your pudding.' She grinned. 'You've got a big day tomorrow.'

4

Converging Explorers

'I can see doing this for the fun of it, but there must be better ways to make a living.'
— Rick Ridgeway, *Ascent of K2*

Punta Arenas is a tiny naval town stuck on the bottom of South America. Despite wonderfully friendly people and a long and varied history, it's a place where almost nothing of interest ever happens. The town itself is halfway between the Third World and the first, and combines the worst parts of each in a rather dull grey colour. It reminded me of Rotherham.

At the turn of the last century, Punta Arenas became the staging post for some of the old explorers on their way down south. This was to be their last sight of civilisation for the two to three years their expedition would often take. In the main square is a large statue of the explorer Magellan, and somehow, over the years, it has become a tradition for those going to Antarctica to kiss his foot. Much to the bemusement of the locals milling around, one of the first things we did upon arrival was kiss his unhygienic-looking big toe.

After we had stowed all our kit in a B&B near the centre, we strolled through town wondering how best to pass the time. With not a great deal going on, we decided to eat our way through the afternoon and looked for a restaurant. After trying five different places, the only thing on every menu seemed to be some sort of eel dish with rice. We resigned ourselves and settled down to eat, but not long after the food arrived it was obvious our stomachs wouldn't stand a chance against such local delicacies. With much polite smiling and a few gesticulations, we pretended the portion was just too much for us and ordered coffee instead.

The ANI staff had repeatedly told us to be patient when flying to Antarctica. They took great pains to explain how the flight in was entirely weather dependent and often a week to ten days would go by without a sufficient break. They explained how there have to be clear skies over both Punta Arenas and the landing strip in Antarctica, and often the weather can force a very expensive return by closing in during the five-hour flight.

Tom told me about how the previous year a

three-man team hoping to ski to the pole had been forced to wait for five consecutive weeks. I looked at what was left of the eels and stirred a few around the plate. I would go mad, or at the very least get a lot thinner, if I had to wait here for all that time. The previous year had been especially bad, though, as there had been a complication with the Chilean authorities. They had decided that they wanted to check that the Russian cargo plane used by ANI was up to scratch in terms of airworthiness.

In response, ANI stated that they would be more than happy to assist, but asked whether the inspection might be done at the Chileans' earliest convenience, because bad weather had already hampered the first of the flights and they were running a bit behind. It was then that the authorities admitted that they didn't actually have anyone in Punta Arenas qualified to inspect the Russian jet and that they were going to have to train someone up. The staff at ANI thought they were just going to have to write off the rest of the season when, a week later, the Chilean authorities proudly announced that they had fully trained an inspector. He promptly made a cursory tour of the plane before pronouncing it, in his expert opinion, airworthy.

I returned to the little B&B to find a man

sitting in our room, waiting patiently. He stood up to greet me, and I saw that he was roughly my height, although a touch stockier, and had deep lines on his face from years spent outdoors. The man introduced himself as Paul Landry.

He looked to be around forty years old, but it was difficult to tell given the lifestyle he obviously led. He had a calm but incredibly resolute air about him. It was as though there was something fundamentally important he had to achieve, but he didn't want to tell anyone what it was. As I introduced myself, he smiled, in a crooked, knowing sort of way. For a moment I thought I might have something stuck in between my teeth, but later I would learn that it was just the smile of someone deeply comfortable with who they were.

Most people are slightly wary when meeting someone new. Entire books have been written explaining how the strength of a handshake or the use of direct eye contact can give the right impression. Effortlessly, and with a natural ease I have rarely seen, Paul could have been a case study for anyone reading a self-help book. He just was. Everything about him seemed entirely unpretentious and self-assured, to the point where it made me feel rather uncomfortable talking to him. Usually, in these sort of situations, I say something stupid — today was no exception.

'I've got three barrels of equipment,' I said, meaning hello, nice to meet you and when would you like to go over the kit we've brought with us.

'Well done,' Paul answered, the grin widening slightly. I hoped that the old adage concerning first impressions wouldn't hold true. Fortunately, before my mouth opened once more, Tom and Andy arrived and Paul's unblinking stare was distracted.

Over the following weeks I learnt a great deal more about Paul. It was fascinating to become friends with someone who had chosen an entirely different way of life to what most of us call 'normal'.

Originally, Tom and I had wanted to do the expedition without a certified guide. However, Adventure Networks had explicitly stated that without the added security of someone experienced in polar conditions they would double the price for each man going. They deemed unguided expeditions to be far more likely to require an expensive rescue, and the unavoidable truth was that we simply couldn't afford to pay the difference. Much to the relief of my mother, we agreed to go for a guided trip, and Paul was contacted and asked whether he would lead us. Without an alternative, there was little point in debating the issue further, and we soon forgot our original high-minded thoughts of completing the expedition entirely on our own.

Paul lived with his wife Matty in the small Canadian town of Iqaluit in the High Arctic. Running a dog team on the frozen sea ice, Paul spent almost his entire life in temperatures cold enough to freeze diesel. Not even trees grow so far north, and consequently their home town has everything from timber to fresh vegetables flown in on weekly cargo flights. Iqaluit is also 70 per cent populated by Inuit, whose rather more spiritual outlook on life has certainly shaped the way Paul and Matty are. When you have to dress in full caribou fur just to pick up your morning paper, it is obvious that this is a lifestyle you have to really want from the very beginning.

Over coffee, Paul explained how he had just returned from an expedition to the North Pole. Just prior to this, during the previous winter, he had led an Australian and a Finn to the South Pole. I did some calculations and realised that for the last year and a half, Paul had almost exclusively been living on snow and ice. Given the twenty-four-hour daylight at the polar regions, in all that time he would scarcely have seen the night sky. No wonder his face looked a little haggard. There is enjoying your work and then there is being obsessive. I think Paul, in his own quiet way, leant more towards the latter.

I had read about Paul and his expedition to the North Pole in 2000 in a couple of magazine articles. They clearly expressed the kind of mentality he possesses, as he was attempting to settle the long-running dispute over whether the American Robert Peary did succeed in reaching the North Pole in April 1909. Polar historians, newspaper editors and even a considerable number of politicians have, over the near-century since the claim was made, hotly debated whether he actually reach 90 degrees North. The problem was a combination of insufficient information from Peary and a rival claim by another American, Dr Frederick Cook.

Cook was a charismatic explorer, but later proved to be of dubious credibility. He had made his name by claiming the first ascent of Mount McKinley, the highest mountain in northern America. He was widely believed, until someone spotted that the summit photo looked remarkably like a much smaller 7,000-foot peak a few kilometres away. Later, one of his fellow climbers would admit that the whole thing had been a sham. Cook then turned his attention to Arctic exploration and, after setting out a few years earlier from Greenland, claimed to have reached the Geographic North Pole on 28 April 1908. His stylish prose and moderately humble description of reaching the pole (humble in relation to Peary's own account, at least) captivated the American public. 'In my own achievement I felt, that dizzy moment, that all the heroic souls who had braved the rigours of the Arctic region found their hopes' fulfilment, I had realized their dream.'

Meanwhile, the American naval officer Robert Peary returned from his own attempt at the pole a year later. He was furious. A huge man, with an almost pathological desire for fame and recognition, Peary had spent his entire adult life in the High Arctic. He had fathered children there, lost the majority of his toes and slowly gone half mad from the effort. For him, the attainment of the North Pole was the culmination of his life's work and he'd be damned if someone else was going to take the credit. His description of that quintessential moment certainly hints that he wasn't prepared to share the laurels, even if they did happen to be with another American. 'The pole at last. The prize of three centuries. My dream and goal for twenty years. Mine at last!'

Back in America, Peary vehemently disputed Cook's claim, mainly on the grounds that the latter refused to deliver any substantial proof of his accomplishments. His journal and all-important latitude readings were in Greenland and, no, it wasn't convenient for anyone to read them this year.

On closer inspection, Peary's own proof wasn't exactly conclusive. Those opposed to his claim cited his own less than meticulous records of his progress north. Besides the large omissions and sketchy sextant recordings, they claimed that Peary's purported distance of 133 nautical miles in four and a half days was simply impossible.

They also examined Peary's final team, which dashed the last two degrees to the pole, and claimed that it consisted of people specifically chosen because they were unable to verify the navigation records. Excluding Peary, there were four Inuit and, very unusually, a black man called Matthew Henson, who was an able polar navigator but, given the era they were living in, was not considered 'reliable'.

Rather surprisingly, the exact North Pole is actually very difficult to find. Unlike something tangible such as the summit of Mount Everest, the pole is an abstract point, which looks uncannily similar to the rest of the

Arctic, and the ice has a habit of moving around each year. At extremely high latitudes and longitudes, compasses need to be adjusted on a daily basis and the twenty-four hours of sunlight can be more than a little disorienting.

Unlike Antarctica, the Arctic is a frozen sea, which makes the ice subject to currents and drift. Many of the earlier expeditions trying to reach the North Pole found themselves in the terrifying position that, when they were returning home, they were actually drifting back faster than they were walking forwards. Understandably, in an effort to avoid being lynched, their leaders elected to keep this rather vital information from the rest of the men.

Living in the Arctic surrounded by polar history, Paul was fascinated by the whole debate and spent years reading the various arguments and counter-arguments. One day, he put down his pen, returned the books to the library and went to see for himself. While bespectacled historians continued to leaf through dusty volumes and argue their point with their colleagues, Paul untethered his dogs and headed north.

With friend, he set off on almost exactly the same day as the 1909 expedition, with a fully laden dog team and a copy of Peary's notes. For weeks they ran beside the dog sleds, scrabbling over monstrous pressure ridges in minus-fifty-degree temperatures. After a couple of near-ruinous incidents when they fell through the ice and into the water, the pair arrived at the pole in forty-two days, utterly exhausted, but only four days behind Peary himself.

When taking into consideration the seasonal fluctuations, the enormous support lines Peary could rely on and the fact that he was unhealthily obsessed with reaching the pole (in any normal society he would have been sectioned), Paul's expedition certainly proved he could have made it. And here, standing before me in Punta Arenas, days before we headed off to Antarctica ourselves, was that same man; a man who had set out to recreate a seemingly impossible journey, just because he could.

★　★　★

The little room in the B&B was awash with an impossibly large amount of kit. Everything from skis to medical supplies, jackets to ski boots, lay on the floor in some long-forgotten stacking order. Paul cast his eye over it all, but before going through it with a fine-toothed comb he opened up a plastic bag he had been holding and passed us each a fur ruff to go on our jackets. The fur is supposed to seal the jacket's hood and protect your face from the wind. We had heard that it didn't really do a great deal and the main reason people wore it was simply to look good for the camera. Later we were to find out that it was one of the most essential items we possessed for protection against frostbite.

'Paul, what kind of fur is this?' I said, running the wonderfully soft fur between my fingers.

'Husky,' he replied.

I thought about the dead dog and knew I was going to ask a question that would make me sound utterly pathetic, but I couldn't help myself.

'What was the dog's name?'

'Slow dog,' he said, deadpan, and for the second time in a couple of minutes I started to feel a little uneasy.

Over the next few days all our time was spent weighing each item of equipment and food. Every single wrapper was removed to lessen the weight and every gram of food precisely measured to last us exactly to the pole. On Paul's advice, items of clothing were discarded, specialist bits of kit modified and the lightest possible combination of provisions taken. Absolutely everything had to be hauled behind us in sleds, and so every gram would count. We had heard stories of the more hard-core expeditions sawing their toothbrushes in half to save weight. I looked at the little complimentary toothbrush I had stolen from Lan Chile Airways and decided I'd probably be able to pull the extra weight. I definitely wasn't in the same category as the kind of people who forgo the luxury of a complete toothbrush.

As we went through the massive inventories of kit, Andy's fastidious pen hovered uncertainly next to the word 'skis'. He went over to double-check, then quietly, so Paul couldn't hear, caught our attention and pointed to the solitary ski bag on the floor. I shrugged and nodded that the ski bag was indeed mine, but Tom stared blankly and then slowly began to shake his head as the realisation dawned on him. There were supposed to be three ski bags, not one. He cast his mind back to Andy's flat in London, where, tucked away in the corner, just by the stairs, were two large ski bags with little white 'Antarctica' tags tied round their handles. He shut his eyes at the horror of it all. We were skiing across Antarctica and had forgotten to bring our skis.

Our immediate reaction was to be mature and sensible about the situation. First, we agreed that under no circumstances should anyone tell Paul. Second, we were going to scour Punta Arenas and the neighbouring countryside for skis and pay whatever amount they cost. We had all just met Paul, who was to be our guide and mentor for the next sixty days, and the last thing we wanted to tell him was that we were so deeply incompetent that we'd forgotten to bring our primary means of transportation.

With an early-morning phone call to a friend in England and some cashing in of favours, Tom managed to get the skis sent by FedEx to Punta Arenas that day. We hoped that the notoriously delayed flight to Antarctica might actually work in our favour, and then there'd be a good chance that Paul would never have to find out about our little miscalculation.

That night, Paul invited us for dinner. As we walked down the steps to the restaurant, we approached a table full of men, with one woman sitting in the middle. The woman turned out to be Matty, Paul's wife, who was in Punta Arenas to lead the other expedition that was skiing to the pole. A couple of years previously she had become the first woman to guide a commercial team to the North Pole, and despite her diminutive stature she looked as hard as nails.

Sitting beside her were two Spaniards who, although unable to speak English, enthused much good intention through a series of wild gesticulations and big smiles. They were both apparently hotshot climbers, who had three Everest expeditions under their belts and were in search of a new challenge. One, Angel, was compact and determined, whereas the other, Willy, was a monster of a man. He had the kind of build that made him look as if he had been training for something from the moment he reached adolescence, with the same sinewy forearms that farm workers get from years loading hay bales and a wiry strength that could never be obtained by working out in the gym. I went to shake Willy's hand and watched my own get lost somewhere inside his giant paw. It was like trying to be formally introduced to a polar bear.

Next to them was a man called Geoff Somers, whom we had previously met in London. He was an absolute legend in polar exploration, having been awarded an MBE for an expedition that traversed 3,700 miles of Antarctica. Despite having broken almost every polar record at some time or another, he was just about the most modest and gentle man I had ever met. He seemed to brush all his own accomplishments to one side and was fascinated by the slightest achievement of those around him. He was in Punta Arenas a little earlier that season, as he was paving the way for a BBC film crew who were due to be filming the Emperor penguins.

Next to Geoff sat two Englishmen. The first introduced himself as Graham, and he seemed down to earth and again extremely modest. He had just returned from running the 'Marathon des Sables', a race through the Sahara desert, where the competitors complete the equivalent of five marathons in as many days. Although even more masochistic races have subsequently been devised, the 'Marathon of the sands' was, for a long time, billed as the toughest land race on earth. Intrigued by how the race was organised and what it felt like to run through the Sahara, I pestered Graham with questions over dinner. Like Geoff, he smiled and gently changed the subject, obviously a little reluctant to broadcast his achievements across the table.

The final person present was Andrew Cooney. I had guessed we would probably run into him some time in Punta Arenas. A little over six feet, with dark hair and dark eyes, he shook everybody's hand slightly hesitantly. He was wearing a black fleece emblazoned with dozens of sponsors' logos, which were neatly sewn on across his chest and all the way down his arm. In large print at the centre was one reading 'Andrew Cooney — South Pole Expedition 2002'. As we sat down to eat, he leant across to Tom and, nodding his head in a self-assured way, said, 'Yeah, really looking forward to having a crack at bagging the South Pole.'

I looked across at Paul, engaged in conversation just across the table, and then slowly back to Andrew. In the dim light of the restaurant, Paul's face looked dark and weather-beaten from the years he had spent out in the cold. Deep lines were etched around his eyes and forehead, and, like Willy's, his forearms were sinewy from thousands of hours of relentless exercise. Andrew, on the other hand, had just arrived from the drab British winter and, like us, looked fresh faced and pale.

Talk of 'bagging', 'conquering' or planting flags in things always makes me feel a little uneasy. It's interesting to see how those with the benefit of experience don't feel the need to advertise any such notion. More often than not they say how lucky they were to have been to a certain place and return unscathed. It is like people talking about conquering Mount Everest. Usually, they just crawl up one side of it and then get down as fast as possible. It's been sitting there for a few million years and somehow I don't think spending twenty minutes on the summit really qualifies.

As we left the restaurant, Tom, Andy and I walked down the street, excited and all talking at the same time. We each felt that we had so many things to say and talked over each other in our mutual enthusiasm. Conversations that night with Geoff, Paul and Matty had fired up our imaginations, as they had actually been to Antarctica and could answer every one of our questions. Like petulant children, we had quizzed them all through the starters and main course and were trying to get a few more answers over coffee before they politely declined and went off to bed.

The night had thrown fuel on imaginations that were already ablaze. With each answer the realisation that Antarctica was just around the corner had become all too clear. It was no longer an abstract notion to be loosely pondered in the warmth of an English pub; our departure was only a couple of days away now and we knew it. It's all very well knowing there is a wolf somewhere in the woods, but when the thing is scratching on the door, it's a different matter entirely.

The other cause for excitement was that Andy and Tom had both felt that the gauntlet had been thrown down with regard to Andrew Cooney. For them, it seemed, the race was on.

Quite uncharacteristically, I was far more cautious. Partly, it was the fact that I was seriously worried about how we would cope in Antarctica, given the books I had read and a few of the conversations I had overheard that night. Also, I didn't like the idea of engaging in a race purely to satisfy our own vanity. It seemed pointless and, more importantly, dangerous in terms of our own chances of success. If Andrew Cooney and the other team turned out to be extremely strong and we pushed ourselves hard over the first few hundred miles, desperately trying to keep pace, then we could easily burn ourselves out. I had seen it before with inexperienced marathon runners, sprinting off at the start, just to collapse around mile twenty.

Fear and a little good sense were holding me back, and both Andy and Tom agreed to let the issue drop.

'OK, we'll take the moral high ground, be mature and stick to our own natural pace,' said Andy a little reluctantly. We fell silent for once, nodding in mutual agreement. 'But it would be nice to rub his nose in it a bit,' he added, grinning mischievously. We all laughed and then agreed that we would keep our natural pace, but not be too bothered if by sheer coincidence that happened to be just a little faster than Andrew Cooney's. Christ, I thought, who's suffering from an inflated ego now?

Over the next few days, we tried to find out where our skis had got to. They had been loaded on the plane in London, arrived in Buenos Aires (not the right country, but close enough), and then been flown all the way back up to Colombia. The Punta Arenas deliveryman said it with such casual ease that for a moment we stood in mute agreement, thinking that this was probably the most obvious thing that could have happened.

In the meantime, Tom and Andy had decided to bite the bullet and asked ANI whether they had any skis kicking around from a previous expedition. After ploughing through the storeroom, they found two pairs of slightly antiquated but pretty sturdy skis. With any luck our original ones would come to rest somewhere in South America and then they could be sent out on a later flight to Antarctica and we could pick them up at the resupply point.

Matty's team had been set to leave for Antarctica about ten days before us, but weather had delayed the flight. Everything was rescheduled for 9 November, and it looked as if we might be ready in time to join them and so get going a little earlier.

We had been sitting for hours in the B&B, surrounded by crates of food and measuring every last item to the nearest milligram. Breaking the silence, the phone suddenly rang in the corner of the room. Paul spoke briefly and quietly into the receiver, while the rest of us fell silent, craning our necks to try to overhear what he was saying. He turned round to face us and smiled. 'We're on,' he said simply.

We ran back to the B&B and furiously packed loose items of clothing. The truck would be arriving in a few hours to take us to the airport. In a blurry haze of panic, important decisions were made in split seconds, as equipment was either bundled into large blue barrels for Antarctica or duffel bags to remain in Punta Arenas. The sweet lady who ran the B&B poked her head around the door and shot a few worried glances at us.

As I put on my Gore-Tex trousers and massive yellow ski boots, she came over and said something in Spanish with a highly aggrieved look on her face. I looked blankly back at her. We had paid her the money, said our goodbyes and spent a long time

119

communicating in a mixture of broken Spanish and mime that we were off to Antarctica and would be back in a couple of months. She kept on talking, getting more and more worked up, until Tom came over to speak to her.

'She thinks we are going to the hostel down the road because we don't like her service,' he translated, and carried on stuffing socks into a barrel.

I stood in my cold-weather clothing, beading with sweat, a pair of skis in one hand and a bag with 'Antarctica' written across it in the other. I would have understood her confusion, but we had spent most of yesterday explaining it all to her, even going so far as to unroll a few maps. Admittedly, some of our impressions of pulling sleds might have been a little cryptic, but she should have got the gist of it by now.

'Tell her we are going a lot farther south than the hostel down the road,' I said bluntly.

Tom did, and she shook her head woefully once more, thinking we would soon be staying with her competitors on the other side of the docks.

5

God's Great Ice Machine

' . . . a country doomed by nature never once to feel the warmth of the sun's rays, but to lie buried under everlasting snow and ice, whose horrible and savage aspect I have not the words to describe.'
— Captain Cook

For a little airport in the dead of night, Punta Arenas was busy. Dressed ready for the Antarctic weather, we all impatiently padded around the departure lounge in our thermals and ski boots, trying not to break into a sweat. The final weather clearance was granted and we started to file down the emigration line. I handed over my passport and, with a resounding thump, the official's stamp declared that I was no longer on Chilean soil. Owing to the fact that no single country owns Antarctica, for the next three months I would be 'officially' disappearing off the face of the earth.

Outside, the wind was gusting across the tarmac. Before us stood a vast Russian cargo plane, its tail open and a forklift loading barrels inside. The words 'Kras Air' were stencilled in turquoise ink across the outside of the fuselage and, as we clambered up the metal stepladder, I realised just how large the plane was. I wasn't sure what I had been expecting, but this plane was the same size as a jumbo jet and we would soon be landing in Antarctica on a runway consisting exclusively of blue ice.

Inside the main cargo hold, netting held down hundreds of barrels of fuel, and towards the front seats had been bolted down for the passengers. For some disconcerting reason, heavy electrical tape had been wound around the majority of the plane's internal components. Looking around, I could only think that the whole thing had a decrepit, post-communist feel about it. It was like one of those grand hotels in the old Soviet bloc which had fallen on hard times and been allowed to gently fall apart. Some generous benefactor had obviously come in at the last minute with a hell of a lot of capital and a few hundred rolls of electrical tape. It didn't exactly inspire confidence.

The fifteen or so Russian crew members smiled hospitably as we took our seats. They seemed well suited to the general surroundings, as they were dressed in a mixture of official 'Kras Air' uniforms and normal clothing. It was as if, at the last moment, someone had asked the captain to share his outfit with the rest of the flight deck. With a small present of some earplugs, we buckled up securely and hoped the safety talk wouldn't be in Russian.

In my limited experience, I have found Russians to be a curious race of people. Whenever I had come across them in the past, they had struck me as slightly arrogant and dismissive. There was always something in the way they spoke that made them seem defensive, as if they were holding on to some sort of guilty secret. However, I soon realised that this first impression was pretty misguided.

As soon as they get to know you, they bring out the vodka and things change for the better. Five shots later and you're being hugged like a long-lost brother, with much slapping of backs and loud laughter. Then they invariably get more drunk, philosophical and slightly weepy.

Since the Soviet collapse, they have had to become resourceful. State-of-the-art planes and computers, which were designed to compete with the West, suddenly had their funding pulled. So, with an ingenuity that would make the A-Team proud, they maintain and service equipment without a penny from their impoverished government. Complicated navigational systems are only kept working by the clever use of a soldering iron and the leads from the back of a video player. It's incredible. Looking around me on the plane, I just hoped their creativity would be enough to get us the five hours across the Southern Ocean and on to Antarctica itself.

Once in the air, the noise of the engines was loud and intrusive. The earplugs helped, but restricted conversation to simple shakes of the head. We all just sat waiting and let our thoughts wander to what we were about to see. Normally the heat and dull sodium lights of the cabin would have made me feel drowsy and sedated, but with anticipation rising I felt more awake than I had done in years.

As we moved farther south, the night sky of Chile would soon be giving way to the harsh sunlight of Antarctica. The southern stars that surrounded our plane would be slowly erased by light, bent and diffracted by the millions of tons of ice, sitting on the horizon, only a few hundred miles away.

★   ★   ★

Antarctica — the seventh continent, the dry, white desert.

Tucked away at the bottom of the planet and thousands of miles from the nearest land mass, Antarctica usually just pokes its fingers around the underside of any map. Just as an iceberg floats with only its tip above the water, so the real nature of Antarctica is hidden from view. It has stood alone for the last 25 million years, surrounded by the most inhospitable seas on earth, far beyond the knowledge and imagination of the human race.

People around me sat in silence. As to what they were thinking, I have no idea. For me, I began to realise that the hopes I had been harbouring for the last year were suddenly becoming something definite and physical. With such doubtful sponsorship, I had refused to let myself think past this point. I just didn't want to build myself up, only to watch everything fall apart at the last minute. In my mind, the plane from Punta Arenas had been the cut-off point, and now it seemed, with each mile south, the boundaries were expanding.

Antarctica seems to affect people quite differently from other continents. Somehow, the enormity of its proportions and the rawness of its beauty seem to conjure up all sorts of strange feelings in the people who go there. In almost every account I have read, there is a recurrent theme; people claim to have been in some way 'touched' by their experiences on the ice. Some even go farther and describe how, when they returned, they found it hard to integrate themselves back into normal life. Antarctica, it seems, had had some sort of life-affirming effect on them.

Although it all sounded rather clichéd and melodramatic, I couldn't ignore the fact that even the most travel-hardened adventurers kept reiterating this theme. I couldn't understand what it was about Antarctica that was having such an effect on people. As my curiosity grew, I realised that one thing was for certain: I wanted to know the reasons why these people had experienced such depth of emotion, why, indeed, they had felt 'touched' by what was simply a lump of ice, albeit a very large one.

Since it was first discovered, Antarctica has inspired a disproportionate number of books. Many of them romanticise everything from the landscapes to the great explorers, but even if you just look at the bare statistics and leave human emotions out of it, it's not hard to appreciate that it is a place totally unlike anywhere else on earth. It is so unique and on such a massive scale that people tend to get a little weirded out by it all.

For instance, the ice cap that flows over its

surface, at its deepest point, is 4.7 kilometres thick. Standing on the surface and looking at your feet, you would have to drill a hole almost the height of Mont Blanc (4,807 metres), or ten times the height of the Empire State Building, if you wanted to get to the land underneath.

The continent is 1.5 times the size of America, and during the winter, when the seas around it freeze, Antarctica, as a whole, effectively doubles its size. Of the permanent ice, there are 7 million cubic miles of the stuff, which represents over 80 per cent of the entire planet's fresh water supply.

When trying to put this amount of frozen water in perspective, I thought back to a time, four years earlier, when I had been trekking in Zimbabwe. I had been following a trail through the bush for some hours when I started to notice a low rumbling sound. With each step forward it seemed to grow in intensity, until, a few minutes later, we rounded a bend and there were the Victoria Falls.

The scene was simply massive. Sheer black cliffs, glistening in the sun, cut away in a sheer drop below me. The calm, flat water flowing sedately at the top, past the cliff edge, suddenly began accelerating downwards. It fell for hundreds of feet, turning an angry white against the black cliffs and gathering momentum all the way.

As the inevitable happened and it crashed on to the rocks below, the millions of litres of water emitted a dull, churning noise that made it almost impossible to hear the person next to you. A warm mist floated back up the cliffs and I stood and stared, as thousands of other people have done before me, at the incredible power of the scene.

As I looked in mute amazement, the only thought that came to me was how on earth did the river not run dry within a few minutes? I just couldn't imagine how it could sustain such an enormous volume of water.

With this in mind, I tried now to imagine the amount of fresh water sitting quietly in the Antarctic ice cap. After a short while, my imagination simply gives up. The sheer scale of the ice cap affects every element of the Antarctic environment. In short, it makes it the highest, driest and coldest continent on earth.

During the winter of 1983, a Russian scientist stationed in a desperately remote base in eastern Antarctica put his thermometer out at the window. It was mid-winter on a polar ice cap and he knew it was going to be cold, but what he didn't expect to see was the specially designed thermometer reading −89.2°C (−129°F). That day he noted the coldest temperature ever recorded on the surface of the earth.

Since man first came to Antarctica, the intense cold has been a subject of huge scientific interest. The early explorers described how their breath froze instantaneously in front of them, falling to the ground 'with a soft tinkling sound'.

Seventy years later, the same Russian scientist was experiencing cold so severe he could have snapped a steel bar as if it were a pencil. The simple reality is that Antarctica is just bizarre. Things can happen there which don't occur anywhere else on earth.

When the US government decided to launch their space programme back in the 1960s, NASA used the dry valleys in Antarctica to test their equipment. This is an area of Antarctica near McMurdo which has not seen rain for 2 to 4 million years. The valleys are not covered in ice, as the water simply evaporates, making the area one of the driest on the planet. This was the closest environment NASA could find to the moon's surface. Even now, polar expeditions conduct physiological tests designed to help astronauts understand what will happen to their bodies in such extreme environments.

Although the Americans, and for that

matter any other country, can use Antarctica for scientific research, the continent itself is the only land mass that is not officially owned by a single nation. Even the vast Sahara desert has imaginary and utterly pointless borders criss-crossing its interior. An Antarctic treaty allows scientists, explorers and a growing number of tourists to go on to the continent, but prevents any corporate nasties from landing their oil rigs and mining equipment. Unfortunately, this treaty may be reviewed in 2048, and the temptation to delve into the continent's untapped resources must be huge.

I find it extraordinary that Antarctica still remains unmolested by the corporate world. Western society is hardly renowned for its ecological sensitivity, and yet it was only comparatively recently that Antarctica became a protected area. Even as early as 1907, a few sharp-eyed entrepreneurs were looking south and wondering what might be found. The explorer Ernest Shackleton, in a desperate bid to raise money for his expedition, agreed to sell any potential mineral rights to mining speculators in the UK. Only the fearful seas of the Southern Ocean and Antarctica's relative inaccessibility have stopped the potential exploitation.

Ex-polar explorers, such as Robert Swan,

have devoted their lives and most of their savings in trying to ensure the world's governments renew the conservationist treaty. Whether this unspoilt continent will suddenly be covered in a maze of scaffolding rigs and drill bits in 2048 remains to be seen, but for the moment it remains uniquely free of political borders.

Some maps of the continent delineate different areas, which are 'unofficially' owned by some of the treaty's signatory nations. So far no one has pushed the issue and anyone can pass from one area to the next, but if one country starts flexing its muscles and planting flags in everything, it's pretty much inevitable that the others will loudly protest and then do the same.

Looking at these maps, I found it difficult to appreciate the scale of Antarctica. The many-digited numbers seemed to blur together, and after a certain point, started to lose their significance. As when contemplating the distances between stars, there is only so much you can take in before it all becomes pretty meaningless.

At the various lectures I had been to in the past, I had seen photographs of Antarctica's landscape. They showed horizons stretching off indefinitely in all directions with nothing but hundreds of miles of maddening ice. I imagined if you got separated from your teammates it could get pretty lonely out there.

The only time I had ever seen such a uniform landscape was while working on a rhino conservation project in south-west Africa. The wildlife park was right on the edge of the Namib Desert, and when tracking and tranquillising the rhino we would often venture into it. Early on in my time there, the park warden had dropped me off to fix a wooden observation post that had been smashed up one night by a particularly disgruntled rhino.

After a few hours of working away, I finished the job and sat down to rest. It was midday and, unsurprisingly, the desert was stiflingly hot. I got out a water bottle, drank a few mouthfuls and looked around at the scenery before me. The sand dunes stretched off into the horizon, shimmering in the dry heat. The glare from the sun reflected off the white sand, creating a hazy stillness which made it hard to judge distances. Only the dirt track we had driven up a few hours previously gave the eye any sort of anchor point. Cutting right through the dunes, it looked like an umbilical cord reaching out to the outside world.

Sitting there, with nothing to do but wait to

be collected, I realised that this was the first time I had ever been alone and in such a vast space. In every direction there was simply the same thing endlessly repeated as far as the eye could see. Without any means of contacting someone and insufficient water to walk out along the path, I felt incredibly vulnerable, sitting alone and waiting. Time passed slowly. Barely able to move in the heat, I found that stupid, irrational doubts started to come into my head. It must have been only an hour or so later, but when the park warden finally returned to pick me up I could have kissed the bugger I was so relieved to see him.

From the photographs, I imagined that Antarctica would hold a similar sense of enormous nothingness. I had been in the desert for just the briefest of moments; in Antarctica it was going to be for sixty consecutive days. Sitting on the plane, only a few hours before we landed in Patriot Hills, I wondered whether the same irrational doubts I had experienced in the desert would revisit me now. Sixty days seemed like such a long time to be out there, skiing with a few friends, hundreds of miles from the nearest person. On the other hand, I consoled myself, maybe I would feel different from that time in the desert. One thing was for sure — there'd be about a 100 degrees difference in temperature and a distinct lack of rhinos.

Despite the timeless and unchanging nature of a desert, Antarctica's climate has altered in recent years. Scientists, desperate to understand what's going on, have been monitoring a number of icebergs that have broken off from the Ross Ice Shelf. Understandably, icebergs are a pretty common sight in the Southern Ocean, and the odd one bobbing around should hardly set alarm bells ringing. That is until the satellite imagery manages to calculate the size of these things. The latest one to break off was called 'B15' and stretches for nearly 300 kilometres. This 11,000-square-kilometre block of ice is the size of Jamaica and contains enough fresh water to put Evian out of business for the next couple of thousand years. In the three weeks after B15 calved off the ice shelf, it was joined by three 'baby' brothers, all of which would have made the iceberg that sank the *Titanic* look like a toothpick.

In terms of global warming, the amount of frozen water locked into the ice cap, if melted, would flood the world on a biblical scale; a fact that makes the 4,000 heavily bearded and slightly weird scientists who inhabit the continent more than a little jittery.

The Antarctic Peninsula is the most northern part of the continent and, over the last decade, it has experienced one of the highest temperature increases on the planet. With enormous icebergs breaking off from both the Ross and Ronne ice shelves, scientists thought the fluctuations in temperature might well be having devastating repercussions.

These two ice shelves, both larger than France and Britain put together, are hemmed in between the vast continental ice sheets of western and eastern Antarctica. The concern grew that if they broke up completely, then sea water would rush in beneath the ice, forcing western Antarctica to break off from the land underneath. As it slowly floated away, broke up and began melting, the world's sea level would rise by approximately twenty feet. London, New York and Holland would then need to get hold of some seriously good water pumps.

Another theory suggests that these ice shelves act like a bath plug for the significantly larger eastern Antarctica, regulating the flows coming off the ice cap. As improbable as it is, if this side of Antarctica were to melt, then there would be very big problems indeed. With a 150–200-foot global rise in sea levels, it's probably fair to say that the predominant race on earth would then be Sherpas.

However, scientists have realised that, although the peninsula is warming, the interior of Antarctica has actually got colder. The exact reasons for why this is happening have been explained to me on several occasions, but the only bit I really understood was that the temperature changes are most likely seasonal and on a comparatively small scale. Essentially the message was there's no need to start buying canoes and stockpiling baked beans just yet.

As the scientists delve more deeply into Antarctica's secrets, they are realising how much more there is to discover. Even now, there are vast tracts of land that have not been visited by man. Antarctica still remains one of the last true wildernesses left on the planet.

Towards the end of the nineteenth century, Jules Verne wrote *Journey to the Centre of the Earth*, and in his wild imaginings he came up with the idea of a great subterranean lake. Over a hundred years later, scientists were flying across eastern Antarctica firing radio waves through the ice when they obtained some rather confusing data. Utterly baffled, they retested it and finally came to the conclusion that their equipment must be right. At the same Russian station where the coldest temperature had been recorded, there appeared to be a vast freshwater lake sitting nearly two and a half miles beneath the surface of the ice. At over 200 kilometres long and 700 metres deep, it is one of the largest lakes in the world. After some more research, they realised that this sub-glacial lake was not alone; there were dozens of them.

One of the first questions on everyone's mind was how had the lake remained unfrozen, given that there were a few million tons of ice on top of it. Although still contested, one theory suggests that the heat flow from within the earth and the pressure of the overlying ice may have allowed this to happen. Despite the temperature being −50 degrees at the surface of the ice, it might be much warmer lower down; possibly only one or two degrees below freezing.

Undisturbed for millions of years, this pristine environment may well have all sorts of incredible prehistoric microbes locked inside it. For the scientists, it is a unique chance to look directly into the past and possibly find life forms that have been extinct for thousands of years.

The Russian scientists took it upon themselves to start drilling a hole, a very deep hole, and after months of work they suddenly stopped, only 130 metres short of breaking through. The problem was they had no idea how to drill into the lake without immediately contaminating it with all the kerosene and dirt on the drill bit.

If they inadvertently pumped the lake full of their own industrial by-products, it would pose a few problems later, when trying to analyse the data. So, in an extraordinary display of patience, everyone decided to wait a few years, until drilling technology advanced enough to offer a practical solution. I can imagine there are quite a few scientists, pacing up and down and going grey with frustration, waiting for some big mining company to come up with a bright idea.

Aside from these sorts of scientific phenomena, Antarctica has many other characteristics which, although more obvious, are no less bizarre.

Each year at the South Pole, there is only one sunset and only one dawn. In summer, the sun revolves around the sky, never dipping below the horizon, and creates twenty-four hours of bright sunshine. In winter, the reverse is true, and not a glimmer of light will be seen for an entire four-month period. If there is anything that is going to mess up a human's biological clock, then having a day that lasts an entire year is certainly one of them.

From what I had read in previous accounts, the twenty-four hours of sunlight barely affected people arriving in Antarctica. The perpetual sun simply caused a few sleepless nights and a general need for a little less sleep. However, the months of complete darkness were an entirely different matter.

'Overwintering', as the early explorers call it, must be one of the most challenging mental battles a human can endure. As the sun slowly dips below the horizon and the last flecks of orange gently disperse into the night sky, the knowledge that the winter cold will make it torturous to go outside until spring must be very hard to come to terms with.

Outsiders, entering a base the following year, talk of the surreal and listless stares of the scientists, as if the entire community had just woken up from hibernation. For months these people have been padding up and down the same small corridors, utterly secluded from physical contact with the outside world. Some accounts describe how individuals had slowly become detached from the others, staking out their own little territory in the camp. Instead of an interactive community, they had become apathetic and isolated, each spending the long months festering in their own allotted place.

Sara Wheeler, in her book *Terra Incognita*, describes the scene when she arrived at a camp. 'When the six people saw me, they fell silent and stared as if . . . I had walked in stark naked. One of them said later, I guess it was like waking up to find a complete stranger in the bedroom.'

Inuit, living in the High Arctic, are well versed in the misery associated with the long polar winter. In modern times, alcohol has been one way in which the less headstrong among them deal with the utter depression it can cause. Humans, deprived of the basic right of sunlight, have been known to simply close down. They become introverted and uninterested, lost in their own private world of lightless suffering.

Inuit refer to it as *perlerorneq*, which means 'to feel the weight of life'. It's no wonder the north of Sweden has one of the highest suicide rates in the world. The experience must be like that of a bushman experiencing solitary confinement for the first time.

The early polar explorer Dr Frederick Cook was one of the first Westerners to articulate the effect the polar winter could have on a person's psyche. 'I can think of nothing more disheartening, more destructive to human energy, than this dense, unbroken blackness of the long polar night . . . The outer world of icy desolation has also descended upon the inner world of our souls . . . the night soaks hourly a little more colour from our blood.'

Although Cook was one of the first to understand the effect, he wasn't alone. In the years to come, expeditions to Antarctica took great pains to try to maintain some semblance of a normal routine throughout the winter. Boredom and isolation could so quickly lead to tempers fraying and, if the captain was unable to maintain discipline, then their micro-society would be in serious danger of collapsing. In an attempt to amuse the men, the ships often contained entire libraries, musical instruments and, on occasion, would even print a regular newspaper. As to what they filled the pages with exactly, I can't imagine, but at least it seemed to keep the men occupied for a while.

The extent to which the captains feared the maddening effect of the long dark is amply attested by an early American expedition led by Admiral Byrd. Rather tellingly, he packed two coffins and twelve straitjackets. Obviously, he believed the challenge of Antarctica would be far more mental than physical.

Fortunately, the lingering torture of over-wintering in Antarctica was not something I would be experiencing. Despite being a little run down, the Russian jet would hopefully be capable of taking me in and out of Antarctica in just a couple of months. The early explorers, on the other hand, obviously had to come in by boat and were entirely dependent on the notoriously capricious pack ice. They had to sail in one year and spend an entire winter sheltering in tiny wooden huts before finally setting out for the interior the following season. A whole expedition often took three or four years to complete. Bugger that for a laugh.

To say that these explorers were tough is a classic British understatement of which they would have been proud. They endured a protracted degree of suffering which would be hard to match in any modern-day society without being arrested. Typical of that era, glory and hardship went hand in hand, and the way all but a few explorers went about trying to reach their goal reflected this.

Although other nations would later show a similar inclination, during the mid-nineteenth century it was the British who drove forward the desire to chart unknown areas. This was a time when the empire was dwindling fast. England needed heroes, but there weren't any decent military campaigns on the horizon. The Establishment wanted to send out a clear message — although not in her heyday, England was still very much a force to be reckoned with.

During this time, the British navy was vast, underfunded and itching to do something worthwhile. With institutions such as the Royal Geographical Society in London egging them on, they turned their hand to exploration. Although not quite as good as musket blasts and cannon fire, exploration and, later on, the attainment of the poles were at the very least considered to be a respectable arena where an Englishman might prove himself.

Soon, men were being sent off into the most far-flung places on earth. With a couple of years' provisions and a sextant, they were told to plant a flag in anything that looked unfamiliar. Enormous wooden ships ventured off into the unknown, had horrendous adventures and often returned with less than a full complement of crew. With each new tale of suffering and endurance, the British public's curiosity grew. Exploration, it seemed, could be just as entertaining as war.

Other countries soon followed suit. In a sort of perverse schoolboy rivalry, but with much bigger boats, nations competed to outdo each other on the places named, the stories of endurance told.

The way the English explored in particular often amuses (and confuses) anyone not born into this kind of culture. The stereotype of the stiff-upper-lipped officer, blindly refusing to look facts in the face, is unfortunately not so far from the truth. The nineteenth and early twentieth centuries seemed to be the heyday of these kinds of men, all stoic in outlook and devout followers of discipline.

One of the most famous examples of the British venturing into *terra incognita* was Sir John Franklin's overland survey in northern Canada in 1821. The three-and-a-half-year journey, covering 5,000 miles on foot, ended in such dire circumstances that the men were forced to live off lichen and by boiling the leather soles of their boots. Cannibalism even occurred before the culprit was executed, and what was left of the original expedition managed to survive thanks only to the kindness of local, but somewhat bemused, Inuit communities.

'Not being able to find any lichen . . . [we] ate a few morsels of burnt leather for supper. Crédit [one of the survivors] . . . brought in the antlers and backbone of a deer which had been killed in the summer. This, although putrid, was esteemed a valuable prize . . . We perceive our strength decline every day, and every exertion becomes irksome . . . but even in this pitiful condition we conversed cheerfully.'

Franklin's book, *Narrative of a Journey to the Shores of the Polar Sea*, 1823, written upon his return, contains stories of hardship and endurance that can scarcely be believed. His classic understatement and unblinking devotion to duty were attributes deemed to be the benchmark for naval officers of his day. As it transpired, this wasn't to be the last of Franklin's suffering, as he was later to disappear with all 135 members of his crew in an attempt to sail through the elusive North-West Passage. However, for the moment the message was clear: the world could be assured that, no matter what the circumstances, British officers did not get rattled.

As more and more expeditions set off into the unknown, the reports as to what was to be found in these bizarre regions gently filtered back to the civilised world. The public's imagination became inflamed by tales of seas so cold they froze ships, of white bears twice as high as men, and strange, dark-skinned people wrapped in fur. Soon the inevitable happened and explorers turned their attentions south. By the mid-nineteenth century, Antarctica had come firmly under the spotlight.

The simple truth is that 150 years ago, no one had the faintest idea what was to be found at the bottom of the world. They were unsure whether there might be a group of islands, a frozen sea or an entire land mass. Most cartographers simply stamped 'Here be Dragons' and left it at that.

However, in London all sorts of theories abounded about what was to be found. The Royal Geographical Society became awash with scientists and fellows hotly debating the issue. A man called John Cleve Symmes even suggested that the North Pole acted as a gateway to an inner world, where the inhabitants kept warm by living under the ice. The earth's poles became a symbol of man's dominance over the planet. Surely, they reasoned, in such progressive times, man could tame such far-flung areas of the globe?

Various expeditions from Britain, Belgium and America went to solve the mystery, but Antarctica proved reluctant to disclose her secrets. A few naval commanders, such as Sir James Ross and Dumont d'Urville, skirted the edge of the continent, naming ice shelves and outlying islands, but couldn't get anywhere near the interior. After their attempts, the most significant increase in knowledge of Antarctica came from the whaling and seal-hunting captains, who ventured into the unknown in search of new fishing grounds. Some, like Carl Larsen, had an interest in exploration, but mainly it was simply a by-product of their commercial pursuits.

In 1898, a Belgian ship succeeded in becoming the first ever to overwinter in Antarctica. Trapped in the pack ice of the Bellingshausen Sea, the crew had a horrific time and only just managed to emerge the following year to tell their story. Despite an entire season on the ice, they had no definitive answers as to Antarctica's true nature. It seemed incredible that in this age of enlightenment, with the invention of electricity, the internal combustion engine and telephones, man still could not determine whether he was one continent short of a planet.

A British torpedo lieutenant called Robert Falcon Scott, desperate for promotion and the chance to make a name for himself, leapt at the chance to settle the issue. With a ship named the *Discovery*, and with a carefully chosen crew, he set sail for the unknown. The date was 1 November 1901.

★   ★   ★

One hundred years later, almost to the day, Tom, Andy, Paul and I were sitting on the plane preparing to go into the interior of Antarctica. While the continent Scott had first seen in 1901 has remained completely unchanged in the intervening years, our own world has advanced at a frightening pace. Technological developments in air travel and computers have compacted everything, diminishing the last great wildernesses. Suddenly, planet Earth is a much smaller place. For good or bad, this fact enables people like me, who are fragile and unadventurous in comparison, to follow in the footsteps of the great explorers and reach for the same goals. We are the product of that advance and piggyback off it to our advantage.

Through the scratched and dirty window of the plane, I waited for my first sight of the ice. I thought about the contrast between my world and the one I was just about to see. While humans had made such changes to the rest of the planet, Antarctica had remained untouched, the winds continuing to blow across its frozen desert, just as they had done for the last 25 million years.

Someone once told me that Louis Blériot, the Frenchman who made the first flight across the English Channel, could have shaken the hand of Neil Armstrong. In a single lifetime, we had gone from flying just over twenty miles across the Channel to the moon and back. The difference is no less startling between the explorers of the early twentieth century and modern expeditions such as ourselves. In ten minutes logged on to the Internet, we could learn more about Antarctica than they could have gleaned in a lifetime's research. They had set off into the unknown, whereas we, on the other hand, knew what we were getting into; we just didn't know whether we would be able to do it.

One hundred years ago, the *Discovery* expedition was the first concerted effort to reach the South Pole. It was also the only time when two of the greatest British explorers, Captain Scott and Sir Ernest Shackleton, would be part of the same expedition.

From the outset, it was obvious they had their differences. Scott was a stoic, disciplined naval officer and Shackleton a charismatic youth who had charmed his way on board the ship. Hopelessly ill equipped and ignorant of how to combat the hostile conditions, they trudged for day upon day. Scurvy, malnutrition and pure exhaustion began to take their toll, and soon after Christmas they made the gut-wrenching decision to turn back. They were 463 miles from the pole. These men had come from a tradition in which they would rather eat the soles of their boots than give up for lack of provisions. For them to turn back, they must have been in a desperate condition.

Upon returning to England, Scott published a book about his adventures and immediately became a national hero. However, this publication aired the tensions that had arisen between Scott and Shackleton all too publicly. Among the stirring tales and dramatic prose was a clear inference that Shackleton had not been up to the challenge. Coughing up blood and, at times, unable to stand, Scott had ordered Shackleton home on medical grounds. Although later there would be evidence of some truth in his claims, the whole episode showed a rather undesirable side to Scott, who appeared to use his position to undermine his subordinates and promote his own ambition.

As was to be expected, this did not go down at all well with the fiery Irishman, and a few years later an advert appeared in a national newspaper. 'Men wanted for hazardous journey. Small wages. Bitter cold. Long months of complete darkness. Constant danger. Safe return doubtful. Honour and recognition in case of success.'

Shackleton was raising his own expedition south.

Hundreds of men answered the advert. Shackleton now had experience and men, but lacked the most important thing — money. Over the next seven months, his drive and resourcefulness were limitless. He pitched to potential sponsors, gave lectures at high-society parties and promised things that were not his to do so. Much to everyone's amazement, the *Nimrod* expedition set sail as planned, a feat that makes our own sponsorship fiasco look like child's play.

Fuelled by the humiliation of 1903, Shackleton's drive was insatiable. In true British style, he ignored the experience of the Inuit and previous polar explorers, opting instead to set off on foot. Despite convincing proof that the use of huskies and skis greatly improved speed and efficiency, he decided to rely on his own two feet. In effect, he was the underdog without the dog.

Although we were travelling on the centenary of the *Discovery* expedition, it was really this later attempt by Shackleton which had most inspired me in my own bid to try to reach the South Pole. His journey into the heart of Antarctica and on to the High Polar Plateau is one of the most incredible feats in recorded history.

After pioneering a new route up the Beardmore Glacier, Shackleton came within 93 miles of reaching the pole. With only five days to go until they finally reached their goal, Shackleton realised they were too low on provisions to continue safely. Where so many would have pushed on regardless, he turned the sleds around, preferring the lives of his men to the glory of becoming the first to reach 90 degrees South. Egos have always proved to be a dangerous thing in the polar regions, and by turning back Shackleton demonstrated that his was not about to sacrifice the men in his command. ' . . . but all is not the Pole. Man can only do his best . . . [later in a letter to his wife] Better to be a live donkey than a dead lion.'

The kind of people traditionally drawn to challenges of this nature are those with an engorged ego to satisfy. The self-confidence and determination required in such pursuits so often go hand in glove with arrogance and overriding ambition. How many times do the climbers on Everest ignore the turn-around times and continue up to the summit? The character traits that propel them onwards are precisely those that bring about their downfall.

Ego is an extraordinary powerful thing, perfectly able to wreck friendships and expose explorers to risks they would never normally take. Yet without its driving impetus half the expeditions would never even get off the ground. It is always that fine balance between channelling the strength an ego can confer and losing your perspective on the situation and destroying yourself and those around you.

As long ago as 1888, the Norwegian explorer Fridtjof Nansen commented on how the human ego can play a part in exploration.

'It is the sad part of expeditions of this kind that one systematically kills all better feelings, until only hard-hearted egoism remains.'

No one likes to admit to such self-gratifying character flaws, but, to a greater or lesser degree, pride and recognition are almost always significant aspects of any expedition. Great wildernesses and Himalayan peaks are places where records can be broken and egos satisfied.

So often, polar explorers focus on the pain and suffering they endured whilst out in these extraordinary places. By talking about the incessant hardships and incredible temperatures, they set themselves firmly apart from the average person. Only a superhuman could possibly attempt the pole and the rest of us might as well stay under our duvets at home.

Ranulph Fiennes, in his book *Mind over*

Matter, says, 'Nature can be wild and cruel in these climes. Most of the eight or so manned bases of the continent are built along the coastline. Even short journeys by the scientists outside the immediate safety of their bases have ended in death by blizzard or crevasse.'

When I first read this, I had no idea about Antarctica or, for that matter, how tough I was. I was a teenager when the book was first published and, looking around the chemistry department that day at school, I weighed myself up against a few of the scientists. Admittedly, the more portly among them didn't look up to much, but here was one of the greatest names in modern-day exploration inferring that normal men could barely make it once round the base without dropping down dead. There are indeed occasions where a blizzard has disoriented scientists and the cold has killed them, but the impression given by such a statement is that only a man impervious to all but Kryptonite could venture into Antarctica's interior.

Maybe that was the case; maybe Antarctica would be as bad as the books said. In the great trans-Antarctic crossing led by Will Steger and Jean-Louis Etienne, one of the men nearly died when popping out of his tent to check on his dogs. It was not as if they were inexperienced tourists, as this team had just spent 220 consecutive days on the ice, travelling over 3,700 miles. Despite this experience, a couple of minutes outside the tent had very nearly killed one of their number. A blizzard had disoriented him and he was forced to spend the entire night in a hole he had dug with a pair of pliers.

Will Steger would later write in his diary,

'Antarctica's terrible interior tries to turn men into its own image — frozen.'

These examples were from people who had actually been there. Combined, they did little to give the impression that a normal person could just up sticks and head south. Even when looking at the outcome of Shackleton's *Nimrod* expedition, any sane person would think twice before they went out and started buying skis.

By the time Shackleton's 'Southern Party' had finally reached the safety of the ship, the men had endured 126 days on the ice. The crew members that watched them clamber back on deck reported that they looked 'more dead than alive'. For me, however, it is the photograph which really tells the story. Gaunt faces, lined and burnt by the wind, stare out in their sadness. Their eyes blaze with an intensity of endured suffering that cannot be imagined. We were hoping to complete approximately half the distance and in roughly sixty days. I wondered whether any of us would have that same raw appearance, the same fierce hardening of the eyes that seemed to convey a mania most would never understand. The same look is in George Mallory's eyes just before his last and fatal attempt on Everest in 1924. He looks like an absolute psycho.

A few years later, Shackleton would raise another expedition called the *Endurance* for which he has subsequently become so well known. This later expedition, although a stirring tale of suffering and bravery, failed in its objective to traverse the entire Antarctic continent. On the final part of this amazing journey, while trying to reach his stranded men for the fourth time in succession, Shackleton suffered so much stress that his hair turned completely grey. Despite his courage and strength, he would never once set foot at the South Pole. He died on the whaling island of South Georgia at the age of forty-seven.

I had copied down into my diary a few lines from Shackleton's account of the *Endurance* expedition. It was a passage that I hoped might remind me of the bigger picture, for those days ahead, when it all got too much. 'We had suffered, starved and triumphed, grovelled down yet grasped at the glory, grown bigger in the bigness of the whole. We had seen God in his splendours, heard the text nature renders. We had reached the naked soul of man.'

Shackleton had been one of those giants from my childhood, an indestructible man with inhuman strength. Sitting on the plane, I wondered whether he might have felt equally apprehensive before his first sight of Antarctica. Things had certainly changed in the last 100 years. For modern expeditions it was all a great deal easier, but the same thought kept on returning — how on earth did we think we could succeed, where giants had failed?

★   ★   ★

A general commotion woke me from all this daydreaming. Light was coming in through the aircraft windows and a few people were kneeling on their seats, craning their necks out of the windows. I unclipped my seat belt and walked up to the front of the plane where I had previously seen a navigator's window. Just like the glass turrets on the Second World War bombers, the window poked out underneath the pilot's cockpit and would give an excellent view of the scenery below.

With eyes adjusted to the dark lighting of

the plane, my first look outside was blurred and confusing. I squinted in the harsh light and slowly shapes started to pull together in focus.

Ice, mile upon mile of it, stretched away in a perfect white expanse. It had a brilliant luminescence, like the sun bouncing off the ocean. This was an ocean all right, an ocean frozen and scoured by the wind and reflecting the daylight like an uncut crystal. I had been too young to really appreciate the first time I had seen the sea, but now, with this landscape in front of me, I understood once again. Cruising along, thousands of feet above the surface, I could see the uniform ice, continuous and unbroken, reaching all the way out to the horizon. The scene was enormous, in the purest sense of the word, and after all these years of anticipation it did not disappoint.

The plane started its descent and the Russian navigator signalled for me to get back to my seat. I clipped in and watched the general activity as the crew got ready to land. It is no mean feat landing a plane the size of a jumbo on a runway made of blue ice. For starters, the runway is not flat. The word 'runway' implies all sorts of standard airport paraphernalia, such as landing lights, smooth tarmac and control towers. As I soon found out, in Patriot Hills they had obviously dispensed with such pleasantries.

The 'runway' consists of a few black dustbin bags, held down with snow and evenly placed around the perimeter. The surface of the ice is so undulating that when a plane comes into land, its tail fin, which is the height of a three-storey building, simply disappears from view. Instead of a control tower, one of the camp staff stands at the start of the runway and, using a small mirror, reflects the sun into the pilot's eyes. It is not exactly a scientific process.

As the surface is blue ice, there is absolutely no point in trying to use the brakes. Fortunately, space is the one thing Antarctica has in abundance, and the idea is just to let the plane come to an eventual standstill. However, as it skids across the ice, the most difficult part for the pilot is trying to keep the plane straight. Often, it veers off at an angle, slewing dangerously close to the mountains on the one side or the soft snow on the other. As they career along, patiently waiting for the minimal friction to take effect, the pilots often have to fire up the engines and correct an imbalance. It looks next to impossible trying to keep the whole thing pointing in the right direction.

But blue ice runways are a necessity.

Without skis on their undercarriage, the pilots have to use blue ice so the wheels can run freely. The problem is that such ice occurs only where there is a great amount of wind, and most planes, including our one, can't land in anything above 25 knots. It's a perfect catch-22.

The Americans have the technology to put skis on their Hercules planes, but refuse to tell anyone how they've done it. They smugly fly overhead, secure in the knowledge that no one else will be able to spend the millions of dollars needed to develop a similar system. Everyone else just has to go and find their own patch of ice to land on. Usually this is right on the doorstep of a mountain range, as the summits act as a funnel for the wind and clear the snow. They also give the pilot something to aim for in the vast white expanses.

The Russians always carry enough fuel to be able to circle a few times and then return to Punta Arenas if the weather remains clouded over. However, with the exorbitant price of aviation fuel, they are often reluctant to make a wasted trip. In the following weeks, while we were skiing south, we would hear reports of dented fuselages or broken undercarriages as the pilots went ahead and landed in marginal visibility. Usually, this would just require a few panels to be beaten straight and the odd tweak with the hydraulics, but with hundreds of barrels of aviation fuel in the cargo hold I can't help wondering if it's purely a matter of time before things go more seriously wrong.

On one occasion, at the end of our season in Antarctica, a scientist was dropped off at Patriot Hills. His aim was to spend the following month building a fully automated weather station. Without the need for human interference, the station would beam back useful reports, allowing the scientists on the mainland to continue with their research all through the winter. He proudly tightened the last of the screws and flicked the 'on' switch. With a smug grin he realised everything was working perfectly.

Then the Russians came. With his bags beside him, waiting patiently on the side of the runway, the scientist watched in disbelief as Kras Air's finest came in to land. Billowing great clouds of smoke and travelling at over 100 miles an hour, the plane came roaring in to land, right on top of the newly finished weather station. According to one of the camp staff, the pilot looked a little sheepish when shown the twisted metal and scattered debris, which was all that remained of the scientist's efforts. Meanwhile, somewhere on the edge of the runway, a man wept quietly into the hood of his jacket.

However, all this was yet to come, and as the plane lowered its landing gear I knew nothing of such certifiable behaviour.

The plane hovered for a few moments and then bounced down on the ice. I could see the dark rock of the Patriot Hills rushing past the window and the engines firing up in reverse thrust in an attempt to slow us down. More bouncing. Then a slightly unnerving graunching sound, followed by a clatter as the fuel cans jiggled up and down in their netting. After a couple of minutes of exchanging concerned but excited looks and a few more bounces up and down for good measure, the plane came to a standstill. The crew member sitting directly in front released his grip on the handle by the door and tentatively stood up. We had touched down in Antarctica.

Cold air came rushing into the cabin. The enormous tail of the plane had opened up and a ramp extended down on to the ice. We clambered past the crates at the back and stood squinting as the bright light flooded in from outside. Just before me was the same vast desert I had seen from the navigator's window stretching off into the distance. I put my foot on the ice, took two paces forward and slipped over, landing heavily on my arse. I had visions of immediately being bundled back on the plane with a splintered coccyx and an award for the shortest time ever spent on Antarctica. After a quick internal inventory, I confirmed that everything seemed to be working and tentatively worked my way across the runway, trying not to look as if I was in pain. Hardly the auspicious entrance I had hoped for.

People on skidoos and huge tracked vehicles zoomed up to the entrance of the plane and began unloading the fuel drums. In the confusion, a woman standing on the back of a trailer shouted and pointed in the direction of a small collection of tents about a kilometre away. The four of us shouldered our rucksacks and trudged off across the hard-packed snow. It was 9 November 2002 and finally I was standing on the biggest lump of ice on the planet.

6

The Big Offski

'If you ever go to Antarctica, don't order your drinks with ice. You'll just look like a tourist.'

Like the ultimate frontier post, Patriot Hills stands alone in the middle of the Antarctic desert. A small collection of tents, a few radio masts and three aircraft are all that one of the main camps on the continent can boast. The tents on the perimeter look out on to a horizon that is utterly bleak and devoid of life. Only the wind sweeping past their flysheets is happy to venture out into this white expanse without fear of getting lost. Everything else is huddled together, neighbours just a few feet apart, all seeking reassurance by their proximity.

We pitched our tents slowly, the cold making us clumsy and badly coordinated. It was a cold that seemed to get in underneath our layers of clothing. Just standing and breathing in the frosty air felt laboured and difficult, while my forehead gently pounded, as if I'd just bitten into an ice cream. Actions that would normally have taken a few seconds took us minutes and were accomplished only with a great deal of concentration. We got ourselves organised in that same semi-confused state in which a drunk tries to drive a car, having to think hard about even the smallest of movements.

Once we were set up, everyone walked over to the communal tent. I went off in the other direction for just a few hundred yards to get a view of the whole camp. With my back to the wind and my fur hood up protecting my face, I stood and let my eyes wander across the tents and the horizon behind. It was bizarre. I was only a few hundred metres out, yet I felt exposed and vulnerable. I now understood how those scientists had got so quickly lost when venturing out from their base. It was that same feeling I get from swimming out to sea, where just a few hundred metres from the shore I feel isolated and cut off. With the sea, though, the feeling is usually combined with my imagination picturing how my legs must look to a shark cruising along the bottom. The film *Jaws* has always played havoc with my enjoyment of summer holidays.

I scuttled back to camp and burst in through the outer door of the main tent.

Inside, about thirty people were eating and generally enjoying themselves. We sat down at a table next to them and started tucking into a hearty breakfast. It was obvious that all the camp staff loved coming in from the cold and shedding the goggles, hats and face masks which effectively isolated them when outside. As in all small and secluded communities, these people had extraordinary patience, and when engaged in conversation gave their undivided attention. Here, time and space were in abundance and stories were seldom interrupted or subjects changed until they had been thoroughly exhausted.

Many of those in the mess tent were pilots or support staff for the planes. Like Paul, they seemed to move between the Arctic and the Antarctic, following the summers and enjoying the perpetual daylight. Flying in the polar regions is certainly a specialist skill and only few pilots have enough experience to land between the pressure ridges in the Arctic and the crevasses down south. As such, they do back-to-back seasons, travelling quite literally to the ends of the earth each year. The only drawback to such a lifestyle I could see was the danger, cold, lack of women, fresh vegetables, culture and clean socks, and the fact that they almost never saw trees or green grass.

As we listened to some stories, it became apparent that many of the staff had worked in Antarctica before. More often than not, they had been with the British Antarctic Survey, and this involved working for a continuous two-year stretch, completely cut off from the rest of the world. Those going would be asked how many cigarettes they might need whilst away and smokers would have to face the horrifying reality of working out how much they really smoked over a two-year period. The communities would often have only fifteen or twenty people in them, and so tolerance of annoying habits was something they all possessed in abundance.

To us fast-talking city boys, with attention spans comparable to goldfish, they all seemed amazing listeners. They didn't try to better a story, interrupt or change the subject to talk about themselves. Silences would appear naturally in the conversation, and instead of feeling uncomfortable it just felt like a natural way for one conversation to end and another to start.

Sometimes, however, you could see that this kind of lifestyle had taken its toll. Sitting across from me was a man called Doug Stern, who was immediately identifiable by the fact that he was the only one dressed exclusively in caribou fur. In styles popular with polar explorers a hundred years ago, Doug sat, sipping coffee, covered head to toe in fur and entirely oblivious to the bemused looks of people around him.

He had a watery but intense look in his eye and a whispered way of speaking which made everything he said sound incredibly earnest, as if he were constantly imparting a great secret. He had spent the last thirty years living in the High Arctic, 100 miles by snow-mobile to the nearest shop, and this definitely showed in any conversation he had. Whether people were discussing satellite phone technology or the politics of the Middle East, Doug would immediately explain how this reminded him of a story about caribou hunting in the Arctic. At first we thought his links were often a little tenuous, but decided to give him the benefit of the doubt. Soon we cottoned on to the fact that it was largely immaterial what you were discussing — there was always going to be something in any conversation which triggered a memory of caribou hunting for Doug.

The simple truth was that he just didn't give a damn about anything else but life in the polar regions. It wasn't in a resentful or bitter sort of way, he just felt that the things people normally value had little relevance to his own way of living. He was the type of person who could look at a desolate Antarctic landscape and bring the whole place to life. He would talk for hours, explaining what was actually happening behind the inert exterior, where most would see just bleak emptiness. I hope he never goes back to living in anything like a normal society.

A man dressed in what can only be described as an adult version of a Teletubbies suit came through the door at the far end of the tent. He was in his mid-thirties, had a calm, trustworthy look about him, and turned out to be the camp doctor, called Gareth.

Obviously slightly bored by the lack of injuries in the last few days, he decided to teach one of the nearby climbing guides how to intravenously inject morphine. With no guinea pig available, Gareth lifted his own sleeve and started to talk the guide through the best angle at which to insert the syringe. The nervous man managed to repeatedly miss the vein and, each time, Gareth would pause to let the pain subside before continuing with the lesson. We all watched, feeling slightly uncomfortable, as the needle finally made contact. I guess in a place like Patriot Hills you have to make your own amusements.

★　★　★

The next couple of days were spent rechecking our equipment and packing our sleds. The sleds themselves were about two metres long with a hard plastic base and fabric stretched over the top. They were to contain everything we would need until our resupply at the Thiels Mountains over 550 Kilometres away. Every bit of food, gas and team equipment was divided up equally and then distributed into the four sleds. From past expeditions, it was clear that a surefire way for dissension to start was for one person to think their sled weighed more than the others.

Paul asked Mairi, the camp chef, to show me the way down to the storeroom to pick up some provisions. We had both started to put on our hats and gloves when she picked up a torch sitting beside one of the boilers. I looked on a little surprised, considering the twenty-four-hour sunlight, but said nothing. Ironically, one of the leaving presents I had been given was a torch, the friend not entirely understanding the whole perpetual daylight thing. We walked about 50 metres out from the camp before Mairi bent down and pulled on a chain, which had been lying on the ground covered in wind-blown snow. A small trapdoor opened up and steps carved out of the snow led down into a dark passageway beneath.

Underneath the surface, dark tunnels led off in various directions. The air was still but incredibly cold, roughly −40 degrees. The light from the swinging torch beam reflected off beautiful ice crystals that had formed on the tunnels' roofs and illuminated rows of provisions stacked against the walls. The walls, in turn, led off into the gloom and it was obvious someone had spent a great deal of time building a little maze of catacombs deep beneath the surface. Mairi opened the conversation.

'You know how a couple of years ago those skydivers tried to jump over the South Pole,' she said while rummaging in one of the boxes.

I had heard something about an American and Austrian team attempting this crazy stunt. The press had reported how it had ended in disaster, with at least two of them freezing in midair and their parachutes failing to open.

'Well, after they managed to dig the dead guys out of the ground, they flew them here to Patriot Hills for repatriation. The only problem was the wind was really strong and the Russian jet couldn't land to take them out to the mainland. They had to be stored down here for a few days.'

I swung the torch beam around the dark corridors of stacked provisions. I could just imagine coming face to face with an ice-covered body, its pale blue lips and frozen features sitting quietly next to the cans of tinned tomatoes. I shivered, half from cold and half from Mairi's casual rendition of a pretty gruesome story. Frozen in the classic 'arch' formation of a skydive, the bodies had been dumped in this subterranean deep freeze. As Mairi gleefully explained, they had to be thawed out in the mess tent for a while before they would fit in the body bags. It must have been a surreal experience walking in one morning and trying to strike up a conversation with one of the 'new arrivals'.

On the surface, the wind had picked up once again. As we tried to sleep that night, the whole tent flapped like a piece of paper held out of a car window, and we soon realised that it was going to be a rough night. Apart from the noise, ANI had provided us with a bright yellow tent, through which the sun shone with dazzling luminosity. It was like trying to sleep inside a light bulb. We had also forgotten our aircraft eye patches and so the only thing we could do was pull our hoods over our heads to try to block out the light.

But the light continued shining with

unrelenting intensity and as I lay in the sleeping bag something inside my body constantly told me to get up and be active. Even at 3 a.m., it would seem, the body felt there was loads more hay to be made.

After turning over for the hundredth time, I had finally had enough. I unzipped my sleeping bag and went through the laborious process of getting enough clothes on to make the dash to the communal tent. As I unzipped the tent door and clambered outside, Tom groaned in a state of semi-sleep.

The wind was whistling through the camp and the snow on the ground whipped up into a dense cloud of particles, swirling in vast eddying movements just above my knees. I leant forward in a cartoon-like pose and, in a desperate bid to get a cup of tea, battled across the open ground to the door of the main tent.

With a steaming mug in my hand, I looked out of the window at some poor sod on the night shift, who was outside near the planes, checking that their anchor points were all secure. A voice from behind me with a pronounced German accent said, 'Windy, huh?'

I turned to see the guide who had had the crash course in intravenous injections. I smiled and nodded. He joined me at the window and we both stared outside, watching the wind gust through the camp, bending everything in its path.

'About two weeks ago, we had wind about 20 knots stronger than this. It was gusting to nearly 95.' One of his hands came up to the window and with a stubby forefinger he pointed out towards the runway. 'That plane over there broke its anchor chains and totally smashed up its landing gear.'

With my sleeve, I wiped the condensation from my steaming tea off the window pane. I peered through the swirling snow at a white plane sitting slightly farther away from the others. I hadn't noticed its awkward tilt before, but now I could see that the wheels had been twisted into the undercarriage in what looked like a fatal blow. A DC-3 starts to fly at around 90 knots. With such strong winds, the airflow over the wings had given it enough lift to snap its solid metal anchor and bounce it off the ice below. The two-million-dollar plane was now effectively worthless, and some time in the future engineers would come to chainsaw off its cockpit and engines for transportation back to the mainland.

What remained of the sad shell would be left where it was, slowly being covered with snow as the years went by. Apparently there were a number of dead planes like this one, scattered around Antarctica, perfectly preserved by the dry climate. It seemed extraordinary that even the relatively mild conditions of summer were easily capable of giving most planes a thorough roughing up.

'The whole campsite blew away as well and we all had to shelter in the underground storage tunnels,' the guide continued matter-of-factly.

With the howling wind just outside, it was easy to picture how terrifying it must have been. The staff had been asleep, securely in their tents, when they realised the wind was becoming too strong. They quickly dressed, clambered outside into the swirling maelstrom and looked for something to give them shelter. Like tumbleweed in the Australian outback, one by one the tents had been lifted up and rolled into the distance. Everyone had scurried to the storerooms beneath the snow and spent hours in the still cold, weathering out the storm. It must have been as disorienting as it was frightening.

Then, as the guide turned to go back to the kitchen area, he laughed, slapping me on the back. 'You'd better make sure your tent pegs are firmly locked down out there,' he joked.

For a moment I laughed too, but stopped quite suddenly when I understood what he meant.

Matty's team had left two days previously, having done all their packing while waiting out the delays in Punta Arenas. We had waved them off from the side of the runway and now it was our turn to climb on board the Twin Otter plane and make our way to the start point. We had just eaten a huge breakfast of as much fresh food as possible, in anticipation of the dried food diet that would be our mainstay from now on. As I helped load our sleds on to the plane, my stomach felt full of eggs, and I clambered on board with a noticeable lack of agility.

Over the last few days I had been a little troubled by the actual mechanics of going to the loo in severe minus temperatures. Ever procrastinating, I had decided to delay the issue further by going an hour before the flight left. With an old newspaper in hand and everything already packed for the plane, I made a conscious effort to enjoy the comfort of Patriot Hills' igloo toilet. With a wooden seat and a little peg to hang my jacket on, I knew that this would be the last time I would be able to enjoy such unhurried luxury.

One of the pilots leant back from the cockpit and started to give a safety talk. The engines were noisily sparking up outside and

I had my fleece hat over my ears. This was the first safety speech on a plane I have ever wanted to listen to, but with all the noise I caught only a few muffled sentences and the words 'homing beacon'. As the pilot turned back to her controls, I tightened my seat belt, waiting for the pre-flight checks to be completed and the propellers to slowly become a blur. With a jolt, the skids started moving forward and within what seemed like just a few seconds the plane was in the air, offering a very different view of Antarctica.

We were flying north, for about 20 miles, to the edge of the continent. At 80 degrees of latitude, this is the point where the land mass, underneath all the ice, actually starts. It's another couple of hundred miles farther north across the frozen sea before you can see the water's edge. Around the coast is the only place where there is any sort of life, with seal colonies and thousands of penguins and whales.

Our start point, however, was a place that looked exactly the same as all the other millions of acres of ice, barren and utterly devoid of life. Some previous expeditions had claimed to see a crack in the ice at this point, with sea ice on the one side and continental ice on the other. As the plane touched down, we saw no such delineation; only the unending horizon stretching off into the distance and the realisation that this was to be our single vista for the next three weeks.

Without speech or ceremony, we attached the rope lines to our harnesses, took a reading from the compass and began the long journey south.

★ ★ ★

The sleds felt heavy when we moved forward. They were fully loaded for the start of the trip and weighed a little more than 80 kilograms. The harnesses tightened around the waist with each step forward and the sleds jolted along behind, reluctant to follow. The ground was not flat either. The centuries of wind had scoured the surface and created wind-blown features, known in the trade as 'sastrugi'. Although sounding like some sort of Italian pasta, the sastrugi was actually hard-packed snow and could be anything up to five feet high. It made pulling the sleds constantly hard on the lower back.

The landscape looked exactly like a choppy sea, instantly frozen in time. The swirling currents and eddying water had stopped in mid-movement, while the millions of years since Antarctica's creation had allowed the frost to permeate through its layers, freezing the water through to its core. It looked basically flat, but the ice rolled in large, imperceptible waves, making the surface undulate and constantly vary in gradient.

We all set off with far too much enthusiasm and the pace was fast. Partly it was the cold which spurred us on, partly the fact that this was our first day exercising for the last week and we were full of beans. It was soon apparent that the surface would entirely dictate how fast we could go. All around us seemed to be endless acres of hard-packed sastrugi.

For that entire first day, the sleds bounced along behind, slewing sideways as they got caught in a rut and pulling us off balance. The harness ropes jolted taut as the sleds hit each new rise, stopping us dead in our tracks and requiring a great heave with the hips to pull them over the crest. Often that wouldn't be enough and we would have to turn round in our skis and pull the ropes with our hands, until the sleds dropped down on to flatter ground.

As we were all fresh and well fed, we got into it and yanked the sleds through the uneven ground with merciless enthusiasm. Sweat poured out of me and I breathed hard, desperately trying to keep up with the others.

Every hour or so, we would ski up to a

great patch of blue ice, its rippled surface shimmering like the scales of a fish. Our skis slipped and skidded across the polished face, so we would stop, strap them to the top of our sleds and continue on foot. The ice fields were streaked by crevasses, which extended for hundreds of metres across our path. The majority of them were just a foot or so wide and so it was no big deal to pull the sleds up close behind, get some slack in the harness ropes and jump over to the other side. Others were a different story.

As we crossed more ice fields, the crevasses got larger and larger. They were all covered in a layer of snow, which extended across the opening and disguised their true depth. After the crevasse training in New Zealand, we all had our rescue techniques down to a T. The problem was that in Antarctica we were coming across them so regularly that it would have taken an impossible amount of time to rope up for each one. From previous climbing trips, I have always been justly terrified of crevasses and yet Paul just seemed to give the surface snow a couple of pokes with his ski pole and then, unsecured, chance it across.

The ice was hundreds of feet thick where we were standing and some of the larger crevasses would undoubtedly extend all the way down to the bottom. As I stepped out on to the snow spanning the walls of ice, my boots made a loud crunching sound. Each time, I couldn't help but wonder if this was the step that would break through the surface and, like a loaded trapdoor, send me down into the crevasse below.

We had one 50-metre rope, which one of us (I can't remember who) was carrying. Most of the crevasses would be ten times that deep. So even if we survived the fall and miraculously didn't get wedged in between the converging walls of ice, there was a good chance that whoever was left on the surface would be hopelessly short on rope for a rescue.

Normally, a snow-covered crevasse would entail the party stopping, getting out a specially designed snow probe and working its way around it. But with this number of crevasses the only option was to hope the man in front went first and tentatively move across it.

I watched Tom give a crevasse an experimental poke with his ski pole. He took a step forward and his leg disappeared through the snow. He swung backwards with cat-like reflexes, pivoting his body round and managing to balance his other knee on the ice ledge behind. In another, frantic second he had completely hauled himself out and stood a couple of feet back from the edge, panting visibly from the shock.

Three times that day, Tom and I would break the surface of the snow when crossing a crevasse. Each time, we would sink only up to our knee or waist, but it was enough to make my heart go straight to my stomach. After every one, I spent the next hour picturing the crevasse I had nearly gone into; its vertical walls and slippery ice offering not the slightest hope of escape.

People talk about a baptism of fire. That first day was definitely the cold-weather equivalent. After six and a half hours, Paul finally held up his hand in a signal to stop. Feeling dog tired, we hunted around for a flat patch of snow on which to pitch the tents and began to set up camp.

As soon as we stopped moving, our core temperatures started to drop. Holding the metal tent poles, even through our padded gloves, sucked the heat out of our hands, and after every action we had to stand and swing our arms to force the blood back into them. Finally the main tent was up and I dived inside to start the stove and begin the laborious process of melting ice for water.

Peeling off my outer jacket, I couldn't believe how much ice had accumulated on the fur hood and on the inside of its lining.

We had obviously been going way too fast. Sweat had frozen as it went through each fleece layer, before finally solidifying on the inside of the outer jacket. It wasn't just around my armpits; the ice looked like a thin coat of chain mail. As my breath had frozen in front of me, the fur of my hood had also been covered in ice. I had never seen anything like it.

Moments later, Tom came crashing in from outside. He lifted his goggles and sat at the entrance to the tent, breathing heavily and looking blankly into space. His eyes looked tired and his face was flushed from the cold and wind. With a spray of ice, he unzipped the top of his jacket and lay back on the piles of equipment stacked in the centre of the tent.

I looked a little more closely at his face and saw two dark patches, about a centimetre wide and three long, on either side of his cheeks. Despite goggles, a fur-lined hood, balaclava and neck warmer, the wind had still managed to get underneath the protective layers and burn his skin. It wasn't so much frostbite, which is where the flesh actually freezes, but frost-nip, caused by the cold wind. Over the length of the expedition, the damage on Tom's cheeks refused to heal in Antarctica's dry environment. In only a couple of days the dead, outer layers of skin stripped away, exposing the raw, red flesh underneath.

Although it was a little unsightly and probably somewhat painful, it didn't actually hamper Tom's progress on the expedition. Owing to the fact that his normal, fresh-faced complexion made him look like a twelve-year-old, he would later consider the frost-nip to be a blessing. The scars could only help in his bid to look, at least a little bit, like a hardened explorer.

As the others clambered into the tent, I saw Andy had the same two dark patches on his cheeks. I couldn't understand it — the wind had felt relatively mild that day and, at times, both Paul and I had pulled back our hoods to allow the air to circulate more freely. I wondered why Tom and Andy had been affected and I hadn't. Paul had skin like leather and spent his life outdoors, so I assumed that only direct contact with a sand blaster would have had any effect on his face. However, my delicate London complexion was hardly used to this kind of treatment, so it seemed extraordinary that I had managed to get through the day unscathed.

As Paul set up the stove and relaxed into his Thermarest, we were all thinking the same two questions — how far had we travelled and was every one of the remaining fifty-nine days going to be equally hard? Over dinner, he looked at our expectant faces and turned on the GPS. We had travelled exactly 9.6 nautical miles. I did some calculations and realised that in six and a half hours of pretty much constant toil we had just broken ten statute miles — a distance that would normally take me about an hour to run.

My diary for that first night reads,

'Having looked forward to the journey for so long, only a day into it and I already have serious doubts. Am I really going to be able to hack another fifty-nine days of this? Pulling that sled over the hard-packed snow is back-breaking work — it weighs a ton! Why didn't I do some more training when I had the chance?

'With so much effort we have done a pathetic 9.6 miles. The distance before us just seems incredible. I've got to start focusing on small goals, goals right in front of me, and just try and ignore the bigger picture.'

None of us voiced any of our concerns that night. Although each of us knew we wouldn't be able to maintain such an exacting pace for the remainder of the expedition, none of us was prepared to admit it. I knew that both Andy and Tom would not utter a word of complaint until it was physically impossible for them to place one foot in front of the other. By virtue of being in the same team, I would have to hold true to that principle. The other thing was that I'd be damned if I was going to be the first to say that it was all too much.

The next morning over breakfast, Paul told us that the climb from Hercules Inlet past Patriot Hills was one of the steepest we would undertake. He also reminded us that our sleds could only get lighter from now on, as we ate our way through our provisions.

'Thank God!' I blurted out, probably echoing the thoughts of the other two, who were morosely sipping their tea and wondering what on earth Day Two had in store.

★　★　★

With such a uniform landscape and so many more miles ahead of us, the one idea we had to cling to was routine. Like a long prison sentence, routine was the only thing that could stabilise the days. Without it, the endless horizons and twenty-four-hour sunlight would blur the unchanging days and time would drift past without even being noticed.

At precisely 6 a.m., Paul would start the day by bellowing 'Good morning!' from the

186

inside of his tent. I suspected that he must have some Swiss blood in him as he was frighteningly punctual. We soon worked out that we had exactly fifteen minutes, to the second, in which to get out of our sleeping bags, pack up our equipment and make enough space for him and Andy to come in and have breakfast.

When wading out into the cold sea, I have never been one of those people who can dive in quickly. It's always an agonising process of inch-by-inch progression, which infuriates almost everyone standing near by. I have to get up to at least the swimming trunk's line before taking the plunge. In the same way, getting out of my sleeping bag was never going to be a fast process. Unzipping too quickly would invite a stream of cold air to come rushing in and, in my pathetic mental state during the mornings, I imagined that such a shock to the system could well be fatal.

Tom and I would wait inside our sleeping bags, the zips slowly creeping down, until the moment when Paul's footsteps could actually be heard crunching across the snow. In a blur of frenzied activity and multi-tasking in a manner which most women would be proud, we would be sitting quietly on our Therma-rests, everything packed, by the time he had covered the distance to our tent. Like guilty children, we would grin inanely as his face emerged from behind the flysheet and he settled himself inside to make breakfast.

With the twenty-four-hour sunlight, the tent would often be warm during the evening. As the sun circled slowly overhead, the radiation would seep through the tent's thin fabric and make it wonderfully warm inside. Our frosted clothing and frozen inner boots were hung against the side walls to dry. The tent was perpetually cluttered with a million items of clothing, attached to almost every piece of fabric in direct sunlight. Our gloves, boots and clothing had to be dry for the next day's march. If not, within minutes of our being outside the moisture within them would freeze and then cold and frostbite would soon take their toll.

However, when the weather clouded over, it was an entirely different story. No sun would beat down on our tent and no warmth would radiate through to the interior. Our frozen clothes would thaw, but not dry, making them dangerously cold for the next day. This basically meant we had far less time to get jobs done without freezing our outer limbs.

In the morning, our combined breath and the steam from the cooking would condense in an icy sheet across the tent walls and ceiling. As we got up and started to get ready, little clumps of ice would fall down on top of us. Even the smallest movement would vibrate the tent walls and a shower of ice would sprinkle down, getting in everything from our eyes to our ski boots. Camping on cloudy days was just unpleasant in every sense of the word.

What amazed me was how quickly we became desensitised to the more unsavoury aspects of life in the tents. Often, during breakfast, one of us could be seen sniffing the air and then looking down questioningly at the bowl of muesli they were eating. It didn't take long to realise that the rancid smell was coming from someone else's hardened, crusty sock, casually draped across their shoulder. Space was pretty confined with four men in such an enclosed area and so it was horrifyingly easy to jog the clothes line and end up with a pair of sweaty inner gloves dipping into your bowl.

Hair, also, seemed to be just about everywhere. Anyone unfortunate enough to examine our tent after a week would justifiably have thought a troop of baboons had been living in it. Hair just seemed to adhere to almost everything we ever ate. Although my manners have sometimes come under fire from my mother, I am certainly not grubby enough to let a strand of pubic hair stuck to a piece of cheese go unnoticed. After ten days in Antarctica, I barely even raised an eyebrow. The glamour of an expedition to the South Pole became steadily diminished, as each day our standards hit yet another new low. I guess that when you're that hungry there is not a great deal that can actually put you off your food.

By 8 a.m., we would have eaten a huge bowl of granola and washed it down with two cups of tea. When climbing, we are always out of the tent and on our way by 5 a.m., so it felt strange to have a two-hour period at the beginning of the day to slowly build ourselves up to venturing outside.

My initial curiosity as to how to go to the loo in extreme weather was inevitably satisfied. Upon speaking to Paul, there were a number of different techniques popular with those in the know. The main concern was the wind. With a wind chill factor as low as −55 degrees, this was not something to be taken lightly, nor was it to be taken slowly, in a step-by-step manner.

The first way of avoiding the wind was to go to the loo inside the shelter of the flysheet. In between the main tent and the flysheet there is an area about the size of a large suitcase, and here it's possible to dig a hole and get on with it. Although definitely the best way to avoid freezing your nether regions, it did have two rather large downsides.

At the first attempt, it soon became apparent that you needed the balance and flexibility of the average contortionist just to manoeuvre your bum into the right place. The layer of condensed ice on the inside of the flysheet would shower down on you as you tried to steady yourself against the thin fabric of the tent. Owing to the fact that the others didn't want to go outside into the freezing weather until the camp was ready to be dismantled, they would be sitting only inches away. If ever there was a moment for stage fright, then this was it. I don't care how friendly or close you may be to a person, going to the loo in front of them is a boundary that I am reluctant to cross. Even zipping up the inside tent wall did little to help, because, although you were out of sight, the thin fabric meant that when the light shone through a perfect silhouette was formed. I am not sure which was worse — seeing a friend go to the loo so close or seeing a shadow-play version of it.

As only the British can do in such situations, we would try to make polite conversation and act as if not the slightest thing irregular was taking place. Only when some unfortunate noises interrupted someone speaking would we look the other way and desperately search for more conversation. Fortunately, I had some lip protector that tasted of incredibly strong mint. With the same technique they use in autopsies, we would smear the lip balm under our nose to shield us from the smell. Streaming eyes and a resonating minty freshness seemed infinitely preferable to the alternative.

Unsurprisingly, this method was unanimously banned after the first few trial runs. A couple of times Tom tried to get the ban repealed, but to much objection from the remainder of us and a threat from Andy to set fire to his sled if he tried it again.

This left but one option — the 20-yard dash. We deemed this the minimum safe distance from the camp, to avoid any horrendous accidents involving one of us inadvertently stepping into a hole. With toilet paper pre-folded and tucked into our top pocket, we would get out of the tent, grab the shovel in one deft movement and sprint across the snow. The only hurdle was that we would be wearing our camp boots, which are the polar equivalent of slippers, being soft and difficult to run in.

At the minimum distance, a single hefty swing with the shovel would usually do the trick and make a big enough hole. Sometimes, however, the metal blade would hit ice and ping backwards, sending us off balance and often resulting in the loss of a camp boot. The backs of our ski pants had a specially designed zip, running all the way across the bum, which could be opened in a microsecond and a squatting position then adopted.

The wind, streaming across the ice, was a constant incentive to be quick. Within another couple of seconds, we were sprinting back towards the tent, a shovel load of snow loosely tossed over the shoulder to hide the evidence and maintain Antarctica's pristine environment. Before the others had barely had enough time to raise a cup of tea to their lips, you would be back in the tent, furiously rubbing your hands together and shivering uncontrollably from the cold.

We also discovered that a number of past expeditions had elected not to take any toilet paper whatsoever and had adopted a technique known, rather graphically, as the 'snow wedge'. Some people argued, quite correctly, that this method was more hygienic, better for the environment and saved on weight. However, I just couldn't bring myself to change from soft, white toilet paper to a horrendously cold block of ice. It was enough of a shock to the system to expose my naked bum to the breeze, without adding insult to injury and plastering it with freezing-cold snow.

Most of the time I would definitely consider myself to be environmentally friendly. I buy recycled writing paper, make donations to Greenpeace and even do the odd trip to the bottle bank. All of which has virtually no effect on the world's diminishing resources, but generally serves just to make me feel good about myself. What is interesting is seeing how far these environmental principles go. In the biting cold of Antarctica, I would quite happily have used an entire tree's worth of toilet paper if it would have made the process any easier. Snow wedgies seemed like a really bad way of complicating an already difficult situation. We had precious few luxuries out on the ice and I'd be damned if toilet paper wasn't going to be one of them.

After only a few days on the expedition all our biological clocks were in sync. It was like that strange phenomenon whereby women living together all get their periods at the same time. At exactly five-minute intervals, and with a regularity to set a watch by, we would all go in turn; Paul, Andy, Tom, then myself. It got to the stage where we knew that we were running late that morning if Andy had been to the loo before the second cup of tea was ready. I don't think I want to be so in tune with three other men ever again in my life.

After the morning ablutions and breakfast, we would get all our outer clothing on. This often resulted in knocking into each other and kicking things over. After a couple of near-catastrophic incidents when one of the pee bottles was nearly spilt, we quickly learnt to do things in an orderly fashion. At the beginning of the expedition, each of us had five stuff sacks in the tent, full of different bits of equipment and all badly marked. If you needed a pair of pliers in a hurry, it could take ten minutes of asking the others to move to the side while you went through each bag in turn. After a day of hard skiing, any disruption to lying utterly still and giving your legs and back a well-earned rest becomes intensely annoying.

Although not naturally inclined to careful organisation, I soon saw the merits in knowing exactly where everything was kept. Initially, we poked fun at Paul for being so anally retentive with his kit, but within two days we all had followed suit. We became organised to the point of mild obsession, and could find a pair of pliers without having to move so much as a single butt cheek.

By 8.15 a.m., we would be outside and packing up the camp as quickly as possible. After the warmth of the tent, the cold and wind were usually a shock to the system, and it was essential to get the body working to keep warm. Paul would lead the first session, setting a relatively slow pace, and we would fall in behind him. In the infinite space of Antarctica, it seemed positively comical that we would ski one behind the other with only a couple of feet between us. Maybe it was for exactly that reason; Antarctica is just so enormous that we naturally came together and moved as one cohesive unit. Maybe it was a subliminal fear of being separated, which made us act like convicts in a chain gang, our steps perfectly coordinated, our skis moving in time.

The net result was that when the person leading suddenly stopped to check the compass, the remaining three would often crash into the back of the sled in front. It was like the elephants marching in Kipling's *Jungle Book*, and every time it happened it brought a smile to my face.

The first session was always two hours long. Then we broke the day up into one-and-a-half-hour sessions with ten-minute breaks in between. We had planned to do only seven and a half hours in total each day, and so the last session was only one hour long. It immediately became known as 'happy hour', but from the word go it was obvious that it would be anything but.

The first two-hour session, despite being the longest, always passed quickly. At this time in the morning the mind still dozed, blissfully detached from the harsh surroundings, while the body carried out the simple task of putting one foot in front of the other. After the first hour, I would take the lead from Paul and that would again help the time pass swiftly.

When leading, it was important to set the right pace, to navigate in an exact straight line and to steer round the largest bits of sastrugi; all of which gave purpose and responsibility to an otherwise largely unentertaining day. Although leading would give the mind something to focus on, it meant that you always had to be right there in Antarctica and entirely conscious of your surroundings. Every couple of minutes it was important to check that our shadows were at the correct angle and the compass needle straight, and this gave no respite. When following, the relentless rhythm and steady plod would allow the mind to wander and, while the body suffered through the day, your mind could be anywhere from idyllic memories with your girlfriend to the latest plans for world domination.

A good session was one where the pace was not too fast. Then the mind didn't have to concentrate too much on the actual mechanics of skiing and, as when cruising along on the motorway, could wander freely. The open space of the Antarctic landscape was like a blank canvas for the imagination to run wild on. Sometimes it was wonderful to have such freedom and a clean space in which the mind could work. At other times the bleakness was almost unbearable, with not a single changing element to trigger a thought. Like a painter perpetually staring at the white canvas and unable to decide where to start, we sometimes found that our imaginations would just run dry. Then, the sessions would each last a lifetime.

On many occasions I fought for what seemed like an hour to resist the temptation of looking at my watch. This battle didn't help my peace of mind, as it made me constantly think about time, when time was the one thing I wanted to slip past unnoticed. I would finally give in and pull back my outer mitten, expecting at the very least that forty-five minutes would have passed. The minute hand would barely have hit ten, and the bewildered depression this could cause was sometimes so strong that I would happily have lain down in the snow and told the others to go on without me. Even in countless good sessions, where my mind wandered almost the whole way through, there was not a single occasion during the entire expedition when I looked at my watch and found that I had skied past the allotted time.

I was surprised at the kind of thoughts that went through my mind. Each of us had his own mental battle out there on the ice, and I am sure different things kept each of us going. For me, one of the main reasons for taking part in these types of expedition is the perspective it puts on life. In normal society I find it so easy to get wrapped up in the business of paying bills, worrying about my career or being anywhere on time. Out in Antarctica, such things are meaningless. There is simply no place or relevance for them, and I find this a very liberating feeling. Suddenly, years of high-stressed London living drop from my shoulders and the single, overriding priority is trying to reach the South Pole. To have such a clearly defined and focused objective is freedom in itself. To be able to justifiably negate everything else that has been so important only a few weeks ago means that life becomes incredibly simple and, in a strange sort of way, content.

The other aspect is that an environment such as Antarctica makes you put normal life on a pedestal. Things that really weren't that great before suddenly become fantastic. The denial and general discomfort a person has to tolerate when skiing to the pole make even the smallest creature comfort appear wonderful by comparison. You know that when the thought of eating a tomato makes you salivate uncontrollably, it's time to go back to civilisation.

Will Steger, who, on his great trans-Antarctic crossing, spent 220 consecutive days on the ice, said, 'I spent my days designing houses, plotting expeditions to come and trying to recapture sensory impressions so absent from this bare white world: the night sounds of summer, the smells of a forest, the touch of the morning sun in May. I dug deep into my mental filing cabinet for such ordinary moments; here they were precious jewels.'

I had originally thought that our breaks would be pleasant affairs. After two hours skiing in mutual silence, it's forgivable to think that we would chat away in the ten minutes we had together. Regrettably, this just wasn't the case. On the odd days when the weather was still and the sun out, we would talk a little or enjoy a joke. Most of the time, however, the incessant wind prevented any real conversation. We would pull the sleds into a horizontal line and then sit with our backs to the wind. Sometimes one of the others would slap you on the back or lift their goggles and smile, but mostly we just sat, enjoying the feeling of not pulling the sleds and the quietness of the landscape.

If it had been cloudy the night before and our gloves and boots were still damp, the moisture within them would instantly freeze during one of our breaks. Having been working hard for the last two hours, and on the brink of breaking sweat, our bodies would cool within a few moments of sitting down and resting. Some explorers put on their heavy down jackets during breaks, but to us that didn't make sense. Rummaging through the sled five times a day in an effort to find the damn thing would add about half an hour to each day. Time I would much rather spend in the warmth of the tent.

With damp clothing, we would sit out the remaining minutes of our break, in desperate need of a rest, but feeling our hands and feet slowly freeze. Often we would want to adjust some clothing or change the tape in our Walkmans and this would further expose our hands to the cold.

When we started off again, we had to ski fast to build the temperature back up. It was like running a car in the cold — it has to reach a minimum temperature before everything works properly. As we clipped on our skis and picked up our ski poles, the problem only got worse. Although padded, the metal ski poles literally sucked the heat out of our hands. After every single break, there would be at least one of us who would stop for a couple of minutes, whirling their arms round and wincing as the blood came back into stiff fingers.

On our last break, we would sit exhausted and wait for Paul to get out his GPS. To keep the batteries warm, he always had it tucked under layers of clothing, and it would take him an age to finally tell us how far we had gone. Like a commentator in a darts match, he would announce the total with gusto and, depending on the results, caused either spontaneous joy or, more commonly, abject despair.

It actually made no difference if the total was more than we had anticipated or not. Either way, we always got up from our sleds for the last time that day and made a concerted effort to up our pace for the last hour. If the mileage had been good, it inspired us to get as much distance behind us as possible; if bad, then we had to make up the deficit.

Invariably, by about halfway through 'happy hour' I was begging for it all to end. I would try to tuck myself in behind someone else and then do anything to keep up with their moving sled. Like a donkey trying to catch the carrot, I found that the sled in front always seemed to be just out of reach. It bounced along ahead of me, threatening to pull away at any moment and leave me leaderless, wallowing in exhausted self-pity. With the morning's speed and enthusiasm long since departed, there was now nothing left to rely on but brute stamina.

That final hour was bearable only because it was the last. Paul would lead this session, and for what seemed like hours I would stare at the back of his head, willing him to stop. Eventually he would ski off at a different angle, looking for a flat patch of snow on which to camp, and I could finally breathe once again — it was over. We would come together, exhausted, but happy that another day was done, and begin setting up the tents.

Just take it one day at a time, I would say to myself each evening. Just one day at a time.

7

Plane Days and Birthdays

*'May God defend me from my friends; I
can defend myself from my enemies.'*
— Voltaire

By the time the Patriot Hills had slowly
disappeared behind us, we had been going for
four days. After the initial problems with
steep climbs, blue ice and crevasses, we had
levelled out a little and were starting to get
into a rhythm. These familiar mountains had
been the only feature on a horizon that was
utterly flat for 360 degrees. Now only the
sight of four men and the noise their skis
made running over the snow broke the awful
monotony of an empty landscape.

With the route stretching off indefinitely, I
set my mind to thinking about how I was
going to deal with the distance that lay before
us. To compartmentalise everything seemed
like the only solution. I couldn't focus on
reaching the South Pole yet; it just seemed a
lifetime away. Instead, I broke the distance
down into manageable chunks and decided

that I would concentrate only on the one immediately in front. Although this was a little like putting my head in the sand, by doing this I had a series of goals that at the very least would be within my grasp.

Working on degrees of latitude, our journey could be broken down into ten segments. The distance to the pole was 600 nautical miles, making each degree a total of sixty miles. If we averaged ten a day, then we would arrive at the pole in the expected sixty days and pass a new degree of latitude every six. Everything thus became geared to a six-day cycle; our food, our fuel supplies, even our week.

On that fourth day, the wind had died down and Antarctica felt like an entirely different place. It was still and vast, but in a wholly unthreatening sort of way. My initial concerns about feeling isolated proved to be totally unfounded. There were no agoraphobic panic attacks or feelings of doubt, only a wonderful realisation that we were attempting to cross an immense desert on foot.

As we changed the lead during the day, we had to quickly learn the best ways to navigate across such a featureless expanse. In sunny weather, the simplest thing to do was just to follow our shadows. At exactly midday, we knew that they would be pointing due south. Every hour before or after this time would move our shadow 15 degrees right or left of this midway point, and we would simply take an approximate bearing from that. Although it all sounds a little random it did work, and just to make sure we checked with one of the compasses at the beginning and end of each session.

Despite the simplicity of such navigation, occasionally the terrain would become seriously confusing. Having skied for half an hour in exactly the right direction, I would look up from my shadow and feel as if the whole landscape had swivelled 90 degrees. Lumps of sastrugi, which had been a marker point for the last ten minutes, seemed to have moved in a split-second glance and were now sitting on the wrong side of my skis. With no mountains to take a bearing off, the unwavering horizon would run the length of my vision, giving not the slightest hint of the way ahead. It felt as if someone had just played an elaborate practical joke and managed to turn the whole world the wrong way round.

I would stop suddenly and dig inside my clothing for a compass to take a bearing. Caught unawares by the unscheduled break, the others would invariably bang into the back of my sled. They would wait for a couple of seconds, wondering what the delay was all about, before pointing with their ski poles in the same direction we had been following for the last half-hour. I know it all sounds like pretty moronic behaviour, but staring at such a uniform landscape sometimes plays havoc with the mind. It was like one of those pictures that you have to stare at for five minutes before the actual shape reveals itself. Those kinds of things have always made my eyes water and given me a slight headache.

Two days later we crossed our first degree of latitude. On the last break, Paul brought out the GPS and with characteristic flair announced that the 81st parallel was exactly 135 feet behind us. We shouted for joy and hugged each other in congratulation. The smiles were broad and genuine, as it was the end of a long and very hard day. The first marker had been reached, the first goal attained. We all realised that there were another nine to go, but for now our myopic hopes were satisfied. If there was ever a case of people trying to be of the 'glass is half full' persuasion, then this was it. We brimmed with weary self-congratulation, despite the fact that at this stage the glass barely had a single drop in it.

I looked back at the patch of snow 135 feet away. As you might expect, it looked exactly like all the other patches we had passed over the last six days. It seemed so stupid to be celebrating the crossing of such an entirely abstract point. It wasn't like the summit of a mountain or the finish line of a race; it was an entirely human invention in a landscape that had no notion of segregation.

Such philosophical ramblings didn't last for long and I helped set up camp feeling thoroughly pleased with myself. Already the days of continuous exercise were starting to take their toll, and when we unzipped our outer jackets a waft of stale sweat would seep up through the windproof layer. Often the smell would catch us unawares and come as a rather overpowering surprise at the end of a long day. Even the calming effect of the severe cold could mask the smell for only so long. We therefore decided to celebrate the crossing of every new degree by having a bath.

We didn't want to waste heavy fuel on melting snow, so a 'snow bath' was the only alternative. I had heard Geoff Somers talk about the importance of washing on expeditions. Aside from the fact that your teammates are more inclined to talk to you, it also prevented sores from developing in areas of skin that rubbed against the harness. The general feeling was that every week or so was enough to stay relatively hygienic and prevent the appearance of any nasty rashes. One of the Russian teammates who accompanied Geoff on his great trans-Antarctic crossing had wandered around naked in the snow every single morning for weeks on end. Cigarette in hand and his bare buttocks exposed to the breeze, Victor Borarsky had apparently woken everyone up each morning, no matter what the weather, in nothing more than his birthday suit.

We were still warm from the day's skiing and so shedding our clothes inside the tent wasn't too bad. As I unzipped the flysheet and stepped out into the snow, the heat just drained out of my body. It was skin-tighteningly cold.

Outside, I could see Andy, butt naked and trying to sum up the courage to smear snow all over himself. Paul was just about to get undressed himself and was standing by the entrance to his tent, looking on, amused by Andy's obvious reluctance. The sight of two of them, the one dressed in full Antarctic clothing, the other without a stitch on, was a caption competition waiting to happen. I leant back inside the tent, grabbed my camera and, to loud protests from Andy, took a photo. The cold wasn't exactly making him, or for that matter the rest of us, proud men, and he had no wish to be reminded of that fact later on, when I showed all our friends the holiday snaps.

In a flurry of snow and a blur of activity, I washed like a demented man covered in mosquito bites. I rubbed the snow over my body so fast that I probably managed to take off a few layers of skin as well. All the while, the wind seemed to go straight through me, stripping the heat away. After about a minute of some of the most unrelaxing 'bathing' I have ever had the misfortune to experience, I bolted back to the tent. Like a hippo heading towards water, I remorselessly trampled underfoot anything that stood between me and the shelter of the tent.

Once I was fully dressed, the shivering had subsided and I had a couple of sips of whisky inside me, I was prepared to admit that Geoff was right and the snow bath had been worthwhile. I definitely did feel a little cleaner, but as a means of celebrating a happy event it was right up there with country dancing for pure masochistic pleasure.

Our days of fine weather were numbered. While we slept, a weather front came through and we woke to the wind howling across the camp. After hours in the warmth and shelter of the tent, to emerge into the swirling snow was deeply unpleasant. Katabatic winds, emanating from the high ground at the South

Pole, flowed the hundreds of miles across the barren surface of Antarctica's interior and hit our little collection of tents with indifferent hostility.

We pulled our fur hoods tight around our faces, got out the large down mittens and trudged off slowly into the gloom. As always, we travelled directly into the wind, keeping our heads bent low against the oncoming snow. The ground beneath our skis had become a great moving cloud, flowing past at 30–40 knots and making the march forward feel surreal and detached.

Suddenly our clear, serene landscape had been replaced by a horizonless blur. In the dim light, it was impossible to see more than a couple of feet ahead. The gusts of wind bellowed up against our windproof clothing, slowing our pace even further, and any loose straps or bits of fabric vibrated furiously in the rippling wind. It would have been impossible to stop and pitch the tent for shelter as the flapping fabric would simply have been pulled out of our hands. The only option was to keep going and hope the weather blew itself out by the evening.

Despite the cold and the unsettling noise of the wind, I still didn't feel any great sense of panic or anxiety to return to civilisation. My only thought was that the wind was hampering our progress. By midday we were moving painfully slowly. Breaks became difficult, the cold numbing our hands in just a few moments. Andy seemed to suffer a little more than the rest of us with cold hands and would wolf down his food in order to get moving again as soon as possible. A couple of precious minutes early, he would be clipped into his skis and checking the compass. The rest of us understood his desire to start exercising again, but didn't want to sacrifice the remainder of our break.

Unable to go for fear of being separated, he would stand with his back to the wind, shivering in the cold. The moment one of us got up to leave, Andy would set off at a furious pace, and we would all rush to follow. Owing to the fact that his goggles frosted up while he was waiting, he would tear off at a 45-degree angle, only to stop a hundred yards later, recheck his compass and then blitz off again in the other direction. On such occasions, the rest of us would usually hang back a little and try to plot a course somewhere in between.

Paul was just a rock when skiing south. The goggles and windproof lining designed to shield his nose completely hid any expression on his face. It was the same for the rest of us, but somehow we would give off hints as to how we were feeling through our body language. With Paul it was impossible to tell. His skiing style never once altered, and with remorseless and sometimes infuriating uniformity his ski tips moved forward regardless of the weather conditions. At the end of the day, inside the tent and with his gentle smile, he would occasionally confess that he had found the skiing hard work and had had a few problems keeping up with one of the faster sessions. This always took me completely by surprise, as the rest of us would subconsciously hang our heads or ski a little more clumsily when tired. Paul, on the other hand, never gave so much as a hint that he was even breaking sweat.

Owing to a wealth of inexperience and our high metabolic rates, Andy, Tom and I would usually start the day skiing off at a very quick pace. With misguided thoughts of breaking records and arriving at the pole before Christmas, we would egg each other on, our skis becoming a blur as they swished back and forward.

'Come on, come on,' we would shout at each other, and whizz off towards the horizon. Andy never listened to music while we skied and instead occupied his time by making complex mathematical calculations involving our distance, speed and time.

During some of the earlier breaks he would occasionally share his thoughts. 'If we average 15.27 miles per day and have no days lost to storms, we could reach the pole faster than any other team.'

In the early morning, we would nod in agreement and believe that such a target was attainable. At the back of the line, Paul would say nothing, silently keeping up with us and patiently waiting for the hours to pass. By the fourth session, both our speed and our illusions of grandeur had come grinding down. We skied with our arms by our sides, shuffling along in a weary sort of delirium. Like children who have been scolded by their parents, we followed the lead man, begging for the day to come to an end. It seemed utterly farcical that only a few hours ago we had even entertained the idea of breaking records. By now, it was simply a case of placing one foot in front of the other and forcing ourselves to move forward, always forward.

At twenty-seven years old, Tom, Andy and I are a few years off reaching our prime in terms of physical endurance. Although our sexual peak was years ago (according to a few magazines I had read at the hairdresser's) we would reach our optimum endurance level only somewhere between thirty-five and forty.

That's why the world's top endurance athletes are all decidedly middle aged. They have experience combined with a frightening level of stamina, which a teenager could simply never match. At forty-seven, Paul was technically the other side of his prime, but owing to his exceptional lifestyle probably only just. It was remarkable to notice the difference between the age groups, and how we really couldn't match him for brute endurance.

I think it's safe to say that Tom and I were pretty evenly matched in terms of stamina. We had climbed together before and each of us had a fairly good idea when the other was having a tough time. However, I always remembered an occasion when he had proved himself to be considerably stronger than me.

We had both been climbing for about ten days on one mountain. After being beaten back from the summit, everyone had trundled back to advanced base camp and reluctantly dismantled the tents in preparation for the long walk out. Two weeks previously, we had ferried in all our equipment in several loads. Now we were carrying a lot less food and so decided to take everything out in one big hit.

The packs were so heavy we had to help each other lift them on to our backs. Immediately after setting out, I realised that the ten-day climb had sapped my energy, and I looked up at the high mountain pass with weary eyes.

There was no path, only acres of loose scree. As we plodded upwards, little rocks slid down the slope, taking us gently backwards with each step forward. I had simply nothing left in me and could barely face the prospect of the long walk ahead. Tom, on the other hand, had obviously found something extra and slowly climbed up the mountain pass, pulling away from me with each step. By the time I finally reached the top, he had been waiting for about twenty minutes, and I found him leaning against his pack, looking as if he had just walked to the garden shed and back.

I grabbed one of the little rocks lying on the ground and cursed it for the pain it had caused me over the last three hours. In a torrent of abuse, I hurled it down the mountainside and turned to face Tom, who was reclining casually, eyeing me with mild curiosity.

One of us had to go a longer way back to collect some empty barrels we had left on the walk in. We should both have gone, but I was utterly exhausted and stood bent over, wheezing for breath.

'Why don't you go directly back? I can pick

up the barrels by myself,' said Tom gently.

I wanted to refuse and demand that both of us go, but I knew all too well that I had nothing left in me.

'Are you sure you can manage them by yourself?' I said reluctantly. 'What about the extra weight?'

'If you take one of my walking boots then we'll be carrying about the same,' he said, and started rummaging around in the top of his pack.

It was hardly a fair trade, as both of us knew, but Tom, ever diplomatic, was trying to save me a dent to my pride. I felt pathetic standing there, the sweat running into my eyes and my legs feeling like lead. To shirk a job that was rightly mine really grated on my pride and confidence. As a consequence, I always train incredibly hard for expeditions. I just never want to feel that pitiful reliance on someone else ever again.

It was, therefore, with considerable relief that I realised in Antarctica that I could keep up with the general pace. After the first hundred miles or so, it was clear that Tom and I were definitely travelling at similar speeds and would get tired at about the same point in the day. Andy, however, was a different matter.

Originally, we had been a little concerned

as to his qualifications for undertaking such a trip, but, as the New Zealand training proved, he could ski well and was in good shape. In Antarctica, we soon discovered that when Andy took the lead he liked to race off at what seemed to us a stupidly fast speed. As with marathon runners in a pack, it is more efficient for a team to travel together, and Andy seemed to be setting a pace that we could barely maintain for a couple of minutes, let alone an entire session.

The increased speed put daydreaming out of the window and made us sweat profusely. After a few of these sessions, I became seriously concerned as to whether we might burn out in the first half of the expedition. None of us knew what Antarctica had in store for us and only Paul had experienced the dreaded High Polar Plateau, which was something we would be climbing on to soon after leaving the Theils resupply point. I felt we needed a steady pace that was quick but left something in reserve, as there was no use being totally spent by the halfway marker.

On occasions, when we were all feeling fired up, Andy's fast lead picked up our spirits and gave us the impression we were scorching across the ice. There was nothing better than getting the GPS out after the last session and discovering we had broken yet another personal best for the distance covered in a day.

However, this was not exactly the norm. A faster pace almost always meant a hard session for everyone else in the team. To be fair to Andy, he was not the only one guilty of leading too fast. As each of us would take the lead, we found the focus it required would snap us out of our daydreaming. The renewed concentration we needed to navigate and route-find would often mean that subconsciously we moved the pace up a gear.

The main difference was that, although the rest of us tried to curb this natural impulse, Andy seemed to press on regardless. As he skied off into the horizon, the team would start to spread out and the rhythm, which kept us all trucking along, seemed to break up. Often, either Tom or I would have to shout ahead or, owing to the noise of the wind, break ranks and ski alongside him to tap his leg with a ski pole.

It soon became a touchy subject. Andy felt he was pushing the team on and getting good mileage, while Tom and I thought he was being an insensitive bastard and burning us out for the march ahead. While he sat on his sled during a break, waiting for us to finally arrive, we would pull up next to him and have to restrain ourselves from lancing him with a ski pole.

In retrospect, it really wasn't a big deal, but with a bleak Antarctic landscape for inspiration the slightest annoyance can escalate into frightening proportions. The mind's boredom tries to feed off something, and the hours of solitude only augment what was once a petty grievance of no importance. There are stories of North Pole expeditions, which have to carry a pistol in case of bear attacks, actually electing to throw the gun into the water and chance it with bears rather than face the certainty that one teammate will kill another over whose turn it is to do the washing up that night.

Paul never really said anything when we had one of our very occasional barneys. Although he would hate the idea that he was old enough, we did all regard him as a mildly parental figure, and he could easily have stepped in to adjudicate. I think he wanted us to work it out for ourselves and therefore vent whatever we needed to say.

Most expeditions have blazing arguments and vehemently hate each other by the end. With us this was simply not the case. We had so few disagreements it was quite incredible. Even if we had a little jibe at each other on the ice, the moment we got into the tent the bad feelings evaporated, lost in our collective relief to be coming in from the cold. Like the steam curling up from our cooking pot, animosity gently filtered through the tent flaps and became frozen in the swirling winds outside.

After a week or so, Andy did agree to make an effort to slow down the pace. With just a simple nod of his head, he signalled his agreement and the hours of frustration, which I had been carrying around like emotional baggage, dropped away from my shoulders. The next morning, in the knowledge that I wouldn't be sweating so much or desperately having to try to keep up, I started the day with a spring in my step. As soon as my lead finished, the other three pulled up next to me as usual.

'Jesus, mate. What are you trying to prove?' asked Tom, wiping the sweat out of his eyes.

'What do you mean?' I said defensively.

'I mean that the last hour is about the fastest session we've ever done. It's nine thirty in the morning and I'm already covered in sweat.'

Both Paul and Andy mumbled their agreement and general discontent. If they didn't kill me for leading too quickly then I was sure the irony would. I trudged over to where Andy was resting and slapped him on

221

the back. Despite his goggles, I could see that he was grinning smugly.

★ ★ ★

When the sun shone and the wind was low, Antarctica was an easy place. On such days, it seemed extraordinary that Captain Scott had managed to die out here, and we would ski along, feeling good about life in general. When the weather fronts came past, such secure and comforting feelings were lost in a second. On these days, almost nothing we did could be described with the word 'easy'.

In Punta Arenas, Geoff Somers had jokingly told us about what his team had nicknamed 'plane days' — days where everything seems to be going wrong. The hypothetical dilemma is simple — if a plane landed next to you, would you get on it? If some kindly pilot landed near by and offered an easy route back to warm duvets, fresh vegetables and a break from the skiing, would you be strong enough to resist? Without the danger of it ever actually happening, we deemed it safe to put ourselves through such a test of moral fibre.

On 20 November 2002, I had the Mount Everest of plane days.

The wind had dropped so it was eerily

quiet, and the cloud level reached all the way down to the ground, making it a white-out in the complete sense of the word. Our skis and ski poles seemed to crunch and squeak in the absolute silence and, despite the lack of wind, it was cold. It was my twenty-seventh birthday that day and previously I had wondered what it was going to be like spending it in Antarctica.

Ten minutes after setting off in the morning, I realised it was going to be rubbish.

The white-out meant all navigation had to be done with a compass, but the severity of the conditions made it impossible to take a bearing then lock on to an object in the middle distance. We couldn't even see a few feet ahead of us. Instead, we had to continually check the compass, looking down every twenty seconds or so to take a reading.

Our sleds caught on unseen pieces of sastrugi and suddenly, for no apparent reason, we would feel ourselves being yanked off balance. We fell over, clumsily and slowly, unsure of anything with such uneven ground. My sense of humour left me somewhere around fall number five, and after that my bad mood plumbed new depths.

Sometimes a sled would turn over completely, stopping us dead in our tracks. We would tug hard on the line, assuming the sled to be caught on a rise in the sastrugi, before turning round to see it completely upended.

Just in front of me, I saw this happen to Andy, and watched while he went through the rigmarole of trying to right it. With the rare calm of someone used to having their patience sorely tested, he turned himself round and sorted out the problem. Not for the first time I thought how level headed he was being. I just assumed he must have a lot of older siblings.

In direct contrast, I have a habit of throwing all my toys and working myself up into a massive frothy. I hate trying to be quiet and calm about the whole situation and would much rather shout a long string of obscenities and give the sled a damn good shoeing. People telling me to calm down only makes it worse, as if I don't get the frustration out of me I'd probably burst in one angry puff of smoke.

I wouldn't be half so confrontational, nor for that matter brave, if it weren't an inanimate object. Seeing as I am not going to hurt anyone's feelings, and I am making myself feel a good deal better in the process, I think the whole process is actually quite therapeutic. My father used exactly the same technique at the start of our family holidays, although often the recipient check-in girls couldn't quite be considered entirely inanimate.

If my sled turned over it was no big deal; with Andy there was a potential for disaster. He was carrying all the fuel for the expedition. Despite the reinforced metal containers, some might leak out, and that was something that has cost a surprising number of expeditions their chances of reaching the pole. Unzipping the sled cover and giving it all a cursory inspection, Andy thought that everything looked a little rattled, but still properly sealed, and we continued on our way.

That night, as soon as Andy unrolled his sleeping bag, we realised something was amiss. With a couple of suspicious sniffs, he discovered that the kerosene had leaked after all. It wasn't as if his sleeping bag had been doused in the stuff, but it was enough for us to recommend that he move back from the cooking stove and not play with any matches. With any luck, it would all have evaporated by the next day, but as the evening progressed and the noxious fumes circulated slowly around our little tent, we didn't so much fall asleep as gently pass out.

As the day continued and the white-out showed no sign of lifting, my ski boots decided to compound the general misery by applying painful pressure under my toes. I trundled along at the back, wallowing in a pathetic, self-pitying mess. I had placed a special moulded plate in the bottom of my ski boots, which was designed to follow the exact contours of my foot and help reduce blisters and pressure. It wasn't working.

Both Tom and Andy had exactly the same boots as me and they had not had so much as a single chafe. They had no such moulded plates and, now that I look back on it all, it seems somewhat surprising that it took me eleven whole days of deep discomfort to work out that it might be more comfortable to take the damn things out altogether. Sure enough, as I consigned the £60 worth of latest shoe technology to the bottom of my sled, I skied along in blissful comfort for the remainder of the expedition.

Paul was having no such luck with his feet. A few days later, while we were eating some breakfast in the tent, he pulled back his socks to reveal two extraordinarily large blisters on his ankle. The skin had been stripped away and only raw flesh remained. The wound looked angry and slightly septic, with no chance of healing in the dry Antarctic climate. Every step must have made him wince in pain, but in a gesture typical of Paul his only reaction was a small grin and a slow nod of his head. It had obviously happened before and would probably happen again.

By now, we had been skiing all day in the white-out. At this stage I had no idea that the moulded plates were the source of my discomfort and I continued on in the gloom, cursing the pain in my feet. The day just didn't show any sign of ending, and by mid-afternoon I felt utterly desperate.

My diary describes the effect the weather was starting to have on me.

'It's like being blind. The greyness of the landscape seems to get inside your mind. Nothing to judge distances off and nothing to help with balance.

'It just wears you down. Slowly, minute by minute, the dullness seems to grow in intensity until it completely absorbs you. Even the bright colours of our jackets seem to bleed off into the landscape.

'How deep you have to dig on days like this! I know there are very definite limits to how much longer I can do this. I just don't have the strength to do it day after day.'

Before I left for Antarctica, Robyn had written a few lines from Rudyard Kipling's poem 'If' on the cover of my journal. I now found myself repeating the words over and over in my head. As if repeating a mantra from some sort of religious cult, I would mumble for hours on end.

I was so tired, however, that I just couldn't seem to remember it correctly. Half-finished sentences would blur together, and no matter how hard I tried I couldn't get it right. Again and again, I would start the poem afresh, only to get confused after the first or second line. The frustration simply added to my despair, and my morale started to sink even lower. The actual passage goes like this,

> *If you can force your heart and nerve*
> *and sinew*
> *To serve your turn long after they are*
> *gone,*
> *And so hold on when there is nothing*
> *in you*
> *Except the Will which says to them:*
> *'Hold on!'*

When Paul held up his ski pole finally signalling a stop for the night, the 'plane day' scenario had been tested to the limit. The whole way through happy hour, I had been deep in the moral dilemma and, much as I hate to admit it, if the pilot had landed within a couple of yards of where I was standing, I would probably have clambered aboard. Any farther away, I simply wouldn't have made it to the plane.

With a body that ached in every possible muscle and a layer of ice stuck to my face, I helped set up camp with listless exhaustion. Once the tents were up, I waited a few moments for the others to get inside, as I wanted to speak to Robyn on the satellite phone without the others breathing down my neck.

The line was bad and we had a broken conversation, which ended prematurely as the battery froze in just a couple of minutes. I had been looking forward to speaking to her for the last couple of weeks, and to be robbed of the chance seemed monstrously unfair. On the back of such a rotten day, this emotional wrangling nearly finished me off completely. It took another couple of minutes before I could get myself together enough to face the others in the tent.

I broke through the flysheet, grumbling loudly and flinging my painful boots against the side wall. I turned to see that the others all had little paper hats on their heads and were beaming big smiles at me. 'Happy birthday,' they each said in turn. A couple of balloons floated around the tent and they each presented edible presents ranging from South African biltong to French-Canadian peanuts. It was like some sort of dreadful rendition of a nativity play. They looked utterly ridiculous, unshaven and grubby from the last ten days of the expedition, but dressed in what looked like the remnants of a seven-year-old's birthday party. You couldn't help but love them for it.

With a couple of shots of whisky and the little edible luxuries added to our evening meal, my birthday went from practically suicidal to deeply contented. I smiled and looked around the tent at the other three. I was so lucky to be with people who could bring out the best in even a day as grim as this. Although this party featured four people of the same sex, an eighth of a bottle of whisky and one tiny bag of peanuts, we consoled ourselves with the fact that, for the first time in our lives, we were undoubtedly having the best party for hundreds of miles around.

8

Focal Points

'The man who views the world at fifty the same as he did at twenty has wasted thirty years of his life.'
— Muhammad Ali

It wasn't just the birthday we were celebrating that night, it was also the fact that things were going better than we had anticipated. A week ago we had been happy for our daily mileage to break into double figures. Now we were consistently hitting around thirteen, and there seemed to be no reason why we couldn't do more. It felt good to watch our goalposts constantly change.

Before setting out, I had been expecting to be in sheer hell almost every minute of every day. Everything I had read focused on the complete misery of polar travel, yet despite the harsh weather and a couple of days when it had all been a bit much, we were starting to realise that we could cope.

Although the last 'plane day' had been a particularly trying time, it was past and I had got through it unscathed. I knew that I would probably be able to cope with another one if it came along, and that assurance seemed to boost my confidence. I knew it was still early days, but I couldn't help feeling that others may have exaggerated the severity of the climate.

Don't get me wrong, Antarctica isn't exactly a warm and cosy place. I was exhausted at the end of each day and, with my hands either freezing or thawing on a continual basis, I always looked forward to getting out of the cold. However, I am definitely no great athlete, nor am I particularly tough, and yet I was feeling that I could withstand the rigours of polar travel. With careful management and the odd trick or two learnt from previous expeditions, the cold could definitely be kept in check. The sleds felt heavy, but they too were manageable, and we were starting to average some respectable daily mileage.

The other thing was that we were skiing only seven and a half hours a day. Although a reasonably long time, it was definitely not the most we could do. If required, I was sure we could push harder. Over the ten days we had been travelling our routine had settled down, and each day we would cover a little more distance. With the diminishing food supplies, our sleds were becoming lighter and our speed increasing accordingly. Without any extra effort, we found ourselves in the enviable position of having a reasonable amount left in reserve.

The next morning the white-out had evaporated. The gloom-filled skies had turned back to their deep, resonant blue and the wind was 15 knots or so. It was only -18 degrees outside and we were all in a good mood, generally enjoying the sensation of being somewhere so exceptional. As we sat sipping tea in the tent, I mentioned to Paul my thoughts about whether past explorers had exaggerated the severity of it all. He seemed to consider whether he wanted to share what he was thinking with the rest of us, then, after a few moments' pause, said rather sternly,

'The simple truth is that expeditions need to make it into the papers, otherwise they'll have their funding pulled. Most explorers have legally binding agreements with their big corporate sponsors and have to guarantee them some exposure. If nothing exciting happens and everything goes like clockwork, then it's not exactly going to make the front page of the paper, is it?'

I thought back to the Norwegian explorer Roald Amundsen, who had beaten Captain

Scott to the South Pole in 1911. After decades of various expeditions failing in their attempts, Amundsen had used huskies and his considerable polar experience to complete the journey without a hitch. While Scott died tragically in a blizzard, Amundsen returned to civilisation and wrote a thoroughly unentertaining book about his expedition. It wasn't so much his dry prose or the fact that Scott's death overshadowed his achievement, it was the fact that it had all gone way too smoothly. As Amundsen said himself, 'Adventure is just bad planning.'

There had been no eating of leather boots, no tales of unimaginable hardship, nor, for that matter, a single toe amputated. To the public, it barely seemed that the Norwegians had broken sweat. Consequently, interest in the whole adventure died almost as fast as Scott. Amundsen, it seems, had just been that little bit too good.

There are very obvious parallels between this story from a hundred years ago and the situation modern-day expeditions often find themselves in. Despite a desperate need for exposure in the press, they soon discover that their exploits are only reported if something goes desperately wrong or a world record is broken. This helps to explain why some of the great names in polar exploration are so pedantic about the exact nature of their expedition. With many of the big prizes already gone, they have to find harder and more elaborate ways of doing the same journey in order to make it into the papers.

Obviously, this is not the sole rationale, as many of these people are the kind who will always push back the boundaries and do things in harder ways. However, it is surprising how often financial motives are at play. By aiming to complete the first ever British, unsupported, solo ski to the Magnetic North Pole, they will break a new record and the dollar bills will come flying.

However spurious it may seem, a potential new world record draws the media. Despite the fact that ten other people may have done the same expedition the previous year, but were just not British, the expedition has still got a good chance of making the papers. While more worthy explorers attempt greater feats, unless they can market themselves effectively the column inches and the sponsors will often elude them.

Paul recalled some of his previous expeditions, when he had been sitting in the tent next to one of his clients while they were speaking on the satellite phone to a press agent. As he stirred the cooking pot in silence, he would listen to them exaggerate the severity of the temperature or turn a minor incident into a life-threatening ordeal. He understood the mechanics of it all, they needed press coverage and things were going too well, but it always caused a lump in his throat.

I wondered whether these people actually needed to embellish their stories. Antarctica is already an extraordinary place without the need to exaggerate and cloud the truth. By hamming it up and describing such an alien environment, all they are really trying to do is set themselves apart and suggest that only they could cope with such extremities. Aside from pandering to a press hungry for tales of adventure, this kind of thing serves simply to satisfy the vanity of their own convictions.

The reality is that it depends on how far you want to go. If you want to traverse the entire continent unsupported, then it is true, only very few can follow in the footsteps of people like Borge Ousland or Ranulph Fiennes. But for other, less ambitious expeditions to imply the same kind of hardship and danger, purely to satisfy their egos and sponsors, tilts the scales and gives a confused picture to those without the benefit of experience.

While we patted each other on the back and sighed in relief that Antarctica wasn't the living hell we had been led to believe, we were reminded of a rather substantial qualifier.

'The other thing is that we're only ten days into the expedition,' said Paul. 'It's true, everyone is coping well right now, but things have a habit of changing when you've been out here for a longer time.'

We all nodded rather solemnly and, in silence, started to clamber out of the tent for another day's march. What Antarctica had in store for us nobody could say, but one thing was for sure, in the future I would make up my own mind and not scare myself witless with the inflated opinions of others.

*   *   *

As we continued skiing south, we saw massive chunks of sastrugi stretching off all the way to the horizon. From the reports of previous expeditions, we had expected much flatter conditions and, much to our disappointment, this just wasn't the case. Although it was hard on our lower backs, the main problem was the beating it was giving our ski bindings. As they twisted and flexed over the uneven surface, our weight and that of the sled put massive pressure on the joints. After only ten days or so, the strengthened metal started snapping with alarming regularity, and although we had packed a few spares we were fast running out.

Most days, one of us would break something on their binding. If nothing could be done on the march and it needed to be completely reassembled, we would either try to use a spare ski or continue on foot. Given the hard snow, walking wasn't too bad and sometimes was even preferable as it used slightly different leg muscles and gave them a bit of a rest.

In Punta Arenas, in an effort to strengthen the bindings, we had superglued all the screws in place. Our inexperience now came back to haunt us, as the sheared-off screws were almost impossible to twist out. In the evenings the tent looked more like a mechanic's workshop than anything else, with skis constantly being passed in from outside to be serviced by an over-enthusiastic South African. Like a child with his first Lego set, Andy would dismantle the bindings with military precision, using a box of matches to slowly melt the glue so that he could force out the broken screws. Despite never having touched a ski binding in his life, Andy would dismantle it in seconds flat and be hammering away with the pliers as if he had designed it himself. Like all South Africans he had that superb 'move over and let me have a go' attitude that most British painfully lack.

Within the first few minutes of the bindings breaking, it became abundantly clear that neither Tom nor I had the faintest idea how they worked. The simple truth was that we shared a general ineptitude when it came to all things mechanical. Andy seized the advantage and immediately relegated us to the lowly position of tool-passers.

We would both look on in a helpless sort of a way, thankful that he appeared to know what he was doing. Paul could hold his own for a while with any talk on the inner workings of the plastic composite Rotterfeller ski binding, but when Andy started getting technical even he had to bow before such an onslaught of mechanical knowledge.

After a while, the metal inside the bindings had been rebent and re-formed so many times that it had entirely lost its strength. Tom, Andy and I all decided to walk most of the time, either out of fear that the binding was about to break or because this had actually happened during an earlier session. Walking was fine while the snow remained hard, but if it suddenly turned soft a hundred miles down the route we would be in serious trouble. Our only hope was the skis we had forgotten reaching Punta Arenas and being flown up to the resupply. Owing to the fact that they had last been seen somewhere in the Colombian rainforest, our hopes weren't high. Then again, there wasn't really anything we could do, except keep plodding on for as long as we could.

As the metal mechanism thingy from the inside of my binding pinged out once again, I prayed to the god of registered package deliveries that our skis would make it to Theils. If not, we were going to have to see whether anyone at Patriot Hills played tennis and try to strap a few racquets to our boots.

We were now twenty days into the expedition. The sun had revolved around our heads for all that time, never once dipping below the horizon and never once hinting that it would do so. Slowly we became convinced that something was sitting on the horizon to the west of our position, so faint it was almost impossible to see. As when you stare out across a field in the dead of night, the shape revealed itself and then vanished when we tried to look directly at it. But after an entire day of skiing, we became certain that there was definitely something there.

With nothing but a straight horizon for the last sixteen days, to see something, anything at all, was strange indeed. Although an odd sensation, it was not an unwelcome one, as according to the maps there was only one thing it could be — the Theils Mountains.

That morning in the tent Tom was strangely quiet. During the previous night I had woken to hear him groan loudly. I opened my eyes and squinted in the bright sunshine. I couldn't focus on much, but across the tent I saw Tom wincing and rustling in one of his stuff sacks. He had a pained expression on his face and was moving awkwardly. In a manner of which a bear with a sore head would have been proud, I said, 'Shut up and stop bloody fidgeting around.' I heard a few more groans and swivelled round in my sleeping bag, tutting in a heartfelt way. As I went back to sleep, I vaguely remember him saying, 'Just going outside to get some fresh air.'

Despite the fact that it was the middle of the night, about minus twenty below and there was more fresh air in the tent than in the whole of Greater London, it didn't strike me as odd that he should be going for a stroll. The next morning I had a vague recollection that I had been woken up during the night, but couldn't remember why or what had happened. As the others came into the tent for breakfast, they both noticed that Tom was obviously feeling decidedly scratchy. He merely grunted if asked direct questions and refused to utter a single word. Not wanting to annoy him, we all let him be and silently packed up the camp for another day's skiing. All through the day, he made not a single noise and skied with a stoic, unhappy air about him. It was only in the evening, after we pushed the issue, that he let on as to what had happened.

We keep all the things we need for eating and general tent life in little pouches that are sewn into the tent's lining. Rather than repacking everything into the stuff sacks, it's a great deal easier just to tuck them into these little caches. During the night, Tom turned over in his sleeping bag and managed to dislodge his thermal mug, which had been neatly stowed away above him. When he turned over once again, he rolled right on top of the handle, which, in turn, caught him squarely in his balls. In the type of exquisite pain that only half the world's population can truly appreciate, he had woken up from his peaceful shut-eye, desperately trying to work out why it felt as if Mike Tyson had just given him an illegal punch.

In a general state of sleepy disorientation, he clambered across the tent, frantically searching for some painkillers to try to ease the gut-wrenching feeling steadily building in his stomach. It was then that I had woken to find him rummaging through the medical kit.

As any man who has two older sisters knows, taking a hit in the family jewels is utterly debilitating. The pain is quite unlike anything else I have ever had the misfortune to experience. Six painkillers in quick succession (a dose that would tranquillise an average horse) didn't help Tom. He scrambled out of the tent and promptly vomited in the snow. The next morning he had been in such a bad mood, not just from the hours of gently throbbing pain, but also because he was finding it difficult to walk. The injury had swelled during the night and the thought of having to be evacuated due to an oversized left testicle had kept him awake until dawn. He knew damn well that he would never live it down when he got back to England.

There is a story of a British climber who had spent years trying to raise enough money to climb all fourteen 8,000-metre peaks. On about his third mountain, he was at base camp, just about to tuck into a local chapatti, when some of the dry flour on the bread made him sneeze. In excruciating pain, he quickly realised that the sneeze had caused him to slip a disc in his back and he needed immediate evacuation. Years of training and raising money went down the tubes and, no matter what he accomplished in the future, his name would always be synonymous with small pieces of Indian bread. It was like Elvis dying on the toilet, for Christ's sake.

To his great relief, Tom discovered that the motion of skiing didn't exacerbate the problem too badly. Although somewhat tentative at first, he had been able to move without causing himself too much discomfort. From then on, we all treated his thermal mug with the respect it obviously deserved.

★   ★   ★

The Theil Mountains seemed to be getting no closer. Despite entire days of skiing and record mileages achieved, they adamantly refused to get any larger and just sat on the horizon taunting us. I started to wish that I was the Muslim prophet Muhammad and for once the mountains would come to me. Much to my disappointment, but not my surprise, they didn't, and the only option was to keep on walking.

We had all noticed how, over the last twenty days, Andy seemed to be almost constantly eating. We were all hungry coming into the tent at night and it did take some commitment to get the requisite 6,000 calories a day down our necks. But he was at it almost continuously. Even after our massive evening meal, we would hear little rustles from his side of the tent, as another packet of biscuits was opened, another piece of cheese crammed into his mouth.

Our diet consisted of a series of snacks during the day, such as lumps of cheese, salami and flapjacks, all of which were high in fat content and designed to burn slowly throughout the skiing sessions. At night we would often eat little biscuits, saved from our day sacks, on top of which we would slice thick chunks of raw butter. The biscuits came from British Army ration packs and had all the consistency and flavour of dry cardboard. However, used as a vehicle to cram as much butter into our mouths as possible, they certainly did the trick. Initially, we had all turned our noses up at Paul's suggestion, but after about three days on the ice heavily fattening, raw butter was one of the most satisfying tastes I could have imagined. Our bodies just craved any sort of fat to replenish the weight lost from the hours of constant exercise in the cold.

We would add a little to our specially dried, highly calorific evening meals, which Paul had brought all the way from Canada. From experience, he knew the effect good food could have on morale and had packed a series of six different meals. There was everything from spaghetti Bolognese to couscous, and each one was designed to whet our insatiable appetites.

An expedition to the North Pole a few years previously had brought with them nothing but powdered mashed potato. To vary the meal from day to day, they had packed seven or so different spices to augment the otherwise entirely bland taste. One night it would be Indian mash, the next Mexican chilli. It must have been horrible waiting in the tent each night to discover which mash surprise it was going to be. The idea of eating the same flavourless rubbish for sixty days filled me with horror. There was really no need to be so unimaginative with the food, and although our method meant carrying a little more weight, it was hardly a great deal. Knowing that spaghetti Bolognese was on the menu, all of us, but especially Andy, would start salivating around the second session and ski like men possessed.

It was interesting, when we portioned out the food each week, to note that Paul was eating roughly 15 per cent less than the rest of us. The ultra-fatty salami was just too much for him, and he basically put down to his age and lower metabolic rate the fact that he didn't need as much food to stay warm or keep up with the current pace. The absolute antithesis to this was Andy's somewhat cavalier attitude towards food rations.

Like a giant panda, which has to eat a third of its body weight in bamboo each day just to stay alive, Andy's mouth barely stopped chewing the entire time we spent in the tent. Considering that our provisions had all been portioned out equally, to the milligram, we all became a little suspicious as to how he seemed to have an inexhaustible supply.

We had originally expected to reach the Theils resupply point somewhere around twenty-six to twenty-eight days. However, as a contingency, we had agreed to carry another week's worth of food, in case of weather delays or injury. As it turned out Andy hadn't broken into the group's supplies, which would have been unforgivable, but instead had eaten his own reserve lunches. During the days in the run-up to the resupply, we noticed that at our breaks he wouldn't eat, but instead just sit in silence, drinking from his water bottle. He had almost completely run out of food, but couldn't say anything without letting the cat out of the bag. It must have been utter hell for him to watch us demolish fatty chunks of salami while he was forced to keep quiet and hide the awful secret of his gluttonous bingeing. When it became clear what had happened, neither sympathy nor handouts were in any way forthcoming, as it was so patently his own doing.

At breaks, I would look enviously at Tom, who had an infuriating habit of placing his English chocolate bars neatly on his knee while he decided which one to eat. In Punta Arenas I had been disorganised and managed only to pick up some dodgy Chilean chocolate at the last minute. The dusty, slightly off chocolate was a poor second to Tom's 'Dairy Milks' and Cadbury's 'Twirls'. While I tried not to look over my shoulder at Tom, Andy would be fighting back the tears at the sight of me casually tossing yet another piece of Chilean chocolate in my mouth. He wouldn't have minded if the chocolate had been scraped off the factory floor. To him, at least, it would have meant something solid would pass his lips during the long hours of the day. For a man so dedicated to food and in a near-constant state of semi-starvation, it was a miracle he didn't become deranged and start boiling the soles of his ski boots.

★   ★   ★

The Theil Mountains shone like a beacon ahead of us, and it was wonderful to have a definite point to aim for. The mountains meant we could dispense with compasses or working off our shadows. If our calculations were correct, we had two more days before we actually reached the resupply point.

With bright sunshine and light sleds, we pressed on at a decent lick. During the third session of the day, Paul suddenly stopped, got down on his knees and peered at the ground. He shouted something back at us, but I for one had my mini-disc playing and couldn't hear a word he said. As I came up to where he had been kneeling, I saw he had ringed a patch of snow with his ski pole. In the centre was the unmistakable indentation of a single footprint, a size-eleven Sorrel boot, to be precise. We knew that only Graham in the other team was wearing this kind of boot and the marking looked just a couple of hours' old. I peered into the distance, in the vague direction the footprint was leading, and felt like some sort of bushman tracking an animal's spoor.

It seemed incredible that in such a vast white expanse, with millions of acres of uniform ice, we had stumbled across a trace of another human being. In one way it felt a little annoying that someone had evidently trodden here before us; in another it was rather comforting that there was life outside our small team. There was also one other thing that solitary footprint signified: we were hot on the heels of the other team.

In a rather underhand move, we had got one of our friends in England to text our satellite phone with the position of the other team. Each night, all the teams on the ice would have a designated time to contact Patriot Hills and report their position in what was dubbed a 'Sched' call. The news that we were safe and how far we had progressed would then be e-mailed to our friends and family on a daily basis. We didn't feel too bad about having someone beam their position to us, as we guessed the others would probably be doing the same. It's almost impossible to be skiing concurrently with another team and not be in the least bit curious as to how they are doing.

Each day the satellite phone would bleep and a new message would tell us their position. We noted rather curiously how their progress seemed to be quite erratic. One day they would manage eleven nautical miles and the next they would obviously ski for a few more hours and hit seventeen. We had stuck religiously to seven and a half hours, and over the last week our mileage had increased to sixteen per day and pretty much stayed there. That day we had already known we were closing in on them, but to see the footprint made us realise how close we must be.

Sure enough, as we set up camp that evening, feeling tired but overjoyed to be in the shadow of the mountains, we could just make out a tiny collection of tents a few miles off to the east. We were pretty much level with them, but on a slightly different longitude. There was no point waving or trying to attract their attention, as apart from the distance they were travelling in a time zone two hours ahead of us and would be neatly tucked up in their sleeping bags. We were on what we called 'local' time (when our shadows pointed due south at exactly midday) and they were still on the same time as Patriot Hills. With the sun revolving around the sky and twenty-four-hour sunlight, each team pretty much chose whatever time they liked. It didn't make a great deal of difference to anyone in particular, except, of course, the poor radio operator who had to receive the Sched calls. In the dead of night, he could often be seen padding across to the communications tent, mumbling under his breath and cursing the irregularity of Antarctica's time zones.

We were all really looking forward to seeing the other team, owing mainly to the fact that we had been without any external contact for nearly a month. It doesn't sound long, but we were definitely all tiring a little of each other's idiosyncrasies. Only that morning, someone confessed that they had heard me tell the same story three times already. Thankfully, the prospect of meeting the other team offered a whole new raft of conversation prompts, and for Paul it was a chance to spend the night with his wife. Female contact had been something the rest of us had tried to put out of our minds over the last few weeks, but as Paul's eyes lit up like dollar signs, we all felt a pang of jealousy.

In the tent that night, we were discussing how best to get a game of cricket going at the resupply, when the satellite phone rang. It was Matty, and judging by Paul's reaction she wasn't in a particularly good mood. As she explained, Andrew Cooney had come up to her earlier that day and complained that the two teams were coming into the resupply area together. He felt that this was a 'wilderness' experience and by having other people at Theils his enjoyment of skiing to the pole would be greatly lessened. His real motives were not exactly hard to see, as he was billing himself to be the youngest Briton to ski to the pole. If we managed to get there before him, Tom would be the youngest, however briefly, and Andrew thought this might well steal his thunder in the press.

Somewhat reluctantly, but with the duty of

a guide to a client, Matty wanted to know whether there was a possibility that we might wait a couple of days in the same location. This would then give them enough time to repack their sleds and get clear. The idea of sitting in the tent for two whole days, twiddling our thumbs and dreaming about the clean boxer shorts and fresh food just around the corner, was not exactly a tempting offer. When Paul told us the situation, we discussed the options open to us and, after a few minutes, our reaction was unanimous. We sent back a message intended for Andrew and his concerns about wilderness issues. The message consisted of just two words; one of them was 'off'.

9

Almost Like a Camel

'Before polar expeditions I had no idea what a wonderful invention soap is.'
— Fridtjof Nansen

When Yul Bryner and James Coburn walk down the street in *The Magnificent Seven*, I remember thinking that they must be the coolest men ever to live. Since then only Butch and Sundance have ever come close. Scenes like that leave big impressions on boys growing up, and the four of us skiing into the resupply at Theils were obviously no exception.

We came over the horizon skiing slowly and four abreast. Side by side we approached the impossibly remote camp, our ski tips running perfectly in unison after so many days of practice. There was not a breath of wind, so it was warm enough to take off our protective outer gear and talk to each other while skiing along. We all smiled and joked around, delighted to be so close to the midway point. There were only eight miles to go that day

254

and we could have taken our time, but Andy kept chivvying us along at breaks, the prospect of unrationed food spurring him along.

As we skied the last few hundred metres to the camp, we could see the other team all clambering out of their tents to greet us. With huge smiles we all met, everybody hugging and shaking hands. After the monotony of the last twenty-six days, to meet and talk to other people felt wonderful, and on such a warm day we could stand outside without fear of getting too cold.

While we spoke, I noticed that all of them, except Matty of course, had grown a beard over the last few weeks with varying degrees of success. The Spaniards had full furry numbers, with Angel showing his age a little with a broad streak of grey hair. With a wry smile, I noticed that the others were on the same sort of level as us and had more wispy affairs.

In Punta Arenas we had also decided to grow facial hair, and after just a few days had started to get competitive. With the general appearance of an overgrown twelve-year-old, Tom was never going to be in the running for any beard-growing competition. After weeks of cultivation, he had nothing more to show than a couple of scraggly tufts poking out from the bottom his chin. Using the minuscule shaving mirror, he would study the seven hairs for hours on end, before finally swiping them off with one swift stroke of the razor.

Paul had had more success, but his fair complexion made his growth barely visible. To our combined horror, we noticed that the moment he settled into his tent at Theils he shaved off everything but his moustache. We all loudly protested at the prospect of having our guide look like some sort of blond equivalent of Magnum PI, but it did little good. Evidently, the Tom Selleck look was all the rage back home in Canada.

I think I came second in our little competition. Much to my disappointment, Andy just pipped me to the post. He had a thick chin strap of bushy black hair, which I just couldn't match. Despite this advantage, he grew hardly any moustache at all, giving the impression that he was in training to be some sort of Amish priest. Admittedly, it was not a good look, but it was certainly better than mine. Owing to some sort of strange genetic throwback, my facial hair consisted of a very slightly ginger, Cary Grant-style moustache (occasionally mistaken for a hot chocolate stain) and a few unpleasant hairs under my chin. To tell the truth, I don't think

I have ever really got over the fact that I am twenty-seven years old and am still unable to grow a full beard.

Apart from a few barrels of fuel huddled together off to the east, a lonely igloo was all that comprised of the entire Theils camp; it was a remote place, to say the least. As we all milled around, talking about how we were finding the expedition so far, I saw another figure emerge from the igloo and walk towards us. We were five degrees away from Patriot Hills and the nearest human being, so I was a little curious as to who it could be. Squinting in the sunlight, I caught a glimpse of what the figure was wearing. It was an outfit made exclusively of caribou fur and there was only one person in the whole continent who would be wearing such a thing — it was our old friend Doug Stern.

A few weeks previously, Doug had been dropped at the Theil Mountains by ANI and asked to report on weather conditions — a great deal cheaper than obtaining the satellite imagery each day. Doug sat by himself, hundreds of miles from anything at all, and radioed in a description of what the wind and skies were doing. Apart from the mountains and a small collection of things he had brought with him, there was absolutely nothing in an entire 360-degree radius. He would be able to talk to another person only once a day when reporting in on the radio, and that would be only for a couple of minutes. For any normal human being it would have been maddening. As was to be expected in such a situation, Doug was as happy as could be and came over to greet us warmly.

Despite the lack of wind, all the standing around was starting to get to us and so everyone retreated to their tents. Doug showed us where we could set up ours and pointed out the spot where all our new provisions had been dropped.

'And tonight, I am going to come round and cook you a delicious meal,' he added with a broad smile.

'What you got for us, Doug?' Andy said, obviously picturing all sorts of wonderful delicacies.

'Conger eel, flown all the way from Punta Arenas!'

'Delicious,' I said flatly, my initial enthusiasm having waned somewhat at the thought of eating the rubbery and utterly tasteless fish. Of all the things he could have brought! Somehow, the eel had travelled almost a thousand miles to come back and haunt us.

All four of us went over to the huge boxes that contained the provisions for the next leg of the journey. The barrels had been bound together by the pilots and were half drifted up with snow. With an inventory, we went through each item in turn and discovered that ANI had done their job perfectly and not a single thing was missing. Mairi, the Patriot Hills' chef, had even included some fresh carrots and sponge pudding, and with no need to ration ourselves any longer we got down to the serious business of eating.

While Andy prepared the stove, we had a snow bath, aired our sleeping bags and, most importantly, put on some fresh clothes. Wearing clean thermals and sliding on a pair of soft, woolly socks felt better than words can describe. The lavish comfort only went to show how grimy we had been before, and we loafed around the campsite, revelling in sweet-smelling luxury.

To our amazement, the skis that had been floating around Central America had obviously landed in Punta Arenas and been sent on to the resupply. The ski bag also contained five new pairs of much-needed bindings, and Andy salvaged anything worthwhile from our old ones and combined them. Soon we would be climbing up on to the plateau, and then our only hope rested on this fresh supply of bindings lasting us the remaining distance to the pole.

If things got really desperate, we also had the bindings from our kiting skis. These damn skis had sat in the bottom of our sleds for the last twenty-six days, utterly obsolete in the head-on wind. They had done nothing but add extra weight to already heavy sleds. When we had set out from Patriot Hills, I had considered the kites to be our secret weapon. Only a handful of people have ever used kites in Antarctica, and to me they seemed like a very James Bond way of getting to the South Pole. I had pictured the other team slogging along on foot, while we cruised past under sail, perhaps giving them a cheeky wave as we went past. The reality could not have been more different. We had not had so much as a single gust of wind in the right direction the entire time. Every one of the twenty-six days had seen the wind directly in our faces and the kites firmly rolled up in our sleds. If we had done our research a little more carefully, we could have had our kiting equipment sent directly to Theils and saved ourselves a lot of hard work. One thing was for sure, 007 would never have been so careless.

After another meal and with about 5,000 calories nestling in my stomach, I decided to pay Doug a visit, as I had heard that he had a stash of coffee with him. As I crossed the snow in between our tents, I bumped into

Matty going in the other direction.

'So, how are you finding it all?' she asked amicably.

'Good,' I replied. 'Well, so far, anyway. The last stretch coming into here was great. Light sleds and the ground really hard.'

'Weren't the conditions wonderful? We noticed you guys were doin' some pretty good mileage. Trying to catch us up or something?' It was said jokingly, but as I am sure is always the case in a situation like this, there were competitive undertones a mile wide.

'No,' I said a little defensively. 'We've just been sticking to our seven and a half hours a day.' Changing the subject, I then added, 'It's funny, though, how the hours pass. When you're leading they can sometimes take for ever.'

'Tell me about it,' she said, giving me a heartfelt look. 'I've been leading the entire time. All the way since Hercules Inlet.'

I was amazed. To lead continuously must have been unbelievably tough on her. Matty was pulling a lighter load than the others (quite justifiably considering she was about half their weight), but even so it must have been exhausting to have to concentrate all the time. She had been concerned that some people in the team would set a faster pace than others and so had decided just to do the whole lot herself and keep things constant. It must have been utterly gruelling for her.

As we stood there talking, I had a closer look at the skis she was carrying. She had made some of her own modifications and the kicker skin on the underside of the ski seemed like a particularly good idea. We use a synthetic version of the old-fashioned seal-skins, to stop the skis sliding backwards. With the weight of a sled behind us, if they were like normal downhill skis and had a totally smooth base we would just slip backwards with every step. By having this synthetic fur, the skis ran forward, but didn't slide back.

While our skis had fur all the way down their length, Matty's had just a foot-long patch right underneath where the ski boots attached. This meant the top and tail of her ski glided smoothly and she was fighting a great deal less resistance than us.

She talked me through how she had done it and I turned round, even going so far as to forgo the pleasure of a coffee, and went back to my tent. I explained what she had done to Andy and Tom, and we agreed to do the same. With penknife and screwdriver in hand, Andy set to work with his usual gusto and a couple of hours later we each had a pair of kicker skins. We tested them round the campsite and the skies ran incredibly smoothly across the snow. It was as if the whole time we had been walking across a muddy field and now we were strolling on grass.

That afternoon, Paul came into the main tent. He had found a pair of Tom's boxer shorts in the resupply kit and, amused by the Union Jack pattern, had put them on over his fleece trousers. Like some sort of bad impersonation of an all-British Superman, he sat sipping a cup of soup and went over a few ideas he had been thinking about for the last few days.

Based on the fact that we had been limiting our time skiing to seven and a half hours a day, and Paul felt we were capable of a great deal more, he suggested a revised strategy for the second section to the pole. As always with Paul, the plan had absolutely no half-measures.

'If we ditch a week's worth of food, one of the tents and half a kilo each from our personal gear, we could save about forty kilos from the team's weight,' he said, looking seriously at us all. 'But what you must understand is that the food ration is going to give us totally inflexible deadlines. If we don't achieve our target distances each day, we could easily start to run out of food. We don't exactly have a big safety margin on this one.'

We all fell silent, thinking about what he had just said. Cutting back so drastically would make us considerably lighter but, as Paul had said, it was giving us very little margin for error. Losing the one-man tent was no big deal, as it had been a nuisance to set up in the first place. Although the 'Gunner's Tent', as it was swiftly dubbed, gave one of us a break from our teammates, it added an extra fifteen minutes each day to setting up camp and was so small it was impossible to sit up straight in it.

From now on, Andy, Tom and I would share just one tent. The prospect was a little alarming, as the larger tent had felt pretty confined with just two of us in it, but the inescapable truth was that if we were serious about going fast, then the extra weight had to go.

However, it was the food which was the risky calculation. Now we would have only a few days' contingency in case of injury or bad weather. By cutting out an entire six-day cycle of food, we would be losing a total of 24 kilograms from the group weight. A huge load to be sure, but I did wonder at what price. There would be no opportunity to re-evaluate once we left Theils and if, for whatever reason, we didn't reach our specified targets, then we would be placing ourselves in danger.

Not just in danger of failing to reach the pole, but if we were unlucky with the weather and had a lengthy storm we might well run out of food altogether.

Paul felt the risk was acceptable, as we could ski faster and reach the pole over ten days ahead of schedule. As I had always suspected, he was the kind of person who liked to put his money where his mouth was.

As for the personal effects, we reluctantly thinned out the required saving. It was easier than I had first expected, as over the past month we had naturally developed a preference for certain equipment. Not having skied in a polar environment before, we had originally brought a few variations for protecting our hands and faces. Quickly, we had each discovered that for one of us the face masks were redundant, for others the balaclavas, and so getting rid of a few items of clothing wasn't too hard.

We decided to share one tube of toothpaste, cut books in half and generally get rid of anything we hadn't used in the first half of the expedition. We had to travel super-light to have any hope of achieving the deadlines, and that meant being unbelievably ruthless with what we were actually going to take. Having said that, we all had limits that we would not cross. I was damned if I was going to start drilling holes in my toothbrush or leave the little bottle of whisky behind.

With such savings in weight, Andy was quick to realise that an extra week's worth of food would soon be left in Theils unguarded. While the rest of us debated over whether to pack an extra pair of inner socks or not, Andy raided the breakfast cereal container and packed three kilograms of muesli into his sled. Amused by the lengths to which he was prepared to go to ensure he didn't go hungry once again, we were happy for him to take the extra weight. However, the deal was that if it started slowing him down and he couldn't keep the pace, it would be the first to go. Knowing Andy, the exact opposite was more likely to happen — the calorific boost would probably make him ski faster.

Having originally set out from Patriot Hills with hefty doubts as to whether we would even reach the pole, sitting in the tent at Theils I realised how much the situation had changed. Instead of sixty to sixty-five days, we were now looking to get there before New Year's Eve. This would drop our expected time to just fifty days, a target that made Matty choke with laughter when Paul told her that night. Perhaps she was right and we were over-extending ourselves. Perhaps we were being rash trying to travel so light.

Not for the first time, I looked around the tent at the others and got carried away in the moment. Everyone looked windswept and dishevelled, but their faces glowed in the yellow light of the tent. There was determination in their eyes and a common desire, which swept everything before it. Like a wave sucking the water back from the shore as it gathers height before breaking, their minds were bent on a single focus. The strength of that desire was extremely alluring and seemed to gather me with it in the current. For an entire month, we had been directed on a single point, and now that we were beginning to realise our potential we each felt that it was time to let the fear drop away and really start striding out.

We all nodded solemnly and agreed that this should be the plan for the second half of the expedition. As Andy moved to get out of the tent he jogged into Paul, who in turn spilt his soup all over his lap. Tom laughed out loud as finally it was Paul who was the one to make a mistake. He stopped laughing rather abruptly when he realised the boxer shorts Paul was wearing over his trousers were his, and one of only two clean pairs he possessed. Clean clothes were like gold dust out in Theils, and without having worn them once he was going to have a crotch that smelt of chicken noodle soup for the remainder of the expedition.

Doug banged on the flysheet and came crashing into the tent. His caribou jacket was covered in lumps of ice, as he had spent the day trying to level the larger lumps of sastrugi on the 'runway'. He handed over the conger eel for the evening dinner.

'You know how they go fishing up in the High Arctic?' he said wistfully, his eyes starting to blank over once again. Sensing a monologue coming on, we all settled down and got ready for another story.

'Imagine a landscape totally covered in snow, totally devoid of life,' he said, but then realised where he was and quickly added, 'Kind of like it is just outside the tent.'

Then, with a deep, unabashed love of the Arctic, he described the ice holes the Inuit fish in and the beautiful landscapes so far north. It struck me as a little ironic that he should be describing something so familiar which also happened to be on the other side of the planet.

A little later, he casually mentioned that all the sastrugi bashing was giving him a pain in his right arm. He explained that a few years previously he had had the same problem and eventually had decided to go to the doctor. The doctor had confirmed that he needed to undergo a minor operation and could he please come back again at the end of the week.

'Not really,' Doug explained to the man, 'I live about two hundred miles away.' We all looked at him in mild amazement and thought about what it must be like to live in a place that was three days' snowmobile away from the nearest medical centre. It was only mild amazement, as when talking to Doug these kinds of statements came out with alarming regularity. Not for the first time I thought that Doug was definitely out there, in more ways than one.

Somewhat surprisingly, the conger eel tasted delicious and we all settled back into our sleeping bags, happy in the knowledge that we did not have to ski the next day. We heard a low, distant buzzing sound and Doug explained that a plane was coming in to do a fuel drop tonight. A few moments later, it appeared over the horizon and, without a great deal of evening entertainment in Antarctica, we all clambered out to watch it land. A weather front was fast approaching and, as it came into land, the white plane looked washed out by the colourless sky. Only its flashing lights could really be seen through the gloom, and I wondered how much visibility the pilot needed. With inch-perfect precision, the plane touched down on the uneven runway and taxied straight to the stash of fuel drums to begin unloading. If the weather deteriorated further, the plane would have to be grounded until the storm passed, and so the pilot hurried through the whole process.

He was in such a hurry that he had left the door to the main cabin open and, just beyond, I could see the small rows of comfortable seats within. I stood in the cold and thought about our notion of a 'plane day'. The hypothetical dilemma was here in the flesh and yet not a single muscle in my body moved towards the plane. I realised that it would have needed wild horses to drag me on board, as we had come way too far to take such an easy road out. As the pilot climbed the steps and fired up the engines once again, I began to understand the strength of my own conviction. I felt utterly determined to reach the pole and I waved goodbye to the pilot without a single doubt in my mind.

By mid-morning the next day, we had finished all our packing and the sleds lay ready for the second leg. We had seen Doug Stern up bright and early, waving a metal detector around by the fuel cache, trying to find one of the fuel drums that had been covered by snow the night before. All the fuel used by ANI is flown in and by the time it has reached the resupply at Theils it is worth an absolute fortune. Losing one of the drums would cost ANI hundreds of dollars, and Doug thought it wise to try to find the thing before anyone discovered he'd managed to lose something about a thousand times bigger than the average set of car keys.

We thought it would be nice to see some fellow Brits and so invited Graham and Andrew Cooney round for tea. Early in the afternoon, they both scrambled into the tent and settled down among all the clutter. Graham was wearing a colossal down jacket and a beanie woolly hat that made him look like a giant Smurf. He smiled warmly and then rummaged in the recesses of his jacket and emerged with some boiled sweets.

We had been surprised to see Andrew pitching up, in view of the somewhat frosty radio communications just prior to our arriving, but the whole afternoon he was nothing less than charming. All the pretence that had so aggravated me previously seemed stripped away, leaving a genuinely nice person who seemed finally at ease with himself. Whether it was the Antarctic environment which had beaten it out of him, or whether Matty had taken it upon herself to say a few words, I had no idea, but as we spoke for a couple of hours that day we were all feeling that perhaps we had been a little too hasty in our joint condemnations.

It was interesting to hear them both complain that occasionally they found it hard to occupy their minds when skiing.

'I just find that there are only about five subjects that I can think about for any length of time,' explained Graham earnestly. 'If I try to go for the more material things, like cars or houses or something, the thoughts only last for a couple of minutes.'

'So what are the things you think about?' I asked, wondering whether they might be the same ones that had been recycling through my mind.

'I don't even want to say them out loud!' he said with a weary grin. 'They just go round and round in my head. I swear, it's driving me mad.'

We all nodded in agreement, in a way only someone who has spent a month entirely lost in their own thoughts can do.

While pouring the tea, Tom mentioned that we had seen his footprint a few days previously. Again, Graham laughed.

'I am the world's worst skier,' he explained. 'I know it sounds ridiculous, but I just hate using skis and would much rather walk. Then again, it's hardly surprising. Travelling on foot is a thoroughly British tradition. So, I guess I don't really have any other option.'

It was a tradition that could exact an enormous price, as the soft snow of the High Polar Plateau might prove. If our bindings kept snapping with their previous regularity, good skiers or not, we might well be joining Graham in his bid to make it to the pole on foot.

Regular as clockwork, we got up at the usual time the next morning. The other team were an hour ahead of us and so we could just make them out in the distance, passing round the front of the Theils Mountains. As we readied ourselves to leave, Doug emerged from his igloo and waved goodbye. After a few minutes, he turned round and clambered back in, obviously content with the amount of human interaction he had experienced over the last couple of days and looking forward to some peace and quiet.

The route stretched off before us, as it had done before. The only difference was that this time we weren't aiming for a midway resupply point somewhere in the Antarctic wilderness. This time we were aiming for the very bottom of the planet. We clipped on our skis, fastened the harnesses to our sleds and, like a tiny caravan of camels, set off into the desert once more.

10

Batteries Not Included

They say that when you reach the summit of a mountain you are only halfway there.

Having felt rested and well fed at the resupply point, only three days later I was tired. It was a deep-rooted, debilitating sort of tiredness, which had obviously been festering just beneath the surface. I was amazed at how quickly the change had taken place. Only 35 miles into the second leg of the expedition, I was feeling totally done in.

Our first day after leaving Theils, we had passed right underneath the foot of the mountains. Despite our having camped near them for the last two days, up close they looked utterly spectacular. The rocks towered hundreds of feet above our heads and huge, iridescent slabs of ice clung to their sides. Wind, funnelled and directed by the peaks, came blazing across the surface. It stripped away the top snow, creating vast areas of blue ice, and swirled around our legs like a great streaming cloud. Often the ground beneath our feet became totally obscured, as the snow caught in the wind and rolled across our desolate horizon. To protect ourselves from this sand-blasting effect, we all pulled tight our fur hoods and skied with heads bent low.

Usually, such harsh conditions would make it too cold to take photographs. However, that day we all preferred to let our hands freeze a little longer and try to capture some of the beauty on film.

I kept my camera right next to my body, under all my layers of clothing. Despite this precaution, within seconds of being exposed to the elements the metal would freeze solid. It was infuriating to go to all the effort of peeling back my outer mittens and fishing inside my jacket, only to have the camera ice up and miss the moment. Within about half an hour of putting it back inside my jacket, I would hear it click and wind forward. My body heat was evidently bringing it back to life and resulting in yet another photo of the inside of my thermal top.

Tom had more success and rather over-enthusiastically managed to shoot two entire rolls of film. As well as these delays, he was also stopping a great deal to look at the different rocks that had rolled off the mountain. They lay in their thousands, randomly strewn over the ice, and while the rest of us skied past them without so much as a second glance, Tom would be on his hands and knees, laboriously studying each one in turn.

Our route led us across huge patches of blue ice, and we were forced to stop and take off our skis. With the added glide of the kicker skins, we didn't stand a chance of crossing them normally, and the only way was to teeter along on foot. Our fully loaded sleds would catch the wind and slew to the side, yanking us off balance on the perfectly smooth surface. Owing to weight allowances, we had no crampons and we would occasionally fall and land awkwardly in a heap. Originally, I considered the falls to be nothing more than a bit embarrassing, but it would have been easy to twist an ankle or break a wrist, and that would have resulted in an annoying evacuation from Theils.

With all the ferreting around for rock samples, Tom had dropped far behind. We stopped to let him catch up and I put on my down jacket to keep warm. Peering through the swirling snow, I realised it was going to take him about half an hour to catch up and I was already starting to shiver from the inactivity. In these conditions he would never have been able to follow our tracks, and so our only option was to sit and wait.

Finally, we saw him look up and realise his

predicament. He put his head down and skied as fast as he could towards us. A few seconds later, he slipped on the ice and went down heavily on his shoulder. He got up once again, but even from a distance it looked as if he was cradling his arm. Finally, he pulled level with us and got a reception almost as cold as the weather. If he had been expecting sympathy, it was not forthcoming. All of us were livid for having to wait so long in the cold.

On the back of his sled were about twenty different chunks of granite, and we looked on amazed. It could not have been more than twelve hours ago that we had all made a big thing of travelling super-light. Like a guilty schoolboy, he grudgingly threw the rocks on the ground, but kept one tiny pebble, which evidently had some sort of particular scientific value. Paul looked on sceptically, no doubt believing he had a load more stashed away in his sled.

Along with refusing to use huskies or decent skis, carrying rocks is another strong British tradition. When Captain Scott died in the blizzard of 1912, remarkably his sled still contained 35 pounds of rock samples. He had collected them on his journey to the South Pole, yet despite the prospect of being unable to get back to his ship, he had persisted in carrying them all the way back. When every single mile counts, it seems extraordinary to me that he should have valued scientific considerations so highly.

Historians have calculated that if he had ditched all non-essential items at the first signs of serious danger, he might well have made it to his resupply point. He had previously cached huge supplies of food and fuel at One-Ton Depot, and with lighter sleds and consequently greater mileage he and his colleagues might have reached it. Ultimately, Scott and his companions ended up dying in their tent, only 11 miles away. Although it's unfair to cite this single aspect, and there are a million different factors which contributed to Scott's death, it's an interesting point when trying to understand the mentality of the early explorers.

Stiff from the cold, I got up from my sled and readied myself for skiing once again. As I watched Tom unload the last of the granite rocks, I shook my head and lamented the fact that the British mentality obviously hadn't changed that much in the last century.

With many apologies, Tom set off once more and led the next session at a blistering pace. Although there was no way of knowing yet, both the shoulder and the waiting would come back to haunt us.

* * *

The second day after leaving Theils, the conditions continued to deteriorate. While the wind stripped away both the heat from our bodies and our chances of decent mileage, the sastrugi seemed to grow in size. Soon, the horizon was just a tangled mass of huge, hard-packed mounds of snow, and only with tremendous effort would our fully laden sleds bounce over them.

Our ski bindings were also getting a battering, and after three continuous days of humourless grind I started to wonder whether it would be our bindings or our backs which would be the first to give out.

Sitting exhausted in the tent on the third night, I quietly fumed with anger. The conditions were draining us badly, and it felt like such a waste of our previous efforts. The whole way coming into the resupply at Theils, we had deliberately tried to be careful and keep some energy in reserve. Now it felt as if we had already depleted this reserve and were fast exhausting ourselves. We all knew that the climb on to the polar plateau would begin within the next hundred miles or so, and if the conditions continued to be so exacting we would have precious little strength left to face it.

With our mileage deadlines looming ominously ahead, we were trying to keep a fast pace on the poor terrain, but the effort was draining us. We had averaged just over thirteen nautical miles a day for the last three days, which, in comparison to the last time we had pulled fully laden sleds, was an encouraging sign. Those first few days coming out of Hercules Inlet, we had barely broken into double figures.

On that third day after leaving Theils, Andy decided to share a few of his thoughts.

'The way I see it, if we average 16.7 nautical miles for this second half of the journey, then we would be the fastest team ever to make the pole. But, obviously, this doesn't include a rest day. Nor, in fact, a day lost to weather,' he added quickly.

It was a tall order to say the least, as even with the light sleds coming into Theils our best daily mileage had been 16.4. To average a distance greater than that was something that just seemed to be completely beyond us. After the beating we had taken in the last few days, I was in no mood to start thinking about breaking records. Instead, I was more concerned about just reaching the pole.

However, as with all these things, just the act of sowing the seed is usually enough to pique my curiosity. It did seem as if we were reaching for the stars even thinking about breaking the speed record, but it was tempting to have something like that in our sights. I had already decided that I wanted to arrive at the pole with nothing left to give. I would only ever get one shot at this and I wanted to get there knowing that I had used up every ounce of my reserves, that I had given it my all. I was pretty convinced that wouldn't be enough to break records, but there didn't seem to be any harm in trying.

As soon as we woke up, we all knew that the fourth day was going to be tough. Despite the promise of clear skies the previous evening, clouds had moved in just as we had set up camp, making the temperature inside the tent plummet. Even with hours of cooking and three men sleeping right beside each other, the temperature stayed just under freezing all night. Our iced-up clothing caught some of the heat from the stove, but didn't have a chance to dry properly. Instead, the ice simply turned to water and then remained wet. We all knew that within seconds of venturing outside it would freeze solid once more, the neck warmers and balaclavas rubbing stiffly against our faces. Condensation clung to the inside of the tent in a solid layer of ice, and soon we were completely covered in a dusting of tiny crystals. The first words to come out of Andy's mouth at exactly 6.01 a.m. were, 'We're just going to have to buckle down and get the mileage done today.'

My own diary entry for the morning reads no better, as the long hours of general dampness were obviously starting to get to me.

The cold makes my bones feel brittle — like my fingers and thighs could just snap if I bent them back a little. It's not the effort of doing what we are doing that is the hard part, it's maintaining the mental enthusiasm and facing the struggle day after day. There is just no respite, no coming in from the cold, no night off.

Back in England people seemed to view this expedition as an honourable, worthy pursuit. Right now, I can see no honour in what we are doing and sometimes it's worse, I can see no point. Originally, I believed I was here because I wanted to see Antarctica, but surely if I wanted to do that I would just fly over the continent and be done with it. Is it instead that I am simply doing this to satisfy my own vanity? Is it just that so few others have made it to the pole that I am attracted to such a challenge?

We have only been skiing for just over thirty days. How on earth did the early explorers hack 120 days on the ice? They must have had minds like steel.

PS: Please God, let us have good travelling conditions today or, if you're feeling really generous, how about a north-easterly wind for our kites?

Somebody upstairs was obviously listening, but only for a little while. When we left camp the sun was out and I quickly shed the doubts that had been plaguing me all morning. With clear blue skies we all just got on with skiing south and tried to let our minds wander to more comforting places. However, our damp clothes made the cold a constant menace, never far from our thoughts. It stopped the daydreaming and brought us right back to the present.

If we had to wait for any reason at all, we would swing our arms or ski round in circles, in a vain attempt to keep the blood flowing to our outer limbs. At the last break, Paul delved into his jacket and gave us the results from the GPS. I felt as if we had been going at a decent lick all day and was convinced our total was going to be somewhere near the fifteen mark.

'Twelve point two,' he said disappointedly, his voice lacking any of the usual gusto that accompanied the GPS reading. The sky seemed to echo our general despondency and clouds began gathering over our heads. The prospect of another damp night in our sleeping bags lowered our spirits even further.

During the last hour, I skied behind Andy and watched him fall over on five different occasions. Each time he picked himself up, dusted off the snow and wearily carried on. For some reason I wasn't feeling so bad, but there was nothing I could do to help him. I just looked on passively, willing him to stay on his feet, as he battled piteously against the harness straps.

It's easy to tell when someone is having a tough time of it, as their actions become far more erratic. Big, strenuous movements are quick to tire you and, like a strong swimmer caught in an even stronger current, very soon the only option is to stop fighting. With pure bloody-minded grit, Andy picked himself off the floor once again and patiently counted the minutes down until happy hour finally came to an end.

The evening was cloudy and drab, but it had one redeeming feature. Strangely, the only way I discovered this was due to my complete failure to kick a bad habit. I had packed five cigarettes for the second leg of the journey, which I intended to smoke either in celebration or when it all got a bit much. I had justified them to myself as essential items, to be used purely for medicinal purposes.

That night, I thought about the prospect of another day freezing in damp clothes and reached for the packet. After a couple of drags I began to feel a bit light-headed and thought I should probably put the cigarette out. Tom had just nipped outside to grab something from his sled and came padding across in his camp boots.

'Look at the way you're sitting!' he shouted excitedly.

'What's wrong with it?' I replied wearily, far too tired to deal with this right now.

'No, you idiot. You're facing west!'

Without thinking, I had put my back to the wind, but instead of facing north I was now looking due west. As the smoke from my cigarette proved, the wind had shifted 90 degrees.

The cloud cover we had been cursing for the last few hours was in fact an entirely new weather system. The front had the effect of pushing the southerly katabatic winds round to the east and would have been perfect for kiting, only there wasn't enough wind. It was a light breeze, five knots or so, and as much as we would have loved finally to have used our kites, it would have been impossible to get moving.

For the first time in thirty-two days, the wind had changed direction. It was encouraging stuff, as we could use any wind that wasn't blowing directly from the south. Just the idea of using the kites was enough to get me excited. To let them do all the hard work, while we relaxed and were pulled all the way to the South Pole, was certainly an alluring thought. That night I slept sporadically. Visions of sailing across the Antarctic wasteland filled my head, preventing peaceful sleep.

★　★　★

The next day, we stopped for our usual break at 10 a.m. The wind still blew from the east but, as we had discovered with heavy hearts that morning, had not gained any power during the night. Somewhat optimistically, Paul delved into his sled and began setting up the kite. We all sat on our sleds, doubtfully watching him untangle the lines. The breeze was so gentle that the fur on my jacket barely moved.

'You really think that there's going to be

enough wind to get us moving?' asked Andy hopefully.

'I don't know,' said Paul, twisting the lines round to set them straight. 'Although it's really light down here, it might be a little stronger 100 feet up. Anyway, there's no harm in trying.'

Wind or not, I was happy just to sit there, enjoying the sensation of having a longer break. Without being attached to his heavy sled, Paul managed to get moving. The kite swooped through the air and we all watched in amazement as he actually built up some speed and sailed across the snow. Although he wasn't going fast by any means, one thing was for sure — the theory was sound.

Despite the cloud cover, the light was good and the sastrugi uncharacteristically small. If the wind had been only a few knots stronger, we would have had perfect kiting conditions. Even with the doubtful wind, Paul's little experiment was good enough for us, and we got out the heavy kiting equipment, which had lain dormant for so long.

After twenty minutes of untangling lines we were ready. With the prospect of speeding across the ice, we all stood at ten-metre intervals, impatiently waiting for Paul's signal to launch.

With a wave of his hand, he signalled for us

to go and I pulled back on the kiting handles expectantly. 100 feet away, the kite did nothing more than ruffle a little in the breeze. After several enormous tugs it became airborne, but managed only to drift aimlessly around the sky. I slid forward a little on my skis and the rope connecting me to my sled went taut. The extra 170 pounds of my sled made it pretty obvious that I was going nowhere in a hurry. After huge amounts of effort, tugging the handles back and forth and trying to generate some power, I succeeded in being pulled almost six inches. It was like eating celery — it required more energy than it actually saved.

The others were gaining equally poor mileage and, in the entire time we had the kites in the air, we managed only to move about 200 yards directly downwind. Soon we all realised that it was hopeless and let the kites gently float down on to the snow. The whole morose situation was pretty far removed from the breakneck speeds I had imagined the night before. We packed up, happy to have had a practice and a break from the continual man-hauling, but also hoping that the next few days might bring just a few more knots of wind.

For the first time that night, we talked openly about how it might feel to reach the pole. Again, Paul surprised me by how candid he was.

'Last year, on that final stretch, I would sometimes find myself crying,' he said quietly. 'Thoughts of my family and friends came rushing to me and, I don't know why, but the emotion of it all just got the better of me.' He laughed a little and then said, 'It's been your objective for such a long time and suddenly you realise you're going to make it. The last sixty days behind you and the South Pole station just in front. What can I say, it's emotional.'

We all remained silent, being typically British about such a heartfelt revelation. It felt odd to hear such a confession from someone as tough as Paul. I would have to be threatened with dental torture to admit something so personal. Then again, that's probably the reason my girlfriend says I'm emotionally crippled. Paul, on the other hand, was just built differently. He completely lacked the social inhibitors that so many of us have always grown up with.

In an effort to change the subject, Andy got out the cards for our nightly game. We had quickly found that cards were a good way to try to take our minds off food, which was becoming more of a problem as the weeks went by. Early on in the expedition, strict rules had been invented which included the loser of the nightly card game having to carry all the team's rubbish in his sled. With great ceremony, the previous loser would hand over the slimy, half-torn packets and relish the fact that his sled no longer resembled a skip.

The card games distracted us from food only for so long, and soon the hunger returned with a vengeance. It had become such an issue that we had all previously decided to keep our lunch bags outside in our sleds. After the anguish he had experienced coming into Theils, Andy had been the first to suggest such a precaution. We deemed the thought of getting out of a warm sleeping bag and padding across the snow in our thermals to be enough of a deterrent.

In spite of this, Tom and I had previously learnt to bend the rules a little. The medical kit was not technically under the enforced six-day food cycle and was therefore, in our book, fair game. Just as in the expedition to Kyrgyzstan, the antiseptic throat lozenges were the first to go. While Paul shook his head at our complete lack of discipline, we all sucked on the honey-and-lemon sweets, arguing quite convincingly that it was pre-emptive treatment and therefore essential.

★　★　★

The next day, as usual, Paul came into the tent at exactly 6.15 a.m. With a smile, he announced that we should all dress as warmly as possible. In the 20-yard dash from his tent to ours he had gauged the wind and realised that it had seriously grown during the night. After yesterday's disappointment, I decided to check its strength before allowing myself to get excited, and went outside for my morning pee.

The sky was completely washed out and cloud extended all the way down to the ground. Where the horizon should have been there was nothing but a great swirling haze of white. The colours of our bright tents seemed to wash into the landscape, becoming pale and obscured. A strong 15-knot wind rattled the flysheet and the guy ropes bounced up and down as the gusts hit them at full force. I came back into the tent and raised an eyebrow questioningly at Paul. These were hardly perfect kiting conditions. He continued stirring his hot chocolate and didn't say a word.

It took us ages to get dressed. I crammed as much clothing as possible under my Gore-Tex jacket and, as I waited for everyone else to get ready, soon became hot and

291

irritable. Despite the gloomy, oppressive landscape, it was a relief to get out of the tent, and we all set to work unwinding the kite lines in preparation for the launch. The kites themselves flapped noisily in the wind. The fabric rippled and twisted, making it difficult to stake them down on the snow. As I walked back up to my sled, I looked around for the others. They had become hazy black objects on the periphery of my vision, and I thought about how careful we were going to have to be.

If one of us got separated, they would be impossible to find again. The wind would conceal our tracks in a few seconds and any farther than 40 yards or so and the rest of the team would be out of sight. We had two satellite phones between us (Paul and Tom) and two Global Positioning Systems (Paul and Andy), but they would all be largely academic if we got split up. Although it would have been nice to give someone a call while wandering aimlessly in the storm, it wouldn't have been a great deal of help. The only way to locate each other would have been by aeroplane, and such terrible conditions precluded any chance of take-off.

Even if the visibility hadn't been so much of an issue, we were surrounded by large lumps of sastrugi. With such a treacherous surface to land on and a complete horizonless blur everywhere else, even the crazy pilots at Patriot Hills would think twice about attempting a rescue. There was only one thing for it. We were just going to have to stick within each other's line of sight.

Finally, everything was ready. We stood at ten-metre intervals with the kites rustling innocently in the wind and waited for the signal to launch. Paul lifted his arm and in unison we released the brake lines.

In the murky light, I watched my kite fill with air, rocket straight into the main thrust of the wind and start spiralling round. The kite lines wrenched at my harness and I was yanked forward, my skis accelerating down-wind. Behind me, the slack cord to my sled snapped into life and together we started to pick up an ungodly amount of speed. I looked up at the kite, alarmed, and frantically pulled on the handles in an effort to control it. Not taking a blind bit of notice, the kite continued its random movements, swooshing through the sky in great arcs. With each pass it gained power, and soon I was hurtling along at breakneck speed.

The grey light made it impossible to see the lumps of sastrugi on the ground and my skis bounced up and down with each new contact. With my eyes transfixed on the kite, I had no time to look down anyway. I must have stood upright for about five seconds, lurching backwards and forwards in the struggle, before the inevitable happened and I went sprawling on to my face.

In a desperate bid to activate the brake lines, my hands were still clinging on to the handles, and so I hit the ground hard. A second later my sled came scorching past my face, so close one of the straps actually slapped me across my cheek. It jammed to a halt as the connecting line went taut and I lay in the snow, a twisted mixture of skis and kite lines. It must have looked as if I had been dropped from a great height.

I was shaking slightly. A hit from such a fast-moving and heavy sled would definitely have broken some bones. The problem was getting hold of the brake lines. Our enormous outer mittens gave us all the manual dexterity of a flipper, but there wasn't an alternative. The kiting handles were made of metal and would just have frozen to our hands in seconds. Slowly, I picked myself up, dusted off the snow and tried not to think about it all.

The lines took some untwisting, but soon everything was ready for another attempt. With gritted teeth, I launched the kite once more and immediately rocketed downwind, totally out of control. With a strange sense of déjà vu, I yanked the kite handles from side to side, desperately trying to control it, but succeeding only in angering it further. My right ski tip collided with a large wedge of sastrugi and I went tumbling down once more. Lying on my chest, I looked on in horror as the kite wound itself in as many twists as it could, before I finally managed to force it on to the ground.

Luckily, my frightened synapses were slightly more alert than I. Some sort of primeval self-preservation instinct kicked in and I pulled my legs up behind me. A second later the sled came slamming into my skis, buckling my knees with the impact. OK, I was now properly scared.

One of the main problems we encountered was that our boots clipped into the skis only at the toe. Without ridged boots or, for that matter, our heels being locked down on to the ski, it was very hard to keep control. Unlike downhill skiing, where the firmness of the boot offers support, our system was more like trying to slalom in flip-flops.

I stood up to see how the others were getting on. In the murky half-light, it looked as if Andy and Tom were having an equally miserable time. I saw Andy fall heavily and the sled hit him squarely in the back. As I looked on, he tentatively got up, clutching his lower back, and then slowly sank to his knees again. He would later tell me that he thought that was the end of his expedition, as his legs had just given out from under him.

Paul staked down his kite and trudged over to where I was picking myself up from another high-speed wipe-out. I put my face close to his ear, so he could hear me over the noise of the wind, and shouted, 'I can't launch the kite. It just goes straight into the main power of the wind.'

Paul nodded and then motioned that he wanted to try it for himself. I unclipped the safety line and handed him the kite. With his feet planted firmly in the snow, he leant back and gave the handles a tug. He was immediately swept off his feet by the power of the kite and landed on his back about 10 feet away. Without the extra weight of the sled to anchor him to the ground, he had been picked up like a rag doll and was being pulled downwind in a furious combination of spiralling kite and flailing legs. It happened so fast that I didn't do anything to help and just stood watching, slightly curious as to where he might end up. A few metres farther and he managed to get a firm grip of the brake lines. Reluctantly, the kite dropped to the ground.

Unperturbed, Paul got to his feet and

started to trudge back to where I was standing, untwisting the lines as he went. 'You've got to get it away from the power zone,' he shouted at me. I simply nodded, as given all the wind it wasn't exactly the best time to have a discussion about the mechanics of controlling kites. 'Bring the kite to the side and then launch it away from the wind,' he bellowed, and got ready for another demonstration.

With skilful movement of the handles, he manoeuvred the kite into the perfect launch position and tugged backwards. It immediately ripped back the other way and Paul went careering off into the middle distance once more. I stood by and simply watched the whole thing happen all over again, my confidence in absolute tatters.

For the next three and a half hours this was pretty much how things went. By mid-morning I had become convinced that a nasty accident was imminent, but really didn't want to give up the chance of making use of this easterly wind. Paul had given me his kite, which although technically identical to the one I had been struggling with was much better behaved. Slowly, I was getting the hang of launching the kite and keeping it out of the main thrust of the wind. By pre-empting the movement and reacting fast, it was possible to keep it away from the fatal 90-degree angle, and once in the weaker area of the wind it became far more manageable.

I lowered my kite to take a rest and suddenly Tom came flashing past. His kite tore across the sky, about 10 feet off the ground and precisely in the main area of the wind. As his skis ramped another lump of sastrugi, his body lurched backwards and forwards, sending him completely off balance. His arms pumped the kiting handles in a vain attempt to keep control, but it was only a matter of time before the inevitable happened. He went flying on to his face and I watched the sled ride straight over his back. He lay motionless, trapped underneath, and I immediately thought my earlier fears of a serious injury had just been realised.

Our signal that everything was OK was to wag our arms up and down. In view of the fact that Tom had both his pinned down by the weight of the sled, I couldn't be sure whether he was seriously hurt or not. I peered through the gloom, waiting, but he didn't move an inch. Slowly, I saw one of his hands break free and he weakly raised it in the air. Fearing the worst and with frantic speed, I unclipped my skis, staked down my kite and began sprinting over towards him. In my haste, I had forgotten to unclip the rope attaching me to my sled and after approximately six paces it snapped tight, landing me heavily on my back. Like an upturned beetle, I lay on the ground and desperately tried to wriggle out of my harness straps. I am sure that if Tom hadn't been in so much pain he would have laughed out loud at what must have looked like a surefire winner for any home video awards.

By the time I managed to get over to him, Tom had got out from under his sled and was sitting on it, breathing heavily. Even behind his goggles, I could see that he was fuming with frustration, and he sat motionless, staring fixedly at the kite. He looked exhausted from the hours of falling over and the constant battle with the wind. Paul came over as well and we stood with our backs to the wind, trying to figure out the best course of action. Paul got out the GPS and showed me the results. In four hours we had gained about half a kilometre, and although Andy and I were definitely starting to get the hang of it all, Tom had barely gone five yards without crashing.

'Either we're going to have to go back to manhauling,' said Paul, 'or we're going to have to try and do something to get Tom up to speed.'

'Can we use the rope to tow him?' I asked.

'If you can take his sled, I can rig something up so he can be pulled along behind me.'

It was worth a shot. Anything would be better than going back to man-hauling. Paul attached Tom's sled to the back of his own and set off downwind. Despite pulling himself and approximately 370 pounds of sled, he shot off into the distance.

I hooked the rope on to the back of my sled and tied two loops to act as handles. Like some sort of bizarre waterskier, Tom held on, while my kite rocketed into the air and yanked us both forward.

We set off at a blistering pace. Not through any deliberate skill of mine, but more thanks to the fact that it was just easier to let the wind take you at the speed it wanted to go. We were going so fast that in the first five minutes Tom fell off the back three times in quick succession. Each time I would hear a shout and then turn to see a great cloud of snow being kicked up and the rope flailing wildly in the wind. I was concentrating so hard on keeping the kite airborne that on the first occasion I hadn't heard his scream over the noise of the wind. At the risk of leaving him behind, we agreed that Andy should act as sweeper and stay at the back.

Soon, however, Tom's skill at downhill skiing started paying off and we began making good progress. Ahead of me, I could see Paul blazing ahead, the two sleds bouncing over great chunks of ice and fishtailing wildly behind him. With the prospect of two heavy sleds hitting him, Paul later confided that he had been petrified that he would cripple himself if he fell.

Looking over my shoulder, Tom would shout loudly if I was heading directly for a large lump of sastrugi. With an extra set of eyes looking ahead, I could concentrate more on the kite, and soon we were tearing along. However, at the back, Andy was having a few problems.

He had been battling with his kite when he suddenly realised that he couldn't feel the fingers on his right hand. He dumped the kite on the ground and stripped off his outer gloves, cursing himself for being so careless. A few lines from the kite had wrapped around his fingers and compressed the thermal filling of his gloves. This reduced the padding he had between the metal handle and his fingers, and upon closer inspection he saw that two of his fingers were sheet white and frozen solid. With visions of frostbite and amputation running through his head, he stuck the two frozen fingers in his mouth. It wasn't exactly a textbook procedure, but it was the quickest and easiest remedy he could think of.

He was lucky and managed to catch it in time. The freezing penetrated only the first few layers of skin, which like the patches on his face would strip off over the next couple of weeks. There was no permanent damage to the flesh underneath, but weeks after coming back from Antarctica Andy would still complain that his hands felt horribly stiff.

★   ★   ★

After an hour or so, the cloud lifted a little and the visibility improved to about 25 metres. At the same time the snow also softened and the three of us tore along, blasting straight through the more malleable lumps of sastrugi. It felt wonderful to be gaining so much mileage so quickly. As I had found out from the last thirty days man-hauling, skiing to the pole is mainly uphill; in fact our route was entirely uphill. Suddenly, with the help of the kites, we were devouring rises that would normally have taken us hours to climb. I turned back and watched the sled bouncing along at great speed behind me. With virtually no effort on our behalf, we were going about five times faster than our normal skiing speed.

A couple of hours later and the wind started to die. With the extra weight of dragging Tom, I had to constantly force the kite through the air in order to generate more power. The effort was making my arms burn and I was getting seriously tired. On one of the steeper uphills, there just wasn't enough wind and we started to go frustratingly slowly.

Given the drop in wind, Tom decided to have another go at kiting, and the four of us set off once again. Slowly his confidence and ability improved and soon I could see three other kites tearing across the sky, the entire team powering along in unison. I was amazed at how swiftly the situation had changed. Only hours ago, the kites had seemed like one of the quickest ways to be evacuated with a broken back. By the middle of the afternoon, we were coasting along.

As we were all competent downhill skiers, it was a great help not having to worry about what our feet were doing and to be able to focus solely on controlling the kites. Often gusts would instantly push us a couple of metres downwind, and if we hadn't been so comfortable on skis we would have ended up crashing almost constantly. As it was, our skis glided over the snow and we leant back in our harnesses, just enjoying the feeling of a free ride.

By late evening, Tom started to crash a

great deal more. It was now 10 p.m., and after thirteen hours of constant kiting we were all getting tired, especially him. After some discussion, we decided to press on regardless and try to rack up a good mileage for the day.

However, with the frequency of Tom's falls, we inevitably spent most of our time sitting on our sleds, waiting for him to catch up. Without the warmth generated by man-hauling, we were far more susceptible to the cold. The incessant waiting became simply torturous. We would sit quietly, huddled with our backs to the wind, and wait for him to draw level with us once more. It was so frustrating, as not only was the cold endangering our hands and feet, we were also missing out on a potentially huge mileage for the day. The wind might well revert back to its normal southerly direction by morning, and it just felt as if we were wasting the day and squandering a superb opportunity.

I kited over to Tom and told him we were going to rig up the 'waterskiing' system again. He stared at me with furious eyes, desperately trying to restrain himself from telling me to go to hell. But that was exactly where he was right then, in his own private hell, and deteriorating fast. Not only was there the frustration of being unable to work the kite, he also felt he was hindering the team's progress. Reluctantly, he tethered his sled to Paul's and held on to the rope from the back of my sled.

I could appreciate the dent to his pride and how frustrating it must have been, but this was the only way the team would be able to progress as a whole. There just didn't seem to be any point in continuing with an ineffectual system, just because the alternative might hurt someone's feelings. Also, at that time, I wasn't exactly in the most altruistic of moods. I had been sitting in the cold for hours on end, endlessly twiddling my frozen thumbs.

With a disgruntled Tom in tow, we all set off once more. I soon realised that my heart just wasn't in it. The wind wasn't sufficient for me to generate enough power to go directly south. My arms were exhausted from the last session and the perpetual cold made me just want to curl up and sleep. The only way I could get moving was to point directly downwind, and this inevitably meant going west, instead of due south. I started to lose my temper. After a couple of slow, annoying falls, there were soon two very unhappy people attached to the same sled.

I signalled to Paul and Andy that I couldn't get enough power and was fast running out of patience. By a stroke of luck, Andy broke one of his bindings at that exact moment, and that seemed like a good enough excuse for us to finally stop. Wearily, I collapsed the kite for the last time that day.

Despite the four hours wasted at the beginning of the day, the GPS read 25.4 miles. Nearly half a degree in a single day! We got into the tent that night feeling battered and sore from hitting the ground so often, but there was a smile on all our faces. In the warmth of the tent and with the curative powers of hot chocolate working its magic, we all realised how exceptional the day had been. We had learnt to master the kites and travelled nearly a marathon's worth of distance on steep hills. Miraculously, no one had been seriously hurt or lost, and there was every chance there might be more wind in the next few days.

I leant back and relaxed, grinning like an idiot. I couldn't believe our secret weapons had actually worked. I had assumed we were going to be lugging them all the way to the pole, without a single chance to try them out.

I looked at the others and my smile widened even farther. I knew James Bond wouldn't have gloated as I was then, but frankly I just didn't care.

11

Southern Discomfort

'It's not the goal but the way that matters and the harder the way, the more worthwhile the journey.'
— Wilfred Thesiger

'Bastard, goddam, useless piece of rubbish.'

A long and heartfelt torrent of abuse could just be heard above the wind. Caught by the breeze, the sound drifted over to where we sat, huddled in a group a few hundred metres away. Despite being muffled by the distance, it was obvious that this was the sound of someone having the worst birthday of their life.

Two days after our previous kiting, the wind had wheeled round once more. It was blowing at about eight knots from the east and the conditions were perfect. With new-found confidence from surviving that first horrific day, we all unfurled the kites and started to sail south in a surprisingly orderly fashion.

In just a few hours we had covered seven

miles and rocketed up hills that would normally have taken us an entire morning to climb. We were now constantly gaining altitude, climbing up on to the High Polar Plateau, and it felt wonderful to watch the kites power us forward and the hills effortlessly drop away. As we crested one large rise, Andy dropped his kite on to the ground and signalled that he had just snapped another binding.

Before coming to Antarctica, we had read a report from a guide who had travelled this route two years previously. We had been amazed by the number of bindings he had managed to break and had laughed incredulously as he was forced to radio Patriot Hills and get more airlifted in. This was our seventh since leaving Theils and, if this continued, we would soon be rivalling that score or, more likely, bettering it. Given the soft snow of the polar plateau, the thought of trudging along on foot now seemed even less appealing.

In just the few minutes it took to repair the binding, the weather closed in. The advancing cloud immediately dispelled all my earlier visions of sailing past the 88th parallel and climbing all the way to the top of the plateau. Soon, the sky and ground merged in a single white blur and the visibility went down to just a few metres.

We pressed on in the dim half-light, still making reasonable mileage, but soon came across an area of gigantic sastrugi. The lumps of snow felt bigger than anything we had encountered so far, but in such miserable visibility we couldn't be sure. Alternating between the pull of the kite and that of the sled, we lurched along, bouncing over the sastrugi and crashing every hundred metres or so. It was infuriating to have no horizon to work off and to be constantly forced off balance by the sled. However, even with such regular falls, it was still faster and slightly more preferable to man-hauling.

That morning in the tent we had all wished Tom a happy birthday. With the easterly winds and the prospect of kiting, he had been looking forward to a birthday to remember. As we sat freezing on our sleds, waiting for him to catch up, it was clear that Tom would not be forgetting this day in a hurry. He was normally the epitome of diplomacy and restraint, but the morning had quickly reduced him to a mess of self-pitying frustration.

While we waited, pulling our clothing tight to keep warm, we could see him repeatedly falling over. Either a lump of sastrugi would unbalance him or the sled would wedge itself in a rut and topple him forward. With merciless regularity he hit the ground, and after every fall he would drag himself back up, determined to continue. As another loud string of expletives carried across the wind, it was obvious the hours of constant falling over were starting to take their toll.

As I sat waiting, the cold had begun to get into my boots. I pulled my feet up on to the sled to get them clear of the snow and sat in the fetal position, rocking gently. I was also starting to get worried about my hands, as they had been numb for over half an hour. I turned and watched Tom kite for a few metres and then hit the deck once again. The problem wasn't the regularity of his falls, as we all were falling over, it was the time he took to get himself ready again. While the rest of us would just give ourselves a quick dust down and get on with launching the kite, Tom would make all sorts of little adjustments to his gloves, sledging harness and about thirty other variables. The process seemed to take for ever.

I waited for him to pull level and then work his way past. I thought it better to let him get ahead and then have a prolonged period of activity. Each time I was just about to get up and start moving again his kite would spiral out of control and he would land heavily once more. The visibility could not have been more than 30 metres and yet I saw him crash five times in quick succession.

The last time I said out loud, 'Oh, for fuck's sake.' I hadn't meant for him to hear it, nor was it a particularly sympathetic thing to say when someone is having such an infuriating time. The words caught the wind and floated down to where he lay, crumpled in a heap on the ground. His head snapped round and even behind the dark lenses of his goggles I could see the venom in his eyes. Immediately I realised how insensitive I had been. Although the cold has a way of severely testing your patience, it was no excuse for being so unsupportive and I immediately regretted what I had said.

Sitting waiting, and with the wind blowing the snow against my back, I thought of one of the last diary entries ever written by Captain Scott. At this stage he knew the end was just a few days away and he wrote, 'How much better has all this been than lounging in too great comfort at home.'

I was about a million miles away from such extremity of suffering and yet, right then, I was still finding it very difficult to appreciate the reasons for us being here. Lounging in too great comfort sounded like exactly what I wanted to do. Just five minutes in a hot bath or an hour's sleep in a warm bed — it didn't seem like too much to ask. I just couldn't understand how Scott was still able to romanticise Antarctica, given that it was soon going to be the death of him. I am pretty certain I wouldn't have been so philosophical.

The hardest part of expeditions of this ilk is the fact that there is just no respite from the elements, never once a break from the cold. Even someone as travel hardened as Geoff Somers, on his epic crossing of Antarctica, wrote,

'If you could only hear us groan and moan in the morning. The inside of your tent is covered in ice and your back aches from the cold. All you want to do is stay in your bag, but you have no choice . . . you've got to go on.'

Forcing ourselves on was all very well, but the issue now was how we were going to do it. Did we continue to make use of the wind or simply go back to man-hauling? The latter was safer and also meant the team could travel together at a constant pace. With Tom falling behind all the time, there didn't seem to be much choice.

Half an hour or so later, Andy, Paul and I huddled together on one of our sleds. Tom was still far behind, so we had staked our kites to the ground and waited for him to catch up. We sat despondently, listening to them flap noisily in the distance, when I finally voiced the issue of what we should do.

'How about we rig up the tow-rope system again,' I said to the others.

'Maybe,' said Paul, 'but I don't think it's going to be easy to persuade Tom to do it. He's having a tough time right now. I know it means we can use the wind, but it might seriously affect his morale.'

As on the first day, we all hated the idea of wasting the wind and going back to man-hauling, but there were other considerations at stake. The resentment and ill feeling the suggestion might cause, especially to someone having a day as terrible as Tom's, might well have disastrous consequences. In the long run, a person's sanity was more important than gaining a few extra miles.

Before we had left England, the three of us had used the kites more than Tom, and this was obviously paying dividends out in Antarctica. Kiting is one of those sports which just seems impossible and then, suddenly, it will click. Going through the process in the wilds of Antarctica was certainly no easy way to learn, and had I been in Tom's shoes I am sure I would have felt equally frustrated.

Without a viable alternative, we decided to postpone the decision-making and continue for a little longer. I launched the kite and, with the thought of going back to man-hauling plaguing my mind, carried on moving south. Like a spoilt child, I let it slowly depress me and completely failed to realise that the clouds were in fact lifting and the giant fields of sastrugi starting to flatten.

Half an hour later and even I started to wake up to what was happening around me. Soon, all four of our kites blazed across the sky in unison. They billowed full of wind, pulling us ever forward. Our skis ran easily over the soft snow and the sleds cruised along without any of the usual lurching motion. The change in Tom was remarkable. The feelings of despair lifted with the cloud and I could see he was giving it everything he had to try to stay on his feet. His persistence was eventually being rewarded and the miles started to flash past.

Andy and I took the lead and, side by side, relentlessly pressed on. For hours none of us stopped. We barely fell over and only took breaks that lasted a couple of minutes. In these, we wolfed down the food and seldom talked, everybody far too eager to get moving again. We all knew how capricious the Antarctic weather could be and were desperate to make the most of this opportunity.

By early evening the wind had started to flag and we had to saw the kite handles back and forth to generate enough power. Andy managed to burn through the plastic hook on his harness, he was working the kite so hard, while the rest of us just had arms like lead. With a dying wind, our progress slowed to just a couple of miles an hour. Eventually the kites ground to a halt and we thought it no bad thing to end a little early to celebrate Tom's birthday.

That night, the party hats came out and we all took a slug from the whisky bottle. It had been a hard and difficult day, but, as always, the frustrations seemed to stay outside the tent. We were also consoled by the fact that we had travelled 23.7 nautical miles and not a single one of them by man-hauling. Without the extra effort of having to pull our sleds, we had burnt fewer calories and so felt slightly less hungry that night. With a sigh of relief, I realised that my earlier aspersions about kiting and celery were proving to be untrue.

Unfortunately, Tom's celebrations were short lived. Climbing on to the plateau, we all started to feel the effect of the altitude. Although the top of the plateau is only at 9,300 feet, owing to its southerly altitude it actually feels more like 12,000 feet. Obviously, we weren't about to start cracking open the oxygen bottles, as neither altitude is exactly high. However, when pulling a sled uphill, through soft powder snow, every little counts, and the altitude made us all feel short of breath and lethargic.

After that second day kiting, I had felt as if the pole was just around the corner. There then followed three days of brutal uphill, which could not have put that feeling farther from my mind. As we gained altitude the temperature also dropped noticeably. The snow softened and the sleds sank deeper in powder, draining the strength from our thighs.

Occasionally, we would wake to find that the ice crystals on the ground had frozen so hard that the sleds dragged across them like wood across sandpaper. We would put heart and soul into these days, only to discover that our mileage had just broken a pitiful twelve and we were going to have to increase our hours.

Getting over the apex of the plateau certainly showed how much more we had to give. At various points in the expedition we had thought that we were working as hard as we could, but now those times seemed to pale in comparison. It was back-breaking stuff. All we could do was put our heads down and pray for the time to pass quickly. It soon became apparent, however, that Tom in particular was having a problem keeping pace.

On the penultimate session of the day, Tom was roughly twenty minutes late coming into the break. Owing to the cold, we were all keen to get moving again, and so started getting ready the moment he sat down to rest. The way our cycles of food worked, one person would be carrying a little extra weight for a couple of days before we readjusted and everyone carried the same again. Just by the way the rotation worked, Tom was currently carrying an extra couple of kilos, so I offered to switch sleds for the last session. Wearily he complied and I set off, following Andy's lead.

Having had his hands and feet steadily freeze during the prolonged break, Andy set off at a blistering pace. I knew my morale would sink if I let his sled pull away and so did everything possible to keep up. By the time happy hour finally came to an end, I had sweated so hard that great chunks of ice hung off the hair poking out from under my hat. My eyelashes had frozen to my goggles, making it difficult to blink, and the habitual 'ice armour' lay thick beneath my jacket.

On the last 500-metre stretch, I had also

snapped a binding. Not wanting to spend time in the cold trying to fix it, I got out one of my kiting skis and used that instead. Without the grip of the kicker skin, it slid back with each step and the annoyance caused my mood to plummet. Not for the first time, I was amazed at how close the line was between feeling relatively comfortable and utter despair. In the space of a few hundred yards, it felt as if I had undergone a complete emotional overhaul.

Only a little earlier I had been feeling good enough to offer to swap sleds with Tom. Now, with the sweat beading over my eyes, I felt completely downhearted. I found myself looking jealously at Paul and Andy, as they had already completed the remaining distance and were starting to set up camp. I could only assume that this emotional pinballing was not a good sign. That such a minor hindrance could affect me so badly clearly showed how frail my mental state was becoming.

Inside the tent, and with the stove already burning, I watched Tom slowly wend his way into camp. I had only had to deal with ten minutes of isolation; he, on the other hand, had spent most of his day alone. Later that night, Tom would explain that the fall he had had on the blue ice just outside Theils was causing him pain again. Somehow, the injury had resurfaced and was really starting to get to him.

With this in mind, we all agreed to redistribute the food provisions for the next cycle a day early. This would lighten Tom's sled considerably and hopefully get him up to speed for the following day. I looked across the tent and watched him sipping his hot chocolate slowly. He looked tired and in pain. Then again, there was a good chance the rest of us weren't exactly looking our best. Perhaps he would be fine tomorrow.

The next day, Tom managed to keep up for the first two sessions then completely dropped out of sight. It was a bright, clear day and so he could easily follow our tracks, but I definitely didn't feel happy about him dropping below the horizon. We stopped and put on our down jackets and wondered whether it could be anything more than his shoulder. For the second day running, he came into camp that night miles behind the rest of us. Dejection and pain were etched into his face and the morale in the whole team started to wane. Our mileage was dropping constantly and we were falling drastically behind our revised schedule.

* * *

I peered out of the tent the next morning and smiled. The sun was out and I could see the horizon stretching out in front of me. The surface looked entirely flat, and with pure relief I realised that we had finally reached the top of the plateau. I knew Tom had been focusing on this point for the last few days and, in his mind, it had signified an end to all the suffering. Yesterday's aches and pains seemed to drop away, and for the first time in almost a week I felt optimistic about reaching the pole.

I swapped leads with Tom, so he could control the morning's pace, and he set off extremely slowly. We plodded along behind, constantly feeling cold and unable to build up enough speed to keep warm. Only half an hour in, he stopped and waved for me to take over once again. As I skied past, I saw him reach back into his sled and look around for some painkillers. It was not a good sign.

By the next break he was a small blur on the horizon.

'What do you think it could be?' I said to Andy, sitting beside me on his sled.

'It must be more than his shoulder,' he answered thoughtfully. 'It just wouldn't slow him down that much.'

We waited, but he didn't seem to be getting any closer. Eventually I thought he might be signalling, but couldn't be sure because of the distance. We unclipped our skis and started to retrace our steps towards him.

When we caught up with him he looked ill from pain. His face was pale and his eyes looked hollow and tired. It looked as if he had somehow been stretched by the mental battle of the last few days. He stood swaying slightly on his feet, and it was obvious that we were not going any farther that day. Paul took his sled and Andy went on ahead. Slowly, Tom and I walked back together and I waited for him to speak.

'I just don't have any energy. I watch you guys tear off and try to follow, but there is just no strength left in me.' He sounded more woeful than I had ever heard him, and it was horrible to see him so reduced. His voice was a low whisper and it was obviously a great effort for him even to walk over to where our sleds lay. Andy and Paul were setting up the tent and I could see Tom staring fixedly at them. His only thought was to get inside and finally rest.

'There is also one another thing,' he said slowly and reluctantly. 'Using the snow wedgies each morning has given me horrible pain. I think it's given me piles.' I could now understand why he had become so terribly morose. He had been trying to hide the problem and press on regardless for the last few days. It must have been terrible. Not just the pain, but also the constant worry that this would keep him from reaching the pole.

Tom clambered inside and went directly to sleep. While he took a welcome break from the isolation and worry, we spoke in hushed tones about what was to be done. As Paul explained, it might well be the altitude that was affecting him so badly. The symptoms were certainly there, as Tom had recently been complaining of feeling lethargic and having constant headaches, but I had been with Tom to much higher altitudes and he had never shown so much as a single problem.

It was bizarre. Altitude sickness normally strikes when a person ascends very quickly, but we had taken thirty-nine days to reach this point. With such a gradual gain, we should all be perfectly acclimatised to the minimal altitude of 12,000 feet. We should barely even feel it.

Altitude, however, is an insidious problem that can strike down even the healthiest in a team. It makes absolutely no difference whether you are the strongest, have trained the hardest, or even if you've been high in the mountains before. Altitude sickness can just hit a person out of nowhere. Scientists are still baffled as to why some are affected and others not, and have still not managed to explain it adequately.

Years earlier, Tom had experienced a similar problem, but he had been at almost double the height of where we were currently camped in Antarctica.

While climbing high on Aconcagua, he had been approaching the summit, at about 22,000 feet, when he had felt his whole head start to swell up. His vision had become hazy and fluid seemed to be collecting in his cheeks. He was climbing solo, very early in the normal climbing season, and so there was no one else around to check the severity of the problem. With what he assumed to be the beginnings of cerebral oedema he promptly turned round and began descending as fast as he could. Similar to a pulmonary oedema, the lack of oxygen and air pressure causes fluid to collect on the brain. If the victim is unable to descend to a lower altitude, within a matter of hours it can be fatal.

On his way down, he passed not a single soul. If he had collapsed or lost his vision entirely, both of which are common with this type of mountain sickness, it would have been curtains. Another twenty-three hours later, without rest or sleep, he was finally clear of the mountain. In a tiny village, thousands of feet below the summit, he stopped, safe at the low altitude of the valley floor.

Ascending quickly and at over 22,000 feet, a lot of climbers would have experienced something similar. However, what confused us was that in Antarctica the situation was the reverse. We had spent weeks climbing gradually and were at half the altitude of any reasonable-sized mountain. Andy and I both eyed Paul sceptically. To us it seemed unlikely that altitude was the cause. Nevertheless, Paul was convinced. He went on to explain how one of the skiers with him the previous year had experienced a very similar problem.

The man was a superb skier from Finland called Timo. While climbing on to the plateau, he had been unable to ski during the day, but felt fine when resting in the tent. For three days he had been utterly debilitated and then suddenly seemed to snap out of it and go back to his normal self. This was all very well if the team were under no particular time constraints, but we had deadlines to meet and time was not something we had in abundance.

Including all our reserves, we had exactly twelve days of provisions left. Andy quickly calculated that we were still 117 miles from the pole and, given the current state of affairs, we were not going to make it. In Theils, we had anticipated covering this distance in just eight days. Over the last few, we had been averaging something just above double figures. This meant that if Tom followed Timo's pattern and was incapacitated for the next forty-eight hours, then there were only two options available to us.

Either we could radio for more food to be dropped to us, or request that Tom be evacuated. We knew that Adventure Networks would charge an arm and a leg to have a plane fly over and drop extra food. This cost would come straight out of our own pockets and, given the disarray of our sponsorship efforts, none of us was under any illusions about what we could afford.

An evacuation, on the other hand, would be covered by our insurance. Although somewhere in the region of £50,000, it would not be a cost we would have to bear directly.

Tom had woken and had been listening to Paul spell out our situation. He raised himself on to his elbows and remained silent. He looked a little better than before, but instead of pain there was now a terrible apprehension in his eyes. He looked as if the world had just collapsed around his shoulders, and I could only imagine what it must have felt like to reach 88 degrees and then be told that if he didn't recover in two days his attempt was over. For days, the thought of finally reaching the pole had been his one shining light. Only by imagining the end and having it so tangibly close was he able to force himself to keep moving south.

Just to have the thought of evacuation aired openly in the tent seemed to cast a terrible quiet over us all. We shuffled uncomfortably and wondered what to say. Nothing seemed important enough to warrant uttering out loud. Finally, Paul broke the tension by suggesting that the rest of us take the group equipment out of Tom's sled. This would make it incredibly light and we would just have to see what happened tomorrow.

Leaning over and slapping Tom on the back, I said, 'Try not to think about it too much, mate. I'm sure you'll feel better in the morning.'

I tried to sound positive and chirpy, but managed to completely fail to reassure either Tom or myself. As he pulled the sleeping bag over his head and curled up to go to sleep, I could see his mind was already whirring and any chance of sleep was a distant promise.

★   ★   ★

By the time we reached the top of the plateau, we had all expected our sleds to be

326

light and the going a little easier. With the extra weight of Tom's sled divided between us, we plodded on at a frighteningly slow pace. Having looked forward to pulling a lighter load, it was frustrating to be back to square one again.

Although he had barely slept from anxiety, Tom had emerged from the tent that morning determined to continue. We had previously agreed that while the rest of us took down the camp he would set off straight away and plod on at his own speed.

It didn't take us long to catch him up and we all tucked in behind. The pace made the cold a constant worry, but the reality was that I would not have been able to go that much faster anyway. My sled sank deep into the powdery snow and the extra weight pulled hard on my lower back. It felt as if my spine was slowly being stretched. Tom was having a few problems keeping up and at each break he would arrive a few minutes after us. Somehow he managed to get through that day and, despite the low mileage, it was an encouraging sign.

With not a breath of wind the next day, we set off without our outer jackets. After about half an hour, the sweat had travelled straight through our fleece layers and Andy and I were covered in chunks of ice. At exactly 88°

23', we stopped for Tom to make a call on the satellite phone. He had previously been in contact with the Prince's Trust (as they were the charity we were raising money for) and they had asked whether we would like to speak to HRH Prince Charles. Standing in the middle of the polar plateau, with an utterly bleak landscape devoid of any form of life, it all seemed pretty surreal.

Tom held the phone to his ear and we all crowded round him. Faintly, I could hear a phone ringing somewhere in England. One of the prince's private secretaries answered and Tom gave his name and explained the reason for the call. Just as he was about to be connected, Paul said loudly, 'Is that Camilla who just answered the phone?'

'Shut up,' Tom hissed, waving his hand in annoyance, and then quickly added, 'Good morning, Your Royal Highness,' as the line went through. Despite being unsure whether he had just opened the conversation by insulting the future King of England, Tom made an admirable recovery. He spoke for about ten minutes but towards the end of the conversation, while Prince Charles was recounting an amusing anecdote, Tom started to panic. He could hear the 'battery low' signal bleeping faintly in the background and knew he was about to cut the prince off mid-conversation. In a move that I like to think was the first of its kind in terms of royal protocol, Tom said, 'Yep, that's great, Your Highness, but our batteries are running low, so I am going to have to say goodbye.' With that, he held the phone out in between us and we all shouted, 'Have a good Christmas.'

As the batteries died and the line went dead, Tom said he could just make out the prince laughing on the other end.

It was an extraordinary coincidence that we should have stopped at that point: 88° 23′ was the exact latitude at which Shackleton had turned around in 1909. At that stage it was the farthest south anyone had ever reached, and it still stands as one of the greatest feats of polar exploration.

Originally, I had been amazed by the fact that Shackleton was only 93 miles from the pole and still decided to turn back. Standing at that exact same latitude, it didn't feel so strange. From where I was standing it would have been another 186 miles round trip to the pole and back, and Shackleton still had to get another 700 miles or so back to the coast.

They had all been marching on foot and the soft snow of the plateau must have been almost impossible. Even with the benefit of skis, we were all finding it tiring work. Back in England, 93 miles had seemed like such a small thing. Out in Antarctica I finally understood that it was anything but. Although the polar landscape may seem infinite, man's capabilities are far from it. Every single mile counts in an environment of this kind, and for Shackleton and his men that 'little thing' would certainly have cost them their lives.

As we moved off, I thought about the injustice of what we were doing. Shackleton had never passed this southerly latitude, nor had he ever stood at the South Pole. With just a few more paces, we would reach farther than him. He was a titan of polar exploration and yet, with each step forward, we were bettering his record. A century had passed, making it infinitely easier for average people like myself, but still it seemed wrong that such a great man had failed, where we looked likely to succeed.

A few hours later I noticed that Tom was keeping up with the pace. In fact, while Andy and I were covered in ice, Tom looked as if he was barely breaking sweat. Obviously he was over the worst of the altitude and starting to feel a great deal better. Andy, Paul and I promptly walked over to where he was and with a loud 'thunk' threw the extra weight back in his sled. Tom moved off a lot more slowly from that break, but even with the heavier sled he could just about keep up.

Although he had made a speedy recovery from the altitude, the other problem was still causing considerable pain. That evening in the tent, on Paul's insistence, Tom spoke to Gareth, the English doctor we had met when first arriving in Antarctica.

'You poor bastard,' was Gareth's initial response, when hearing of the effect snow wedgies could have. Understandably reluctant to have his condition broadcast around the Patriot Hills campsite, Tom asked that it be kept under wraps.

'No problem,' said Gareth earnestly. 'Mum's the word. So, what medical supplies have you got with you, and we'll see if any of them might help.' Tom went through the list, but unsurprisingly none quite suited his condition.

With the clearer weather of the last few days, ANI had scheduled some flights to go to the pole. Along with managing the logistics for expeditions such as ours, they also flew a number of tourists directly to the pole. The plane would be there only for a matter of hours, and so the tourists would pile out, walk round the mirrored ball that marked the most southerly point on earth, and then head directly for the gift shop.

Right next to the pole itself there was

apparently a large American science base, which, rather astutely, had decided to capture the market for South Pole souvenirs. With the nearest competition being nearly 700 miles away on the coast, it had not proved too difficult.

In one of the most remote places on the planet, the American gift shop could offer T-shirts with all sorts of clichés and idioms loudly embossed on the front. There were baseball caps, badges and posters, all with a South Pole seal neatly stamped on top and a price to match. It can only be a matter of time before the golden arches of McDonald's get their filthy paws on the pole. Mind you, after fifty days on the ice, even the thought of their processed meat and a lard-filled milk shake would seem pretty alluring.

For approximately $20,000, tourists would have about four hours standing at the lowest point on earth. Dodging the chirpy 'How y'all doin' and 'Missing you already' from the local scientists, they could stroll around the base as they pleased. To me, it certainly looked like a hard way to get value for money, but for others it was evidently a once-in-a-lifetime opportunity. As Gareth spoke to Tom on the satellite phone, he informed him that a flight was due in the next few days and he would try to stow some medicine on board.

As it would turn out the only way for him to signal the pilots was via the normal radio frequency. This was accessible to pretty much anybody stationed on the Antarctic continent who cared to listen. As delicately as he could, Gareth explained the situation, desperately trying not to go into too much detail about the exact nature of the cargo they would be carrying.

It was Christmas Eve and the wind was strong. The skies were clear, but it was seriously cold and we skied along with our heads held low. Having wished Prince Charles 'Happy Christmas' only the day before, I was now feeling thoroughly unfestive. Although it was definitely going to be a white one, me still suspected Christmas was going to be a rather disappointing affair. I had a few favourite mini-discs labelled 'For emergencies only' and one of them was playing right now, while I desperately tried to distract myself from my own thoughts.

I was dreading the idea of Christmas out in Antarctica. I knew my entire family and girlfriend would be out in South Africa and I was expecting the thought of speaking to them to make me feel quite low. I knew they would all be together, having a wonderful time, and this would only serve to accentuate the small pangs of homesickness I was already starting to feel. There are some emotional issues that I find very easy to block out or overcome, but when it comes to family matters that just isn't the case. I have always been very close to my family and Christmas is one of the few times in the year when we are usually all together. I knew that tomorrow I would miss them terribly.

Suddenly, a plane flew past. It was only about 20 feet off the ground and just a few feet off to our right. Lost in my thoughts and with music playing loudly, I hadn't heard it coming at all. I nearly toppled over I was so surprised.

The plane circled low overhead. In the little windows running along the fuselage, we could see the camera flashes of the tourists clicking away. On the second pass, a door at the rear of the plane opened a few inches and a package was thrown out. With a red marker ribbon attached, the projectile landed in the snow somewhere ahead of where we stood.

'Christmas,' I shouted out loud, wondering what presents had just been air-dropped to us. I started to ski over to where it lay, laughing at the thought that, in Antarctica, Santa was evidently forced to travel by Twin Otter plane. The lads at Patriot Hills had obviously done us proud and put together a little collection of goodies to help us celebrate in the Antarctic wilderness.

As the plane dipped its wings from side to side to say goodbye, we all waved our ski poles in thanks. Eagerly, we started to converge on the package. It lay on the snow, its red ribbon catching the wind. Tom was a little way behind, having taken a photo of the low fly-by, and so it was just Andy and me standing around, waiting for Paul to rip open the plastic covering.

A single cardboard box fell on to the snow. Paul reached inside to check there was nothing else and then bent down to see what it was. Wiping the snow off with his glove, he read out loud: 'Suppositories for the treatment of haemorrhoids.'

We shook our heads incredulously. All that effort and they hadn't even included a tot of whisky, a Christmas cracker or a single pair of clean socks. Those utter bastards. Tom skied up to us and, with an air of disbelief, Paul handed him the precious cargo. I watched Tom swivel it round and, like Paul, try to read the writing through the plastic cover. The only consolation I could think of was that at least one of us would be having a more comfortable Christmas.

★   ★   ★

That night we sat in the tent while Tom glumly read through the instructions. With each new discovery of what the treatment actually involved, his face wrinkled further in abject horror. The bullet-like suppositories lay on the floor and we all tried to be sympathetic and understanding. With grave faces, we were trying to sensibly discuss how Tom could get on with the glamorous business of applying the medication without traumatising the rest of us. Catching an accidental glimpse would have been all too easy in the tiny tent.

Finally, Paul burst into torrents of laughter. In between the chuckles, he was trying to suggest that the three of us could poke our heads out of one end of the tent and zip up the door around us. Like men being punished in the Foreign Legion, with only their heads sticking out of the sand, our three ugly mugs would be the only things protruding from the tent.

Tom's stony look started to crease and soon he was giggling as well. A few seconds later and we were all laughing hysterically. If anyone happened to be walking past at that moment, they would have seen a lonely tent, hundreds of miles from the nearest camp, shaking gently, as four men were crying with laughter. It was wonderful to see Tom get his sense of humour back.

Only a few minutes later, while Tom was cursing his use of snow wedges, Andy let it slip that he had been using them the whole time. What was remarkable was that he was still continuing to do so despite the obvious risks involved. I had tried it once and resolutely decided never to put myself through such distress again. Tom had learnt his lesson and had stopped the moment the problems had started, and likewise Paul didn't want anything to do with the whole sordid affair.

The fact that Andy was still prepared to use this technique, despite the alarming, not to mention painful, consequences, made us all shake our heads with disbelief. Our astonishment was only compounded when a few seconds later someone announced that we actually had an ample supply of toilet paper.

'That's just like spinning a loaded revolver,' Tom said with a wry smile.

I woke up to find Andy's face about three inches from my own. It was 6.05 a.m. and, regular as clockwork, he was clambering over me to go for his morning ablutions. With his hairy chin strap of a beard and frostbitten cheeks, it was alarming to be quite so close to him, but a huge smile cracked across his face and he beamed 'happy Christmas' at me.

The solar panels had been working continuously for the last three days in an effort to get the satellite phone's batteries specially charged for the occasion. I phoned Cape Town and after a couple of rings Robyn answered. She told me that there was about an 80-degree temperature difference between us and that she had just settled down to a Christmas lunch with my family. As I flicked away a pair of socks that were right next to my face on the drying line, I thought they were probably having a slightly better time than I. She spared me the pain of describing the food on the table and we tried to have a 'normal' conversation.

Even with the delay on the line, after a while I could hear she was starting to get upset. I missed her as well, but sitting in a tent with three other guys found it hard to say so. There had been a thousand thoughts going through my mind over the last few weeks. I wanted to share all of them with her, right then on the phone, but it just felt impossible. The difference in what we were each experiencing at that moment seemed to be worlds apart. Although the radio waves from the satellite phone could fly through Antarctica's interior, I felt my emotions were just unable to do so. I rang off feeling completely withdrawn and unhappy.

As we emerged from the tent, it felt like one of the coldest days yet. We had previously decided to do only a half-day, but even that was trying. Tom set a slow pace once again and the cold started to make my whole body shake. Towards the end of his session, I was just too cold to be moving so slowly and broke ranks, to speed on ahead. I had been hoping that we would break the 89th parallel, but by the early afternoon it was obvious we were not going to make it. I helped set up the tents, thinking that birthdays and Christmases were definitely best avoided in Antarctica.

From our reserve rations, Paul made some rice pudding and pulled out a surprise bag of Canadian 'turkey jerky'. The dried meat tasted wonderful, and after a couple of shots of whisky things started to look a little rosier. We decided that we would try to stick to our original four-day schedule of reaching the pole before New Year's Eve. At our current pace, this did mean doing ten-to-eleven-hour days all the way, but that seemed preferable to the expedition dragging on day after day.

During the afternoon, Andy and I tried to shave using a cheap disposable razor without any soap. After an hour of slashing away at my face, a strange rash developed under my chin, which the others took great pleasure in pointing out. We played cards and enjoyed the usual banter, but I felt anxious and uneasy the whole day. I could think only in terms of mileage and hours skied and neither was particularly conducive to getting everyone in the festive spirit. Four more days, I told myself. Just four more to go.

As it would turn out all the mental preparations I had put myself through over Christmas were to be unnecessary. It was wonderfully warm on Boxing Day and we all set off without our outer jackets. Halfway through the first session, I felt the wind start to build and with a huge smile I realised it was from the northeast. On the last section before the break, Tom came skiing up beside me and we both talked excitedly about whether the wind was strong enough to get one more day's kiting in.

At the break, Paul wasn't convinced and didn't want to waste a couple of hours trying. We all protested and reluctantly he decided to give it a go. While setting up, Andy managed to freeze two of his fingers, but decided not to say anything. Paul was looking cold and annoyed and might have told us to can the idea if he found out about it.

Reluctantly, the kites went into the sky. With a great deal of effort working the handles, we started moving. Despite there being a total white-out, the surface of the snow was perfect, and we all just drifted along in the gloom, making steady mileage south. The hours passed, lost in the murky surroundings, and barely a sound could be heard over the gentle swoosh of the kites. It felt like passing effortlessly through a cloud. The landscape was devoid of all definition and the fog gently drifted past in its endless stream.

Just as on the previous days' kiting, the cloud started to lift during the afternoon. The sun came out and the ice crystals dazzled with their luminosity. Although we were not moving particularly quickly, we were still moving at double the speed of man-hauling. I leant back in the harness and watched the other three kites gently move through the air.

Looking round, I got an incredible sense of how lucky I was to be doing such a journey. I thought back to that conversation in the London pub and how far we had come since that first inkling of an idea. Only fifteen or twenty people had ever kited in Antarctica, and it was humbling to think that I was now one of them. Before, fear and concentration had prevented any sort of enjoyment, but now, with the milder conditions, I could appreciate my good fortune whilst actually kiting. As the miles to the pole slowly eroded away, all the concerns and tension about keeping to our deadlines seemed to drift off into the ether.

The doubts I had been harbouring for so long had no more significance for me now. The day's kiting had stripped away their potency, and that night we camped at 89° 19′, only 41 nautical miles from our goal. Surely the pole was now within our grasp?

12

Running Out of South

' . . . it is only from a proper focal distance that we can see what things really are. I am not sure that I was, at that moment, in what are usually called high spirits. What I felt was more of the nature of a deep inner soul-satisfaction.'
— Sir Francis Younghusband

The decision was simple. It just wasn't easy.

The day's kiting meant we only had to average 13 miles a day and we would reach the pole on schedule. The whole of the next day I thought about the target and how easily attainable it was. I hated the idea of dawdling along when the pole was just over the horizon. It seemed like such an anti-climactic way to finish the expedition, to drift along, only half trying.

I decided to rehearse a little speech. I thought it made far more sense to push hard today and then go all out with a twelve-hour dash tomorrow. I had presumed that Tom would be the hardest one to bring round to the idea, as the last degree had definitely taken a lot out of him. Strangely, it didn't turn out that way.

At the last break, Paul announced that we had covered 14.7 miles so far and should reach 16.5 by the end of the next session. This was the most we had ever done and I was definitely feeling tired. However, I still preferred to do a few extra hours now and then make the pole late tomorrow evening.

We sat there, resting quietly and chewing on some food. It was time to see what the others thought and, if necessary, bring them round to the idea of going a little farther. As with all these kinds of occasions I knew the words, they just didn't come out in the correct order.

'If we carry on a bit more tonight, then, by pushing hard tomorrow, the pole would be kind of there, wouldn't it?'

They looked at me quizzically. I regrouped.

'What I mean is, we would be able to reach the pole by tomorrow evening.'

'Why bother?'

It was Andy and he sounded annoyed.

'We've got a perfectly good schedule, which we are going to meet. Why do you want to up it again? Is it this sodding speed record thing?'

'No, it's nothing to do with the record,' I

replied, trying to sound indignant.

My statement was only half true. I was prepared to put in the extra effort mainly because I wanted to reach the pole having given it my all, but also I didn't see any harm in having a crack at being the fastest. I was surprised that it was Andy advocating we stick to the schedule. The entire expedition I had been pleading and, at times, begging him to slow down. I had spent hours concerned that his lightning pace would burn us out and now, the one time we could push ourselves to the utter limit, he was electing to take it easy. I was confused.

'I think we should ski the entire way through the night, with another eight, two-hour sessions, and try to reach the pole by morning.'

There was only one person such a comment could have come from. Tom, Andy and I fell silent, each thinking about what that statement actually involved. Paul was suggesting we ski for a total of thirty-six hours, non-stop, and cover 41 nautical miles in one hit. This would be one of the longest polar marches anyone had ever done in a single push. I turned towards him and looked at his face. His expression was completely obscured by his goggles and nose protector. I leant over and lifted the flap. He was smiling.

'You are joking, right?' I said hopefully.

'Nope,' he answered simply, and the smile on his face didn't budge an inch. 'We've got three options. One, we ski all the way through the night, two, we do a little extra this evening and go for it tomorrow, or three, we stick to the original plan.'

We had all just skied farther than we had ever done in a day and I was really looking forward to crawling inside the tent for a hot meal and some well-earned rest. Suddenly my expectations had just expanded and they were bullish to say the least.

'If we all choose to go through the night,' Paul continued, 'we will all probably be more exhausted than we have ever been before. It's a big commitment and we'll only stop for injury or if an extremely bad weather front comes over. Why don't we think about it over the next session?'

We skied off, just as we had done every other day, but this time with a lot on our minds. I liked the idea of reaching the pole in a single effort, but the simple truth was that I was totally unsure of whether I could do it. Over the last few weeks, my deep tiredness had been kept in check only by the thought that the pole was just around the corner. A thirty-six-hour dash at this stage in the expedition might well be more than I could physically take. I was also scared of disappointing the others. It would be terrible for everyone to pack up the tent and go for it, then only a few hours later for me to cough politely and tell them that I couldn't go on.

The last session ended and we stood in a group to tell each other our individual decisions. Tom went first and said that he would prefer the all-nighter option or, failing that, to go for the pole the next day. To me, he sounded confident and as if he had resolutely made up his mind.

'But I'm not sure about it. Not sure at all, in fact.'

Then Andy shared his thoughts. As always it was an all-or-nothing option. He, like Tom, preferred to do an all-nighter, but if not, he wanted to stick to the original plan of three days to the pole. I went next and gave the same options as Tom, but I also added, 'The truth is that I don't know whether I am able to do it. What happens if I can't go on after five hours or so?'

Paul didn't like the sound of this one bit. For him, when a decision was made there was no turning back. He was obviously keen to quash the idea that someone might just give up after a few hours and started to stress that we would need to be fully committed to the idea. So far we had one definite and two others trying to sound definite, but, quite clearly, unable to get down from the fence.

Just as Paul confirmed what we all already knew and said that he wanted to press on that night, Tom said he was feeling light-headed and sat down on his sled. I wondered whether this might make our decision for us, but a couple of minutes later he stood up and said he was fine to continue.

After a brief spell in the tent, we started to get ready once more. Silently, we went through the actions so familiar to us now — packing the sleds, clipping on the skis. Without ceremony or comment, we moved forward across the snow and began the last stretch to the pole.

★　★　★

For the first time since we had been in Antarctica, the sun moved across the sky and started to revolve in front of us. I lowered my head and squinted as the bright daylight reflected off the snow ahead. Normally, when we were heading south, the sun would be behind us, but now everything felt out of kilter. It was like leaving the house to go to work and discovering that the stars were just starting to come out.

The first few hours passed easily. I still had

the feeling of being rested from our brief spell in the tent. I knew that it wouldn't last and the strength was only skin deep, but for some reason it gave me confidence for the hours ahead. After another six hours of endlessly trudging forward, I could do nothing to shake the light-headed feeling. While my body mechanically repeated the same well-practised motion, I just couldn't focus my mind on a single thing. My thoughts seemed to float a little way above me, swirling around in an unsteady haze. My eyelids kept trying to close. Just a couple of seconds, they would seductively say to my brain. Just a couple of seconds and no more.

At the breaks, we sat in silence. There was no slapping each other on the back or words of mutual encouragement. For some reason there didn't seem to be any need. It was like the antithesis of a team-building exercise. We just sat, thinking of nothing in particular, our characters temporarily subdued. It was not in pain or sadness, but just in the knowledge that there were more hours ahead of us. I didn't think of anyone from home or want any of the others to try to talk to me. I just wanted the hours to pass, but even that seemed like a vague sensation.

Then, suddenly, I would be doing something I had done a thousand times before

— clipping on my skis or resetting my goggles — when the tears would come running down my face. At first I couldn't understand why, but then the emotions would surface with a kind of latent power. It was as if they had been there all along, but I had never noticed. They were incredibly forceful and graphic, welling up inside me in an overwhelming surge.

I choked and spluttered for air, confused by where it had all come from and trying to hide it from the others. I would quickly pull the hood over my face and ski off with my head held low. I thought of my girlfriend and my family. There were friends who had said kind words of encouragement, strangers who had in some way helped me in the past. It was vivid and affirming, while the flood of emotion felt like such a welcome relief from the numbness of countless hours past. The emotions kick-started some sort of endorphin rush in my brain, which in turn seemed to lubricate my limbs and, just for a few minutes, my legs would feel supple and fresh. In such moments, I realised that it had not been thanks to my own muscles that I had skied all this way. It had been entirely to do with the strength of my emotions, and they largely fed off the support and caring of the people I knew back in England.

More hours. Our shadows started to turn full circle. The sled in front moved at its slow, relentless pace and I just focused on keeping my ski tips as close to it as possible. By now we were 13 miles away, and Paul had said that last year, at this distance, he could see the shining dome of the American base. I kept looking up and scanning the horizon. Nothing. It must be there soon.

'There it is!' cried Tom and, pointing with his ski poles, he strode off at a faster pace. I couldn't see anything, but just didn't care. We had seen it at last. Another half an hour and Tom's pace had slowed back to our normal rhythm. He stopped and slowly admitted that what he had thought was the science base on the horizon was in actual fact two lumps of sastrugi in the middle distance. We plodded on.

Another half an hour went past. I looked up again and saw black shapes on the horizon. They were about 45 degrees west of the direction we were heading, but they were unmistakably man-made objects. Possibly it was the glare of the sun or the constantly changing longitude which had confused us, but we just didn't care. With a surge of energy, we all wheeled round and made a beeline for the pole.

Having followed a compass needle for so

long, it was incredible to finally have something tangible to aim for. The bearing we had been following since our start forty-five days ago had turned into a physical reality. It drew us towards it, simply by virtue of that fact that it was the only thing there.

Given the undulating surface, the base soon disappeared from view. The surge of energy I had just experienced went with it and the weariness crept back in. Andy and Paul were still hyped up from the sighting and tore off into the distance. The gap between us increased and I felt myself sink into utter and complete exhaustion. It was like one of those dreams where you are trying to run but your legs don't seem to work. Tom was just ahead of me and was obviously in the same sort of state. His pace was almost as slow as mine and we both summoned everything we had, right down to our toes, to continue.

Having been out in the cold air for so long, we all hacked and coughed almost constantly. The cold seemed to strip our throats of moisture and we rasped with a dry wheezing sound. It was fine, so long as we didn't breathe too deeply, but with all the effort of trying to catch up with Paul and Andy the problem only got worse. All I wanted to do was fill my lungs with air, but each time my stomach would clench up painfully and my throat burn in dry pain. Occasionally the coughing fits would stop me dead in my tracks.

I pulled up to where the others had been waiting for the last ten minutes. I had the tent in my sled and so they had no choice but to await my arrival. A few hours previously, we had agreed to put it up for an hour, to have a quick rest and something to eat. I just sat on the cold snow, watching the others in a sort of mute, catatonic state. Andy walked over to where I sat and, without a word, unzipped the cover to my sled and got the tent out.

Once it was up, I crawled inside to join the others. It felt wonderful to be out of the glaring sun and I slumped against my foam mattress. Paul had prepared hot chocolate and I sipped it slowly, wincing slightly as the hot liquid stung my chapped lips. I had started to drift off into a deep, comfortable sleep when suddenly I woke with a start. Paul had reached over and slapped me on the leg.

'Don't fall asleep, Patrick. We've got to leave in half an hour and you've got to eat.'

I toyed with the unappetising muesli in its bowl. Looking across the tent, I could see Tom with his eyes gently closing. His head lolled forward in the same sleepy motion of people travelling on late-night buses and his hot chocolate rested limply in his hands.

Andy, meanwhile, had just polished off his third bowl of cereal. He looked hairy and dishevelled, but wide awake. The plastic spoon went from bowl to mouth in a hurried blur, as finally there were no restrictions on how much we could eat. Even in my semi-comatose state, I thought how he never ceased to amaze me.

After the quickest hour I have ever spent in my life, Paul looked at his watch and roused us all out of the tent. None of us had said a word; we had just sat and concentrated on staying awake. For some inexplicable reason I felt a lot better standing outside once more. Some strength had come back to my legs and I felt ready to go again.

I had presumed that the dip we were in would pass in a half-hour or so. Instead the American base stayed hidden from view for another two hours. I started to get worried. Had we made the same mistake as before? Were we heading in the wrong direction? It felt as if we must have missed it altogether and that we were going to have to retrace our steps. If that had been the case, I would have refused to take a single step farther.

Slowly, the tops of the tallest buildings emerged. They poked out over the crest of the hill and we had something to aim for once again. In an hour the whole base was in view, and even from this distance it looked enormous. There was one main yellow building on stilts, which looked like a giant Portaloo, and an endless scrapyard of piled containers and outlying buildings. As we approached, a massive Hercules plane banked round, leaving a thin vapour trail across the sky, and headed for the heart of the station.

I had been told about the American base before. The vast site was purportedly covered in a maze of machinery, buildings and containers. The thought of having such a monstrous structure literally right on top of the Geographic South Pole seemed like an utterly insensitive and typically American thing to do. Why couldn't they have built their base a mile away from the actual pole? It wouldn't have made the slightest difference to any of their costs or logistics, and it was hardly as if they were stuck for space.

The great mountaineer Reinhold Messner, when he traversed the Antarctic continent with Arven Fuchs, said, 'You ski a thousand kilometres through complete stillness and vastness and suddenly you see domes, containers and masts. Amundsen's ripped tent should stand at the South Pole, nothing else.'

Antarctica is so immensely huge and so

much of it is just acres of meaningless ice. It seemed incredible that the Americans had imprinted themselves so incongruously on the one place that means so much to people. Why should the Stars and Stripes fly over the South Pole, when it was the Norwegians and then the British who had first reached it? This is the one continent on the entire planet not owned by a single nation and yet, at its centre, a single nation had been allowed to plant its own footprint firmly in the snow.

After all I had heard, I had been dreading actually coming face to face with the base. Standing there, resting on my ski poles, however, it felt strangely comforting. Although it was not at all what I had previously thought, it was wonderful to have signs of the outside world. As ugly and ill fitting as the base looked, it was still good to have something tangible to reach for. At the North Pole, there is nothing to differentiate the actual point from the miles of surrounding ice. The only way to be certain that you are on top of the world is by verifying it with a GPS. It was a pretty abstract and man-made goal we were aiming for, and having an important-looking base at the site somehow seemed to give credence to our efforts.

For the next two hours, the base remained

exactly where it was. The weather closed in and we shuffled along in dark cloud. Each time I looked up, I expected the buildings to loom above me, but instead they sat obstinately on the horizon. It took us four hours more to come up to the electricity wires that surrounded the base, and there we stopped for a break. Andy was hunched over and complained that he felt sick from all the cereal he had eaten. I just felt numb. If someone had said we had to camp right there, only a kilometre away from the pole, I probably wouldn't have kicked up too much of a fuss.

As we set off across the compound, I began to feel annoyed with myself. I was frustrated that I didn't feel more excited, that I wasn't savouring every step to the lowest point on earth. To just drift up, without being fully conscious of what was actually happening, seemed like a terrible waste of all our effort. Like a drunk trying to pull himself together for an important occasion, I shook my head from side to side, forcing the sleep away and focusing my mind.

Just then, I heard Paul curse behind me. He had broken another binding. I reached back into my sled and pulled out one of my kiting skis for him to use. Tom was at the front and slowed down a little. The three of us came up level beside him and side by side we crossed the last few hundred metres.

A few scientists were milling around by the edge of the runway, and just past them I could clearly see a small mirrored ball. It was the famous ceremonial South Pole, and in a semicircle around it stood the flags of the Antarctic Treaty nations. Their colours billowed in the wind and, four abreast, we approached. The scientists moved back respectfully as we came past in silence, and then we all stopped. For so long this moment had been rehearsed in all our minds; for so long we had been sharing the same vision of reaching the pole.

We all held on to one ski pole and then Paul said, 'At 3.34 p.m. on 28 December 2002 the Commonwealth Antarctic Expedition has arrived at the Geographical South Pole.'

With that we drove the ski poles into the ground and it was finished. We hugged each other and smiled. I unclipped the line to my sled and sat down on the edge. I didn't feel the quick burst of excitement I had felt so many times before, but instead a slow undercurrent of content, which felt stable and well grounded. It was a happiness that had deep roots, and from it emanated an incredible sense of calm.

It wasn't the life-affirming or semi-religious experience I had read about in other accounts. I didn't feel in any way changed or better. I just felt happy that it was over, that I had such incredible friends to share the moment with, and that we had finally succeeded. What we had done was such an infinitely small thing in the goings-on of the world, but it was something nonetheless. We had made some sort of a contribution, however small and insignificant, and, through this journey, expanded our own horizons. Finally I had seen the Antarctic ice cap first hand, felt the frost on my own skin and been able to experience the very thing that had inspired the early explorers. I was now in a position to judge for myself and make up my own mind.

I can easily understand that to the other six billion people on the planet what we did may have seemed like nothing more than a self-indulgent and pointless waste of money. But standing at the pole, at a place with no more east, west or south, I felt certain that in this one thing I was right. The journey had been worth it. Why? I really had no idea, and frustrating as it may be can still not answer the question adequately. But I do know that it was worth it, every breath and mile.

By then, many more Americans had come

out of the base. They were seventeen hours ahead of us and so it was early in the morning for them. They were there to replant the marker for the location of the actual South Pole. Where we were standing was the ceremonial South Pole, and the exact position of 90 degrees South was about twenty feet away. Owing to the movement of the ice cap, the point changes a little each year.

The scientists scribbled away in notebooks and then unrolled a large, old-fashioned-looking tape measure. A few minutes later a little copper marker, far less grand than the mirrored ball, was firmly planted in the ground. To the nearest millimetre, this was the lowest point on earth.

Just by taking a couple of paces, a person could walk round the world. They would cross every time zone on the planet, traverse every line of longitude. This was the end point, the place where everything converged. How we measure the planet all comes together at this point, and the normal laws of separation seemed to lose their meaning. It was a place where every other single point on the planet, be it Mount Everest or the Mariana Trench, New York or Beijing, was simply North. If any of us had been Muslim, we'd have had one hell of a job trying to pray in the right direction.

Suddenly kindly faces, wrapped in fleece hats and thick neck warmers, came up and introduced themselves. We were the first visitors they had seen all season and the scientists shook our hands warmly. Although their official policy was not to 'fraternise' with expeditions, you can't stop people being curious, and the Americans could not have been more welcoming.

Preoccupied by the notion of actually being at the pole and with the tiredness resurfacing once again, we shook their hands in confused silence. While they slapped us on the back and said 'Good job!' we could only stare back blankly, happy to see them but unable to articulate a single word. After a few more minutes, people started to get cold and they all began to thin out and go inside.

I walked up to the mirrored ball of the ceremonial South Pole and peered into the metal. I saw my own figure reflected and, like something in a hall of mirrors, the image was bent and distorted. This strange, haggard face stared fiercely back at me. Frost covered the cheeks and the fur around the hood was solid from chunks of ice. It was the first time I had really seen myself in all the time I had been away. Instead of a pale, fresh-faced Londoner, what I saw was a face with dark cheeks and lines about the eyes. Hours of squinting in the continuous sun had made me look weather-beaten and old, but it was the eyes which had really changed. They had a deep, hollow quality to them which conveyed an unnatural sort of tiredness. It was a level of exhaustion I had never seen in myself before. I guessed it was probably time to get some sleep.

We camped about 10 feet away from the actual pole and found that on a previous flight ANI had shipped a small box of provisions to us. We ate some food and then phoned the Patriot Hills radio operator to check in for our nightly Sched call.

'Jason, we have a problem. We don't have a southerly position to give you,' said Paul on the satellite phone.

'What's that? Please say again.'

'We've run out of south!' said Paul, and we all cheered in the background.

'You're not supposed to be at the pole for another two days,' came back a confused voice. Then, after Paul had explained the last concerted push, 'Well done, lads, nice one.'

★   ★   ★

That night, for the first time in many months, I relaxed completely. It seemed incredible that we were finally there. Tom had become the youngest Briton ever to ski to the pole,

Andy the first African and Paul the first person ever to ski to three geographical poles in a single year. Having made it in forty-five days and six hours, we also became the fastest team ever to complete the journey.

The last record of the fastest time was more than a little spurious. A Norwegian called Borge Ousland, who is widely regarded as the best polar traveller on the planet, managed to reach the pole in just thirty-five days. As if that weren't good enough, he was also travelling solo and unsupported, aiming to complete a full traverse of Antarctica. For him, the South Pole was just the halfway point, and he ended up reaching his goal in McMurdo Sound after only another twenty-two days.

A few years previously, Ranulph Fiennes had tried to complete the same journey. After ninety-seven days of utter hardship he had called in the rescue plane. Fiennes was no pussycat, and for Ousland to have completed the distance so fast he must have been unbelievably strong mentally or, at the very least, some sort of physiological freak.

We could therefore legitimately call ourselves the fastest team, but we were clearly nowhere near the same level as someone like Borge Ousland. We had arrived a full ten days after him, at which point he had probably been pacing himself for the second leg of the journey. However, he has devoted his life to becoming the best in the world; we, on the other hand, were just a few friends, trying to fulfil a long-standing ambition.

Having said that, I was glad we had reached the pole so fast and felt a few pangs of pride that we had attained some sort of record. However, even then, I knew it was not something I would think a great deal about. I only have to remind myself of what other people have achieved and the whole thing falls into perspective rather quickly.

Nevertheless, Paul's record of becoming the first to reach three geographical poles in a single year was truly remarkable. With all the different poles in Antarctica, it is difficult for anyone not looking directly at a map to appreciate quite how exceptional this is. There are in fact four different poles: the Magnetic, the Geo-magnetic, the Geographic and the Pole of Relative Inaccessibility. It all sounds a little complicated, but in essence only the Geographic is at the very bottom of the world, and it is this one that most people refer to when discussing 'the pole'.

Paul's previous expedition to the South Pole had arrived in mid-January 2002. Straight after that, he had spent the summer months skiing to the North Pole and then flown directly to Antarctica with us. We had arrived before the New Year, making Paul the first man to reach three poles in a single year. Taking into consideration that this entailed three long expeditions, skied back to back and all in the severe polar climes, it was no mean feat. The man was quite simply a machine.

For so many, breaking a world record is the most important thing. As they cross the last few hundred yards to the pole's mirrored ball, the prospect of making the history books seems to be uppermost in their thoughts. As I looked round the tent, it was obvious such things meant very little to my teammates. They looked tired but delighted, and simple things, such as food and sleep, preoccupied their thoughts.

They were under no illusions about what they had achieved. On a personal level it was momentous. In the great scheme of things it was really useful only as a dinner party brag. We all knew that the various records might prove useful when trying to drum up some media attention and keep the sponsors happy, but that was really as far as it went. We were doing this because we wanted to experience Antarctica, and breaking some record was a very minor adjunct. It had just been a bit of harmless vanity which had inspired us to push so hard at the end and attempt to be the fastest.

Our tents were pitched almost directly on the actual pole. We spent a full twelve hours sleeping, with the entire weight of the world on top of us. Amazingly, we didn't even have a headache in the morning, nor had we fallen off the bottom of the planet. Instead, we had slept long and well. There was no more tension and no more doubt. We had reached our abstract point in the middle of millions of tons of ice. We were at the South Pole.

★   ★   ★

That night I was reminded of a Thomas Pynchon quote that the travel writer Sara Wheeler had referred to when she had flown to the pole a few years previously. 'But I had to reach it. I had begun to think that there, at one of only two motionless places on this gyrating world, I might have peace. I wanted to stand at the dead centre of the carousel, if only for a moment; try to catch my bearings.' Also there was Amundsen's reaction when he reached the pole in 1911. He wrote,

'I cannot say — though I know it would sound much more effective — that the object of my life was attained — that would be romancing it rather too bare-facedly . . . The

366

regions around the North Pole — well, yes, the North Pole itself — had attracted me from childhood, and here I was standing at the South Pole. Can anything more topsy-turvy be imagined?'

Topsy-turvy or not, I could imagine how he must have felt. I knew that neither here nor at 90 degrees North would the object of my own life be attained. I had not devoted my life to this expedition, nor sacrificed everything to be where I was just then. Even in that moment of accomplishment, I knew I was just looking into that window for the briefest of moments and catching a glimpse.

The next morning we got a message that the Americans would give us a little speech about the base and what the scientists were up to in Antarctica. Paul had heard it before, but last year had been given a cup of coffee. We had packed none for the expedition and it was something that I had sorely missed. With the prospect of a cappuccino and a warm room, I was happy to listen to them talk about anything they liked.

We walked over to the large Space Age dome, which had been the centrepiece of the American base since it was built in the 1970s. Over the decades it had gently sunk, and there was a huge ramp, cut into the snow, which led to the entrance. Inside, giant timber beams supported the tunnel like a mine shaft, which led to a central area. Once our eyes became accustomed to the dim light, we could see that the dome was in fact just a shell, designed to protect the little huddle of buildings within.

A hundred feet above our heads, shards of light pierced the dome at the centre. They illuminated the underside of the canopy, where great stalactites of ice clung to the metal. We were led up some stairs to a door, which looked as if it had been taken from a butcher's deep freeze. Ironically, the door was designed to keep the heat in, rather than the cold.

The first thing that struck me about the room was the dull sodium lighting. After weeks in the brilliant Antarctic sunshine, the room looked dingy and morose. It took a good couple of minutes for my eyes to adjust sufficiently, and even then I had to squint in the gloom. As soon as the freezer door shut, the heat also got to us. In just a couple of paces the temperature went from an ambient -30 degrees to room temperature and the change made me feel a little woozy.

We took our seats and an American with a bushy moustache and a deep Texan drawl started talking about how environmentally friendly they were. I listened for a couple of minutes, waiting patiently to be offered tea or coffee, but none seemed forthcoming. Another ten minutes into the speech and my expectant smile had faded completely. Having been looking forward to coffee for the last few weeks, I now realised there must have been some terrible misunderstanding. Either that or I had been horribly duped.

While yesterday's half-drunk cups lay tantalisingly close on the table in front of us, there was not so much as a digestive biscuit being handed around, let alone a frothy cappuccino. It was outrageous. I had walked over a thousand kilometres and they couldn't be bothered to put the kettle on. In true British style I sat there stoically and out of principle refused to listen to a single word the man said.

Soon, the lecturer stopped talking and an ungainly middle-aged man took his place. As the 'Vladimir' on the name tag suggested, he was a Russian, who had been working with the Americans at the pole for a number of years. From the outset, it was obvious that he was frighteningly intelligent. He sat rather awkwardly and seemed to take great pains in describing what it was he actually did for a living.

With our wits somewhat dulled by the long hours of solitude and skiing, I wasn't sure whether it was just me or whether any of us could understand a word he said. With alarming regularity he would start a sentence with 'Obviously' or 'As you are well aware' and then go on to explain some theory which lost me after the first couple of seconds. In a doomed bid to impress, Tom threw in a couple of facts he had gleaned at university about subglacial features and tectonic movements. Vlad didn't so much as bat an eyelid. In answer, a barrage of information and technical data came streaming back, which again, went completely over my head.

As I started to switch off and get worked up again about the coffee situation, I began to notice a horrendous smell. I gave a few experimental sniffs, but couldn't work out where it was coming from. Gradually the stench was getting stronger, and if it carried on it would soon be totally overpowering. It then dawned on me that it was my own clothes that smelt so bad.

The heat had warmed up the fabric and the days of exercise were now coming back with a vengeance. An acrid haze of warmed sweat floated gently out from under my clothes. If they hadn't been my own, I would definitely have gagged. Concerned that a couple of the other Americans in the room might catch a whiff, I zipped up my jacket and remained perfectly still. I was soon sweltering in the heat of the room, but it seemed preferable to risking the certain offence I would cause. I started to go red in the face and become uncomfortably hot. Then, over the intercom system, I heard that a Single Otter plane was coming in to land. It could only be for us.

I jumped up and told the others that I would go out and meet the pilots. Grabbing my hat and mittens, I bundled out of the room, trying not to pass too close to anyone else. It felt wonderful to be outside again and I briskly walked up to the runway to greet the plane.

It touched down and two men in matching polar suits came clambering out. They began unloading long twisted pipes and assembling them by the plane. Curious as to what they were doing, I went over to introduce myself. The two men were about fifty years old, with well-lined but benevolent faces. They introduced themselves as Brian and Jamie and explained that they were assembling a kiting buggy, which had been custom made by a Formula One designer to work in Antarctica.

They seemed friendly and said they were hoping to get back to Patriot Hills in around ten days. It seemed an extremely ambitious target, given that neither of them had any polar experience. However, I had never seen these things moving and so decided to take them at their word. In return, I warned them about the horrendous sastrugi they would face passing 85 degrees and, to prevent it being one of the shortest expeditions ever, also mentioned that they should watch out for the power lines that ran just outside the South Pole base.

While our plane sat on the runway, fuelling up in preparation to leave, the others came out of the lecture. They were also curious as to how the buggies operated and Brian and Jamie went over how it all worked. To me it didn't look as if they would have a hope in hell of getting over the sastrugi, nor had they thought about some really basic elements of the design. For instance, the safety handle, which in an emergency would release the kite from the frame, was tiny. Bouncing along at 20 mph, wearing big down mittens, there was no way that they would be able to grab hold of it and activate the mechanism.

However, our expedition was finishing, while theirs had just begun. We wished them luck and loaded our sleds on the plane. As it would turn out, Brian and Jamie were not long in following us back to Patriot Hills. Despite carrying twenty-five days of provisions, they waited for the right winds at the

South Pole for just two days. Their buggies weighed about the same as our sleds, yet they refused to drag them or wait for the weather to change. It must have taken them months to complete the buggy's design and yet, only two days later, they radioed in for a rescue plane. Money for expeditions is hard enough to come by as it is, without people annoying the sponsors and squandering their chances so quickly.

* * *

From the plane, the Antarctic interior looked spectacular. Continuing in a perfect, unbroken layer, the shimmering white blanket of snow stretched north in all directions. Making use of the low katabatic winds, the pilots flew at about 50 feet, scorching across the surface of the ice. Landmarks that had been with us for days now flashed past in just a couple of minutes. Once again our vision had been realigned, and instead of concentrating on just the small patch of snow in front of our ski tips, we could now see the vastness in its entirety. We sat, craning our necks to the windows, and watched the ice glide past.

It was incredible to think that we had crossed every inch of it on foot. Within six hours we would be back to where we had started and then, from Patriot Hills, we would begin the long journey home. I thought back to the early explorers and how, for them, it had not been so easy. While we had just climbed up the steps to a plane, they faced the prospect of the entire return journey. For them, the South Pole was the summit of their mountain and the hard part was trying to make it back to safety.

The American base had been our first sign that there was civilisation close at hand. It signified the first step back into the normal world, and with each hour passing on the plane we would be immersing ourselves further in that normality. For Amundsen there had been no such reassurance. His small team of Norwegians were the first to reach the South Pole and, at that moment, they could not have been farther away from civilisation.

Captain Scott was another man who knew this only too well. After a lifetime of effort, he had finally arrived at 90 degrees South, only to find one of Amundsen's tents already standing there. Scott had no plane to come and collect him, no way of escaping from the reality of his circumstances. He had to suffer the anguish of coming second in a game that meant everything to him. His diary accounts convey a sense of utter dejection and despair which is simply heart wrenching. He knew he had over-extended himself, and the prospect of returning looked bleak to say the least. 'There is very little that is different from the awful monotony of the past days. Great God! This is an awful place and terrible enough for us to have laboured here without the reward of priority . . . now for the run home and a desperate struggle. I wonder if we can make it.'

How easy it was for me to sit in the plane and rely on technology to get me back home. In comparison to the early explorers, I had faced dangers that were barely perceptible. Theirs had been a much greater struggle, a struggle that had ultimately claimed the lives of Scott and all his men. Looking out the window of the plane and watching the endless miles of ice drift past, I thought how lonely it must have been for them to die out here. His dark, stained, canvas tent must have looked impossibly small in such open fields of ice. There would have been nothing familiar or comforting in his surroundings, only an empty white landscape to stare at day after day. I am not sure whether death is any easier in normal, everyday surroundings, but at least it wouldn't entail the doubt of wondering whether the journey was worth it. Or, as the old explorers used to say, whether the game was worth the candle.

Even now, the only way to set out on an expedition is to ignore the base-line risk that you will be exposed to. Obviously, any perceptible danger is limited as far as possible, but there are always risks that cannot be avoided. My own solution is normally just to put my head in the sand and trust firmly in the old adage of heavy smokers — it won't happen to me. But lying in a tent, all hope of rescue and resupply gone, the reality would be there, staring you straight between the eyes. It must be horrendous to realise that these are the last few days of your life, slipping away quietly in a swirling blizzard. To see the end coming so clearly, I think that is what I would be scared of. I don't ever want to be prepared for when that day comes. Just hit me from behind and let my last thought be a happy one.

In 1912, after the loss of one of his teammates in a crevasse, the Australian geologist Sir Douglas Mawson read the following text:

Life — give me life until the end,
That at the very top of being,
The battle spirit shouting in my blood,
Out of the very reddest hell of the fight

I may be snatched and flung
Into the everlasting lull . . .

Mawson went through utter hell on this expedition. He discovered vast new sections of Antarctica, but in the process lost both his teammates. With acute vitamin A poisoning caused by eating his dogs' livers, he survived the remaining 160 kilometres to camp only by sheer force of will. He was a tough, obstinate leader who would undoubtedly have marched until the last. Characters like that are just so appealing. Not only to schoolboys searching for heroes, but to anyone who pushes themselves farther than they previously felt possible.

On the plane, our situation could not have been more different to that of the likes of Amundsen, Scott and Mawson. We all relaxed and enjoyed the luxuries of heating and padded seats. Before long, the pilots signalled that we were coming up to Matty's team, and we piled over to the right side of the plane to catch a glimpse. In a split second they were gone, a blur of people and waving ski poles. Sitting there lazily, eating a tuna sandwich that had been sent along with the plane, I didn't envy them one bit.

The pilots informed us that the Russian cargo plane had come in already and the next one was due on 4 January. Barring weather delays, this looked like our next chance of getting back to Chile. For days, while skiing on the final stretch to the pole, I had dreamt about getting this early flight and then somehow changing my ticket to go directly to South Africa. I knew my girlfriend and family would still be there on holiday, getting fired up to celebrate the new year.

For hours, I had imagined the looks on their faces as I arrived nearly a month early. Considering that most expeditions are held up by weather delays for weeks on end, it was an ambitious target to say the least. However, it had been something that kept my mind occupied and my legs moving fast. When we actually arrived at the pole those precious few days early, although I dared not mention it out loud, I had thought I might make it in time. Sitting on the plane and listening to the pilots, the casual information sank my hopes once and for all. They had been totally unrealistic, but I still felt sad to have the dream finally come to an end.

The plane touched down and the rear door slid open. One of the ANI camp staff stood in the opening, a wide grin spread across her face.

'Jesus, it stinks in here,' she said with a laugh. We clambered down the steps and the first thought to strike me was that Patriot Hills felt incredibly warm. When we had first arrived, I had been slow and clumsy from the cold; now, in comparison to the pole, it felt positively balmy. It seemed incredible that the human body could adapt so fast.

We were led to a large tent and gradually we became spoilt on the luxuries of life. The tent had mattresses to sleep on, there was fresh food being prepared for us and it was only a couple of paces to the wash tent. With a bar of soap in hand, I padded over in my camp boots and stripped off my many layers of clothing. The wash tent consisted of a thermos of hot water, a flannel and a little bucket to stand in. Sighing at the prospect of being able to clean myself at leisure and without the rushed panic of an average snow bath, I pushed the plunger on the thermos down expectantly. To my dismay, it had just run out of water. I picked it up and walked outside to exchange it for a full one.

On the way, I passed a few people who had just arrived from Chile on the last flight in. They were wrapped up in their down jackets, shivering in the cold. I said 'Good morning' cheerfully, but they just stared at me in a slightly horrified way. I returned with the thermos, wondering why they had been so unfriendly. I knew I was looking a bit rough round the edges, but there was no need to be rude. As I shut the door to the wash tent, I caught my reflection in a small mirror hanging on the wall. Aside from looking skinny, with a grimy, patchy beard, I also realised that I had crossed over to the other tents without a stitch on. Having been used to an all-male, close-knit team for the last forty-six days, I had forgotten a few standard Western practices. I had to admit that sauntering across the ice butt naked and issuing greetings might seem a little bemusing for newcomers to a polar environment.

Far from the depressing and rather pathetic attempt at a party I had been expecting, New Year's Eve was actually fantastic. A load of pilots and scientists from a nearby base flew in for the occasion and the Scottish contingent at Patriot Hills got things going with some Highland dancing. There were also some Chilean climbers who had just returned from an expedition near the Ellsworth Mountains and, after sixty days of hard grind, they were up for any sort of party.

Given that I had not drunk more than a couple of sips of alcohol in all my time on the ice, the beer and wine soon took their effect. Attempting to perform the traditional dance of 'Strip the Willow' on an icy floor, wearing ski boots and with six beers inside me, proved to be way too much. Fortunately I was not alone, and while the music pumped out from a tiny radio, our set moves for the dance descended into something that looked more like a Turkish wrestling match.

With people from all over the planet and no particular time zone to work to, shouts would go up at various points in the evening proclaiming that it was now midnight in someone else's country. In the end I celebrated the moment about ten different times and eventually went to bed some time around Australia's New Year.

* * *

Four days later, on the morning the Russian jet was due to land, Matty's team flew into camp. Having last run into them at Theils over a month ago, I was excited to see them all again. The Spaniards looked entirely unaffected by the whole expedition — the only discernible difference was that their English had improved a little. With big arm movements and even bigger grins, they signalled that they had enjoyed the last couple of months. From what I gathered, they had found it difficult to adjust from the varied and dangerous pace of Himalayan climbing to the protracted toil of a polar expedition. Then again, given all the language barriers, I couldn't be sure of what they were saying. They might just as easily have been signalling that my flies were undone.

Matty looked shattered from the ordeal and seemed happy that she would soon be returning to Canada. The stress of coping with an otherwise all-male team and her decision to always lead from the front had noticeably drained her. Her face looked pale and gaunt and she seemed to have lost some weight. Surprisingly, Graham had also lost a great deal of weight and looked especially tired. On top of the general fatigue, he had also had to cope with a stomach bug for the last week and had lost nearly 3.5 stone. Without his usual dry smile, he said that the whole thing had been far tougher than he had expected.

Unfortunately, I barely spoke to Andrew Cooney. Satellite phone in hand, he was talking incessantly to press agents, making doubly sure they had his record-breaking title exactly right. I walked over, waving hello, and he motioned for me to wait a second. A couple of minutes later he covered the mouthpiece with his hand and with upturned eyes said, 'God, there are so many interviews I've got to do back in England. I'm going to have to get myself an agent.'

Evidently the charm we had seen at Theils had been just a momentary lapse. I walked off and left him to it.

★ ★ ★

With great fanfare, the Russian jet came steaming into land. The wheels bounced on the ice and the plane careered down the runway as it had done many times before. We took off, and after a few hours of muggy sleep we heard one of the flight crew saying that we had begun our descent into Punta Arenas and we should all buckle up. A little later the huge tail of the plane opened once more. With a screech of hydraulics, the massive cargo ramp descended to the runway. This time no cold air rushed in and no dazzling Antarctic sun shone through. We walked to the back of the plane and down on to the tarmac.

Colours were simply everywhere. After the endless white and blue of Antarctica, even the drab Chilean airport sparkled in the evening light. The green grass, the advertising billboards, even the clapped-out taxis seemed alive in a myriad of colours. In comparison to the inert Antarctic landscape, everything seemed to have such life and energy. We ambled over to the immigration line to be officially stamped back into the world and just enjoyed the sight of people going about their business. The bustle of everyday life was simply fascinating. I stood there, smiling vacuously at the sight of it all. Only a couple of months ago I would not even have blinked at the things that now caught my eye.

With unrestrained joy, the landlady at the bed and breakfast welcomed us at the door. It was late in the evening and we had obviously just woken her up. Such concerns were of little importance as she obsequiously bustled us through the reception area and into our old rooms. She beamed at us once more and proudly straightened the sheets at the foot of one of the beds. Evidently, we had finally tired of her competitors south of the docks and were now back at the best B&B this side of the Panama Canal.

13

Shedding Our Skin

'The quickest way to a man's heart is through his breast plate.'

Like some sort of bulbous, rosy-cheeked chef, darting from pot to pot in the kitchen, we attacked the Chilean breakfast buffet with gusto. Since we arrived in Punta Arenas, our appetites had just been insatiable. At every meal we had double portions, our bodies craving any sort of sustenance, even, it would seem, the dreaded conger eel. After a shower and wearing clean-smelling clothes, I became concerned that nobody would believe I had been to Antarctica. I was starting to look exactly as I had done before I left. With a few swift strokes of the razor the beard had also gone, and with it any hopes of arriving at Heathrow looking tough and 'explorer-like'.

Both Tom and Andy had enviable frost-burnt cheeks. They would later prove to be well worth all the pain and bother, as Tom used them to great effect when attempting to break the ice with pretty girls. Andy's mother took one look at them and decided to bake a few hundred cakes in sympathy. All in all, they were the perfect accessories for an aspiring adventurer.

In between meals, we decided to have tea at a hotel in the centre of town. Shackleton had apparently stayed there at the turn of the century, and in such a one-horse town as Punta Arenas we thought they might have a few old photographs of him or at the very least some general polar memorabilia. As we walked through the reception area there appeared to be nothing of the sort, but the hotel looked nice enough, so we sat down for some sandwiches.

Paul and Matty came to join us and soon we were all sitting around a big wooden table, feeling a little fidgety in the plush surroundings. After about half an hour, a message came through that ANI had successfully moved Andy's flight forward and he should pack up all his belongings as soon as possible. With a quick shake of the hand and a few smiles, Andy was gone. Looking at his watch, Paul realised that they should probably get moving as well, and he and Matty got up to leave.

In just a few minutes they had all departed and Tom and I sat quietly, feeling a little isolated at the large table. For so long our team had all been living right beside each other, existing in a mutual, almost symbiotic way. I knew this would no longer be required once we got back to the UK. Perverse as it may seem given all the infinite space in Antarctica, we had skied only inches apart, slept uncomfortably close at night and spent all our free time relaxing in the confines of the tent.

In Antarctica we had passed water bottles because subconsciously we knew that the person next to us was thirsty. We had hung jackets to dry with the hoods folded in, simply because we knew one of us liked them to be hung that way. Each of us had been in tune with the way the others felt and, at the time, it had seemed vitally important.

Suddenly, all this was over. The cohesive unit, which had been strong enough to get us a thousand kilometres across the ice, had broken up with just a few casual goodbyes. It seemed sad that something that had been so unshakeable a few days ago should have collapsed so effortlessly. The distance and time would dull the memory sooner than we would hope, but for each of us there would be a residual mark, an imprint that would only fade so far, as what we had been through together had been important enough to shape a small part of our characters.

We finished our cups of tea and started to move outside. As we passed the reception area, Tom walked up to a man in a shiny black suit standing behind the desk. In his broken Spanish, he asked him whether they had any pictures of the famous explorer Ernest Shackleton.

'No, señor, I am very sorry, but we no have a Shackleton staying in our rooms. Will he be arriving later today?'

'It's unlikely,' said Tom, 'but thanks for looking.'

In an effort to get some fresh air and dispel our gloomy mood, we decided to take a walk along the beach by the side of the dock area. It was a drab, pale afternoon, which seemed to reflect our general frame of mind perfectly. Shopping trolleys and old car tyres littered the sand and the whole area looked like a depressing version of Blackpool pier. Neither Tom nor I had a job to go back to and, as eager as we were to see our families, we knew that as soon as we got on the plane reality would hit us hard. Mobile phone bills, long-overdue council tax and job interviews were just around the corner. The bubble was about to burst, and this rubbish beach in the arse-end of Chile looked like the perfect place for it to happen.

As we sullenly ambled back to our B&B to

pack up for the plane the following morning, a massive pick-up truck screeched to a halt in front of us. Fearing an imminent mugging by Chilean banditos, we both tensed up ready to scarper. With a huge grin and a shout of 'Eh, gringos!' Rodrigo, the leader of the Chilean expedition we had met in Antarctica, jumped from the truck and walked towards us. Impossibly large numbers of people were with him in the truck and soon the pavement seemed full of rejoicing Chileans. The little crowd milled around, all showing their devotion to the heroic Chilean explorers and celebrating the success of their expedition.

Rodrigo and his team, having spent sixty days mapping a new area of Antarctica, were quickly elevated to the status of national heroes by the local press. Everybody in Punta Arenas wanted to get in on the action and soon we all piled into a local bar to congratulate them and listen to their stories. Late the next morning, we finally got to bed, happy to have experienced some good Chilean hospitality, but feeling dreadful from the tequila. Over the previous few days I had become bored with being so damn healthy all the time. After the months of training and the effort of having to stay so meticulously fit, it felt fantastic to let the fitness slip away, and we woke up the next morning nursing a horrible hangover.

Four hours later and the excess-baggage lady was proving to be a formidable enemy. Obviously accustomed to preying on Antarctic travellers, despite nearly two hours of haggling she wouldn't budge on the price of US $600 for our excess weight. With alcoholic sweats and a slight feeling of nausea, I was in no fit state to deal with her and so passed the buck to Tom. He smiled, name-dropped important Lan Chile Airways officials and even tried the old trick of unloading a few barrels at the check-in desk. Usually, as the stinking clothes pile up on the polished floor and the queue of passengers behind approach near-riot status, check-in girls just wave you past. The wicked witch of the south was having none of it, but somehow Tom managed to beat her down to US $450.

On the plane, as we waited for take-off, the electrics began going haywire. All the lights and TV screens started flashing randomly and then cut out completely. We had all disembarked to let them check the status of the fuses when an earthquake shook the ground alarmingly. In the departure gate, people looked at each other with that questioning stare that usually precedes open panic.

A little more wary, the passengers boarded

once again, but with reassurances from the captain regarding the state of the plane's electrics they started to settle down. As we taxied out to the runway, we passed another plane that had obviously just caught fire and was being doused down on the side of the tarmac. I watched the fire hoses spray water high in the air and couldn't believe this was happening at the same airport. For the second time in almost as many months, I paid great attention to the pre-flight safety announcement.

Thirty-six hours and four different aeroplanes later, we eventually touched down at Heathrow. My mother and father were there to meet me. As we hugged, I felt an overwhelming urge to express all the thoughts that had occupied me for so long on the ice. All those protracted hours spent thinking about them and the other people who meant things in my life. I wanted to tell them how much I had valued their support. How their affection had been one of the only things keeping me moving on that last desperate night to the pole.

'Nice to see you, Dad. How's things?'

'Good. How was the pole?'

'Yeah, good, thanks,' I said, nodding slowly. With that we walked through the airport and began loading up the car. I might just have been to Antarctica, but that didn't stop me being British.

★   ★   ★

A few days later the snow was falling in big, damp chunks. The tree branches sagged under the weight and the grass lay covered in white. The snow had followed me home and, despite being a familiar sight, it still managed to instil a sense of wonder. I sat at a desk looking out of the window. I had just spoken to Robyn on the phone and she was trying everything she could to get her flights changed. At the moment it looked as if it would be another week before she could get back to England. The homecoming had all seemed a little empty without her and I knew now I would have to wait another week before any sense of normality returned. Only when her plane finally touched down would everything be as it should be.

A small mountain of bills and threatening letters lay in front of me. During the morning I had loosely organised them into piles graded according to importance, but then seemed to lose impetus. Instead I stared out of the window and gradually tried to muster the strength to start the whole process of getting back into a normal taxpayer's life.

I let my eyes drift over the fields of snow and wondered what my next move would be. A top priority was definitely to find some sort of gainful employment. The pile of letters under my nose seemed to be either from banks or equipment stores, and I doubted they had written to congratulate me on my recent achievement. I was in a lot of debt and knew I should get back to a steady job as soon as I could.

One of my friends, on his own personal quest for adventure, had already rung and asked whether I was interested in another expedition to Antarctica. I had said that I would come round and have a look at what he had in mind, but that was all. If it was straight man-hauling then I was happy to tell him to forget it, but if it involved a significant amount of kiting, then that was a different story. When we had finally mastered them, the kites had simply been incredible. The whole concept of harnessing the wind in Antarctica had been exploited in only a handful of expeditions before ours. There was, therefore, a great deal left to be done, and I knew it would be very hard to say no.

Many people, having attained one of the poles, would then face the other way and try the next. For some reason the North Pole didn't hold any great appeal for me. The pressure ridges and open leads of water would preclude any kiting and it would mean another fifty days of hard grind. Possibly, in a few months, I would have been up to it physically, but mentally I was in no fit state to try something like that again. As I had just discovered, the head was the thing which kept you moving, not the muscles.

There was also the issue of being away for so long. To be perpetually off on an expedition would have put a huge amount of strain on my relationships back home. It was unfair to keep asking my girlfriend and family to go through the whole stressful process. If there was another expedition on the horizon, it would either have to be a good deal shorter or I had to think of a way to rope Robyn into it as well. I leant forward and picked up a Biro sitting on the edge of the desk.

'Hot countries,' I wrote on the back of one of the envelopes, and then added a question mark for good measure. That was the way I could pique her curiosity. I had to come up with an expedition to somewhere extremely hot.

After hours of dawdling, I got up and scrunched the envelopes into one large pile. I crammed them into the bottom drawer of the desk and walked outside. In the garage, my barrels of equipment still lay unpacked. After a little ferreting around, I managed to find my skis and lay them on the snow outside. With my trainers jammed into the outer shell of my ski boots, I clipped them on and started skiing off across the nearby field. My parents' dog came bounding up expectantly and together we moved across the heavy snow. In a few minutes we were past the field and into the neighbouring farm.

It was beautiful. The sun shone down brightly on the snow and the air was cold. I skied as fast as I could, trying to dispel the frustration of the morning. After about half an hour we came up to a dirt road and I began taking my skis off to cross it. A local farmer was on his tractor near by and, seeing me, he leant out of the cab and whistled loudly. I stopped, turned round and walked up to where he was.

'You that young fella from round 'ere who's been skiing up near them polar regions?' he asked in his thick Suffolk accent.

'Yeah, that's me. Just got back a couple of days ago,' I said, smiling back at him.

His heavy, weather-beaten face crunched up a little and he seemed to be lost in thought for a moment. 'Antarctica, eh?' he said, mulling the whole concept over in his mind.

'Makes a change, I suppose,' he muttered more to himself than anyone else.

With a turn of the key, the tractor slowly pulled away up the hill. I stood and watched him go, returning his amicable wave as he crested the brow. Evidently polar exploration didn't cut much ice up in the wilds of Suffolk. Then again, I thought, why the hell should it?

Postscript

'So how many cattle can you raise in Antarctica?' The man swung a half-dead fish over his shoulder and looked at me sternly.

'There're no cattle there at all,' I said, smiling back at him. He looked at me quizzically, as if he wasn't quite sure whether I was telling the truth. After all, I had just told him Antarctica was bigger than the whole of North America put together.

'What about corn? You must be able to grow corn there.'

'No, Benjamin, you don't understand. It's all ice. There is nothing but ice over the entire continent,' I said earnestly. I clicked the laptop a few times and a picture of Antarctica flashed up on the screen. Benjamin peered down slowly over my shoulder, until his face was just a few inches from the screen. In the process, I now found myself looking directly at the face of a recently caught rockfish, gulping slightly.

A couple of seconds later he stood up and shook his head in absolute disbelief. He turned to see whether anyone else was around with whom he might share his amazement but, unfortunately, we were the only two people on the lake so early in the morning.

'Patrick, tell me something now. Why on God's earth would you go to a place like this?'

'Well, there are lots of different reasons,' I began a little uncertainly.

Sensing my hesitation, he interrupted, 'I don't think you English can be too clever.' Then, his weather-beaten face cracked into a broad smile. He laughed a deep, self-indulgent laugh that was so contagious I started to giggle as well.

Put like that, I had to admit he did have a point.

For the last three months I had been on a road trip around southern Africa with Robyn. On the shores of Lake Malawi, the local fisherman had seen me each morning, sipping coffee and staring into the screen of a laptop. I had been there for two weeks, every morning until late, trying to complete this book.

Under the shade of a tree, away from the white African sun, I would spend the days writing. It was more than a little surreal to be describing Antarctica's frozen surface while sweltering in the tropics. In Malawi, colours, life and mosquitoes were all around me; the diametric opposite of the featureless ice I had grown so accustomed to.

In just a week, I had undergone an 80-degree change in temperature. My feet still bore the scars of the expedition, my hands still felt stiff from the cold, and yet suddenly, I was in a place of such lazy heat and relaxation. In just a matter of days I had been whisked away from the lowest point on earth and now stood on a beach, the water gently lapping over my ankles.

Some days I would look out over the water and think how different it had been for Captain Scott. No planes, no support, nothing at all, in fact. Only the long walk home.

Each day the fishermen and I had waved and smiled, but Benjamin was the first to pull up his canoe and actually find out what it was that I was doing. In the process he ended up with a lot on his mind that morning. Given that he had left his village only once before, the whole concept of Antarctica was understandably quite a hard one to grasp.

With a laptop in a secure metal case and a huge transistor battery pack, Robyn and I had driven all the way up the coast of Mozambique, stopping off here and there as we went. The metal case was probably not the best idea, as every time I went near an official building the guards outside would start to get nervous and point their machine guns in my direction. Evidently, in a country that has just experienced thirty years of civil war, carrying something that looks like a high-tech bomb is not exactly a good move.

After so many years of war, there is not a single building in Mozambique that doesn't have something falling down or, at the very least, pockmarks from the bullets. I had never seen a country so utterly ravaged by poverty, AIDS and political strife.

At first, whenever I got out of the car and the people from the local villages approached, I was nervous. It seemed as if a tide of people, all moving and shouting, had surrounded the car. For a Westerner, so used to respecting the rules of personal space, it just felt so threatening. Hands would reach out, people would come close, and it was uncomfortable to be the centre of such attention.

I'd lock the doors and keep the engine running. I would be aggressive, defensive, readying myself for the imminent attack.

A week or so later, I finally relaxed.

The villagers in Mozambique are the most gentle people I have ever met. They are naturally kind, generous and, above all, ready to laugh. You'd have difficulty getting mugged even if you tried. Violence is as unnatural to them as pouring away clean water.

While writing this book, I spent many hours in the same place, watching life go by. Often, I would peer over the top of the laptop, absent-mindedly staring into space or watching the people around me as they went about their business. When looking for inspiration, I frequently found myself wandering around the plantations or through local villages. Aside from sharpening my reflexes, as I dodged the falling coconuts, it also meant that I would bump into all sorts of people.

What struck me was how extraordinarily friendly people were. As I walked along the road and waved, women balancing huge woven containers on their heads would nearly spill their contents in an effort to wave back. The stern, wizened faces of old men would crease into huge toothless smiles at the slightest provocation, and the children . . . well, understandably, the children would just break your heart.

When I had flown back from the pole, a friend had greeted me in the local pub by saying, 'The hero returns.' He had meant it glibly, but it was something that stuck in my mind as I spoke to these people in Mozambique.

Those who had jobs would break their

backs working each day. Hour after hour, they would load coconuts on the back of trailers or carry wood down the mountainside. Ten dollars a month was considered a good salary in Mozambique, and out of that a person would have to feed an entire family. The computer I was working on would be able to feed one of their villages for about a year and yet, back in the Western world, it was already starting to become obsolete.

★ ★ ★

In Antarctica I had skied for roughly eight hours a day and had burnt many thousands of calories. I wondered how many calories these men around me were getting through, carrying their loads in the midday sun. There was no one around to tell their story, no one to say to them at the end of each day, 'The hero returns.'

There are heroes out there, I guess, but they have very little to do with people skiing to the South Pole.

Acknowledgments

Skiing for hours on end in Antarctica, there is time to think. Finally, there was time to appreciate just how many friends and colleagues had been utterly selfless in their support of this expedition. They contributed passion and enthusiasm, which became the backbone of our trip, constantly giving us impetus and constantly restoring our faith. Over the last year, my list of debts has grown long indeed. Even in our darkest hours, when the sponsorship faltered or our muscles refused to go on, there was always someone pushing us forward. There is nothing more inspiring than another person who is prepared to put their faith in you. First of all my thanks must go to Tom, Andy and Paul. They showed patience, drive and kindness on so many occasions and in difficult situations. I am also glad we have returned such good friends.

Then, to the people who made it possible. To Amanda Bross and Vanessa Pereira at Artists Independent, to Laura Aron at Flagship Publicity and, of course, Tim Ward at Omega. They rushed through contracts, took risks and put their faith in an unknown. Without your support, I would have fallen at the first hurdle. Also, I must thank Alan Lester and Hugh Morgan at Fishers for their unexpected and kind support. Dr Clarkson at the Scott Polar Institute for setting me straight on some horribly inaccurate scientific generalisations, and Mike Brown for patiently wading through reams of unpolished thoughts. Then, on to family. As they always do, the Garratts instinctively helped in any way they could. They offered the perfect environment in which to write the book and thoughtful advice when I needed it the most. Thank you, Rick and Margie. My sisters I must thank for their near daily help and sound advice. As I lurched from one disaster to the next, they were always there, always helping. I have long given up trying to repay them. The same goes for my long-suffering parents. Despite my countless mistakes and painful inexperience, they have always stood back and calmly helped from the wings. They have gently guided me when I needed it and just shown their love when I didn't. For my part, I can only hope that one day I might be able to do the same for someone else. Finally, to Luke Janklow. I guess it all really started happening the day I walked into your office.